BORN, MADLY

DARKLY, MADLY DUET

TRISHA WOLFE

TRISHA WOLFE
LOCK KEY PRESS

Hell is empty and all the devils are here.

— WILLIAM SHAKESPEARE

PROLOGUE

I, MONSTER

Perfection.

The ultimate assumption that it can be attained if one works hard enough, sacrifices enough, is determined enough to prevail…is the very definition of insanity.

But what is this maddening thing we call perfection?

It's different for everyone.

That one, blissfully high moment of utter and complete satisfaction, of achievement. It's a sweet glimpse of heaven. A split-second where demons depart and the gates inch open, granting us a limited view of something holy.

We have reached the top of the mountain. We have conquered. We reap our reward.

Ah, that reward doesn't come freely. There's a price.

Fear.

Let me rip the Band-Aid off.

Fear governs our life—that soul-sickening dread of loss. Once we've obtained our perfection, anxiety creeps in like the demonic force it is to steal our light.

The truth is a nice dash of salt in a fresh, cavernous wound.

Once we've tasted the sweetest perfection, savoring it on our tongue, everything that follows can only be bland by comparison. Or worse; a sickly sour. Quickly becoming a rotten bitterness that roils our stomach.

The higher we reach, the further we descend immediately afterward. A crushing low.

A torrid pit of hell awaits us at the bottom.

Maybe that's where London and I made our first mistake. Believing we could bottle our perfect piece of heaven. Immortalize it. Exist only for each other.

Maybe we still can.

But the higher we climbed, drugged on each other, ruling over a damned world that bowed and trembled before the god-like monsters we'd become, the harder our fall.

We are perfection.

And we are the fear that lurks beneath it.

We feast on each other and exist only for the highs…and even now as I kneel before my dark goddess and pray for her mercy, I regret nothing.

We truly were *happy*.

Maybe we still can be.

Locks and keys—the symphony of my life. A masterpiece, my design. My fear brought us to this moment.

The razor-sharp edge of the knife presses into my neck and splits my skin, and I release a hiss. I search her gold-flecked eyes for the spark that tells me she's ready. Her eyes are wild, filled with loathing contempt, her chest heaving as glistening beads of sweat dot her smooth brow.

My beautiful angel of mercy, now my vengeful angel of death.

"Do it," I command.

Her hand steadies. The cold steel a tantalizing tease to my heated flesh.

"Close your eyes, Grayson." Her voice is throaty and raw, wrapping me in her cruel, loving embrace.

I push against the knife, drawing blood. "I want to see the satisfaction it brings you."

Her delicate neck pulses with a strained swallow. I feel the force of it in my throat. My thirst for her never quenched. Even now, as she grips the weapon with both hands and begins to drag the blade across my skin, I yearn to taste her one more time.

Death at my lover's hand. The ultimate reward and punishment for our perfection.

I couldn't ask for a more perfect ending.

FLESH OF MY FLESH

GRAYSON

The beat of slow-pulsing music stirs my blood.

There's an influence in it. An air of mystery. That which is too powerful, too ineffable, to describe—you have to *feel* it. That intoxicating rhythm coursing through your system. Adrenaline sliding against your veins. A lover's caress that makes your body tremble, anticipation igniting your skin.

It's the feeling only a truly free person can feel.

Alive.

The beat throbs inside my chest as I move through the club. Bodies pressed thick and undulating on the floor, exposed skin, sweat—the smell of lust and alcohol infuses the air. I watch the body of the crowd rise and fall like the swell of a wave. Crashing and cresting. A siren's call beckoning me closer.

I weave through the dancing bodies, a prowling wolf. As if in slow motion, I walk among them, noticing every lick of the lips. Sway of the hips. Touch to the brow. Dilation of pupils.

It's predatory, this gravitational pull that arouses their curiosity. Men and women alike turn in my direction, their eyes tracking my movement. Hypnotic sex appeal—it's a lure. The hunter doesn't need to stalk his prey. Like the bright, colorful flower that attracts the insect, then snaps its mouth around its meal...

I can feel their draw to me.

That power surges, emitting a pheromone to reel them in. The music choreographs our dance, the composition of hunter and prey. It's electric.

I settle against the back wall of the nightclub, all corners and the entrance in view. I'm dressed in dark clothing, concealing the tattoos that have been circling the news and Internet. I've changed the color of my eyes from blue to brown with contacts. My hair's grown out enough not to match the description of me.

But here—among the other predators—I don't have to hide.

They welcome me.

This is my hunting ground.

The beat changes. Faster. Harder. And my gaze captures the blonde entering the Blue Clover.

My whole body is lit on fire.

Like a moth to the flame, I only see her; her brightness eclipses the dark corners. The club fades away, the music a distant and muted backdrop to the loud *thump* pulsing in my ears. Every muscle in my body tenses, my chest aflame with a scorching ache that sears my throat, my mouth watering to taste her.

Six weeks on the run, and this is the first time I'm in danger of being caught.

She glides around the room like an immortal goddess before her worshipers. She's a sinner and a saint. Her short black skirt a tease for the senses, her angelic brown eyes circled with flecks of gold, her halo to lure you into her gauzy web with the promise of salvation.

And I am lured. Completely. She owns my entire being. Flesh and bone. My black soul belongs to her. With one look, she takes me down. If she demands I kneel right here, I'll drop to my knees, offer penance for my sins as I plead for her to devour me.

She moves closer, keeping me in her sights, and I'm clawing out of my skin to reach her. I press my back into the wall to ground myself. My shoulders ache from the pressure. I'm hard in anticipation as I watch her slender legs eat the distance between us.

With three words I come undone:

"I found you."

My eyes close at the sound of her voice. I capture her neck and pull her to me, teasing a length of brunette hair from beneath the wig. I lower my head to her shoulder and inhale. *Lilacs.*

London's petite body molds seamlessly against mine, making me whole. My other half. Two puzzle pieces sliding together. A perfect fit.

I drag my palm up her thigh, memorizing the feel of her soft skin all over again. "God, you're real."

Her breathy whisper teases my ear. "In the flesh."

I burned my fortress to the ground to set her free. She's innocent in the law's eyes. The fire provided me time to escape, authorities burdened with the task of combing through the ashes as they sifted for my remains.

And for London? It put her above reproach. She's a victim.

Only I know how truly lethal my psychologist is, and feeling her now, her scent swimming all around me…into my veins…I'm under her spell. She's a seductress. Seducing me from miles away, just as she does now.

My thumb finds the beating pulse of her neck. "You did this," I whisper harshly to her. "You brought me here."

Her glossy lips twist into a sultry smile. "I had to."

My heart thunders under her hand. "This is dangerous. You're dangerous." I'm risking everything to be here, but existence means nothing without her. I roam my hands up her body, feeling every inch of her. "No purse."

She narrows her eyes. "No identification. Are you searching for a wire?"

I stop and pull her against me once more. "I would be stupid not to."

"You're paranoid."

I smile. "Is that a diagnosis?"

"It's a fucking observation."

"I'm on the run from the FBI," I say, trailing the pad of my finger across her bottom lip. She melts beneath my touch. "That tends to make one a little paranoid."

"Not about *me*," she stresses. "Don't ever question me. I'm risking just as much as you are, Grayson."

"Noted, doc." She's fire and life. She brings color to my world. I've been waiting a lifetime for her without even realizing she was the missing part of me. Flesh of my flesh. "But you're still dangerous."

Her silky lips find my neck. Her mouth opens to taste me, her tongue slips over my skin, and a hard shiver rocks through me. "That didn't stop you before." Her breathy declaration heats my skin.

I soar under her touch. "It won't ever."

"Grayson," she says, her voice filled with raw emotion. "I found a way for us to be together."

My body tenses. "It's not time."

The music changes beat, a provocative melody, forcing a shift in atmosphere around us. London pushes onto her toes and links her arms around my neck, speaking into my ear. "You have to trust me." Her body sways, and I follow her lead as she guides us off the wall and into a slow dance. "You gave me a choice once, now I'm offering you one."

Her body is so delicate in my hands, I could break her, but I let her lead. "Down the rabbit hole," I say, remembering the moment on the hospital roof when I offered her my hand.

She lays her head against my chest. "Together."

The music swells, taking me with it, ascending higher as I tuck her close, knowing that I'll never be able to leave her now. The choices have always been London's to make. I might've designed the traps, but she guided us there.

She guided me *here*.

She traces something soft along my throat, and when she pulls back, I glimpse the dried clover. A smile curls my lips. The gift I left for her in her childhood dungeon. I gave her one small clue, and she took that frail hint and used it to direct my course.

When she next appeared on the news, she had the clover pinned to her suit. In a newspaper article, she was shown distraught, gripping a blue bar napkin in her hands. To anyone else, these objects would be meaningless. But to me, they didn't belong.

Sometimes it's what's wrong with the picture that captures our attention. And London and I...we're very, very wrong. A portrait of the wicked and sinful. She's the artist and I'm her canvas, waiting for her to complete our story.

Then recently, a broadcast on the Internet revealed the

date: Her announcement that Agent Nelson was traveling to Mize for the reveal of the dead girls' identities.

I followed her story like she knew I would. I followed her to the Blue Clover because we belong together.

And I've waited long enough.

While she was unveiling the horror story of her life to the world, unearthing dead girls from the soil of her childhood home, I was pretty diligent myself, setting up false leads across the country. Dropping little breadcrumbs to keep the FBI taskforce busy.

We'll come back to that later.

Right now, I'm famished. Starved to taste what I've been denying myself for far too long.

London pushes close to my ear. "You're hungry," she whispers. "Ravenous. I can feel your need."

Teeth gritted, I grab the skimpy material of her skirt and bunch it in my fists. I find her eyes—those bottomless browns shimmering with gold—before I take her mouth. I groan into the kiss, the taste of her a drug injected into my deprived system.

The music returns with a roaring crash to my senses. I'm drunk on her and swaying beneath her spell. Only one other indulgence compares to this sublime feeling, and I'm unable to deny myself any longer. I break away and turn her around to face the club.

Securing my hands to her hips, I bring her back against my chest. My eyes shutter as she snakes an arm around my neck, welding her body along mine.

I dip my head low and whisper, "Choose."

Enticing me isn't enough. London thinks she's going to poke the beast with no implications…let's test that theory. If she's ready to bring the manhunt to an end, then she's ready to take lives.

I feel the quake roll over her body. "You don't think I'm ready."

"I think if I've come all this way, placing myself right in the path of bloodhounds, you're going to prove it."

"Didn't I prove it when I dunked a pedophile in a tank of acid?" Her words seethe with righteous anger.

I smile at the memory of our first kill. "Your hands still look clean," I say in a hushed tone. "I want to see them dirty. I want to see them *red*."

Her body responds to my challenge with a hard shiver. Then her hips rock into me, daring me all the same. London and I have been battling for control since I first entered her therapy room. If she only realized just how much control she has over me...the damage she could do.

"This isn't your selection process," she says, a tremble in her voice. "It's too impulsive."

"No...it's new. It's us. This is *our* selection process." And it's sexy as hell. I drag my hand up her thigh, her thin, little skirt nearly ripping under my palm. "You've been selecting your victims for a long time, London." I guide her head with my cheek, our eyes scanning the crowd. "Trust your instincts."

Like a radar, my soul recognizes other black souls. I can spot them in a crowd. Zeroing in on that indefinable thing that makes us alike. Same.

The damned.

Killers.

London has this ability, too. It's what makes her so damn good at her job. Sensing the dark thread woven through a killer's being. Pulling that thread until it unravels. Fraying the end until she has him wrapped around her finger...

She's an artist.

I take her hand in mine, running the pad of my finger over

11

hers as I seek the groove marks that wrap her flesh. They're deeper now. As if she's spent hours twisting her little string around and around, tightening it until her finger throbbed.

My jaw clenches. Our time apart hasn't just been torturous for me.

Her shoulders tense. "Some things never change." She presses back, sending a thrill through my whole being.

I slip a hand beneath her skirt. Her thighs squeeze together as I roam up her inner thigh. She rolls her head across my chest, entranced. As London grinds against me, setting my senses aflame, I tease her panties aside, seeking the proof of her arousal.

Her approval is felt in the heat rolling off her body—the wetness soaking the material of her panties. "Fuck." My teeth damn near crack under the pressure of my clenched jaw.

Self-control is what's kept me hidden this long.

Another reason I had to leave London cuffed to the trap as my lair blazed into the early morning sky.

She makes me fucking reckless.

My erection pushes painfully against my dark denim. I'm tempted to dig the switchblade out of my pocket and trail the steel blade up the curve of her ass, cut her panties away. Become a loosed animal. Wild and feral. I want to drag her over the nearest table and fuck her in front of everyone here.

My adrenaline careens painfully against every artery. Blood roars in my head. As her hips expertly roll across my restrained cock, she raises her hands above her head and dips low, sinfully sliding her body down mine like the seductive goddess she is. Proving I'm just a mere mortal in her divine presence.

A heady groan works its way free. She's breaking me.

I've never danced with anyone before. Never had the chance. Never craved the experience.

Until her.

London makes me desperate to taste everything I've missed…taste it all for the first time with her.

"Touch me," she whispers, taking my hands and bringing my arms around her slim waist.

The raging fire within smolders into a slow burn as I relax against her. My dark lover, and yet, still my sound psychologist. This is why I chose her; she knows what I need.

Because of her, I no longer crave the pain that has always correlated with pleasure. Never one without the other. My body wears the scars of every agonizing slash I inflicted while my victims suffered.

"We can be free," she says, tempting me further.

And like that, the tension coiling my spine snaps, releasing the pent-up rage. My hand clasps her throat as she pushes her ass up against my pelvis. *Christ.* A low growl is set loose.

Sweet. Fucking. Perfection.

We can be free. Free to experience every beautiful sensation that was denied to the both of us.

The music crescendos as multicolored lights swirl amid the smoke-filled room. We're hidden beneath the haze of it all —a part of the scene. And yet we're right out in the open. Above every boring fuck here, taking what we want. Owning this life.

We are gods.

I push her fake blond hair aside so I can claim her skin. My teeth sink into her shoulder, my fingers branding her thigh as I force her closer, rocking against her harder and faster, frantic to be inside her with each hungry thrust.

Her soft moans vibrate against my chest. "Choose," I say.

Fucking hell…as her gaze swings around the club,

13

searching her victim out, I swear to God she soaks my hand nestled between her thighs.

"Him," she says.

Gaze narrowed, I locate her victim right away. He's easy to spot. I've noticed him, too. I draw London even closer as I watch the man dressed in a sleazy metallic V-neck grab a short blonde by the arm. He doesn't manhandle her; not bold enough to draw attention. But his intentions are clear in his rigid frame.

"Perfect." With great difficulty, I separate from London. I put enough space between us to adjust myself with a harsh groan. I'm still too tempted to pick her up and take her right against the wall of the club.

Her sound of protest sends a fiery ache down the length of my body, and I turn her around and pin her to the brick, breaths searing my chest. "The bad things I'm going to do to you…" I assure her.

Her eyes glisten with lust as she looks up at me, then she kisses my neck with the softest caress. I bite my lip, letting the pain ground me. "Don't make me wait. *Again*." She slips under my arm, and I catch her hand.

"Make a scene, baby," I say, letting her fingers go one by one.

I brace my hands behind my neck as I lean against the wall. London's hips sway, effortless sex appeal radiating off her like a neon sign inviting every man here to take notice.

London is sexy. She's sultry sophistication. A breathtaking goddess. But London in disguise…with smoldering makeup and tight, formfitting clothes…is downright evil. If I didn't already know what masquerades beneath, I'd have no willpower to deny her.

I have no willpower now.

Our target has little chance in escaping her snare. She

stumbles right up to him, placing her hands on his chest. A drunken display as she laughs off her embarrassment. She's too sloppy to stand on her own, using his arm to keep herself upright.

He offers her his drink, and she groggily waves it away. She's had enough. His dark eyes gleam in the bouncing lights. She gives him one more drunken stroke along the arm before she staggers off.

His gaze never leaves her backside.

He looks around the club, taking note of anyone who could've witnessed the interaction before he sets his drink on the bar with a crisp bill. Within seconds, he heads toward the exit after London.

I push off the wall. Keeping my distance, I follow him through the club and out into the humid summer night.

My pulse speeds with lust for the hunt, my adrenaline surging with the power.

Alive.

The feeling only a truly free person can feel.

London is the music awakening my soul. She's the reason my heart beats. I'm alive for her—I'm free because of her, and now we're unstoppable.

2

WICKED GAME

LONDON

The balmy night air sticks to my skin, causing my silk blouse to cling to my chest. I stagger my steps, making sure I appear the helpless, intoxicated victim. The closer the heavy footfalls sound, the more my heart rate ramps.

The man behind me is not a victim.

He chose his fate the second he followed me out of the club.

During one of our first sessions, Grayson said his victims were akin to predators stalking the woods in search of prey. If they fell into the hunter's trap, they were in the wrong place to begin with.

For us, this moment is predestined. It was never a question of *if* we would hunt together but *when*.

Grayson understood our dynamic—what we would mean together—before I could even conceive my own truth.

We're an inevitability.

Once I shed every lie, severed every anchor weighing me

down, it was like being reborn. I walked through the embers of one life to another; a new start. A new woman—one who no longer fears the dark corners of her mind.

Rather, the time I spent apart from Grayson only solidified my resolve. Strengthening the bond between us, knowing with each sign I gave him, he was waiting. Waiting for me to fully accept my new reality. Waiting for the FBI to look the other way. Waiting for the perfect moment, when every mechanism he set into motion aligned, bringing us together.

A skillfully planned and manipulated moment of chance.

Always a step ahead, my patient has this world twisted around his finger…and we're all just trying not to be left behind.

Like the man gaining on me now, he's desperate not to be left behind, dominated by a world that no longer belongs solely to the male gender. Anger seethed in his eyes as he scoped out his choice victim in the nightclub. Maybe he's unaware of why he's so hostile toward women; maybe he despises his mother. Maybe he recently suffered a stressor that sent him over the edge—a wife or girlfriend left him. Humiliated him. Perhaps these slights have happened to him all his life…and now he's ready to set it right with me.

No matter what his reasoning, his justification, he won't be given a second chance. Grayson no longer manufactures redemption just as I no longer suggest rehabilitation.

Rehabilitation for the truly deviant and disturbed is not possible.

I feel the man's presence looming, a dark shadow growing and swallowing the light. And when the blackness descends over me, he's there to claim his prize. His arm bands around my waist in a tight vise.

"*Shh*," he coos as he places a sweaty hand over my

mouth. "We're just going to have a little fun, baby. Didn't think you'd put me on frustrate like that and just walk away, did you? Get me all hot"—he rubs his crotch against my ass —"then leave. You know what happens to little cock teases?"

His sour alcohol breath twists my stomach. I shake my head against his hold, maintaining my helpless disposition. Giving him the guise of being in control. Although I'm not sure he needs the reassurance. This isn't his first time.

There's no hitch in his voice. No tremble or stutter to convey the usual nerves that accompany a first-time attack. He's aroused, with no inhibition or worry that he might not be able to perform due to inexperience or his alcohol consumption. Rather, he appears confident. He knows he has enough time.

"Cock teases get punished," he says. His arm is suddenly gone from around my waist, and I hear the snap of a weapon —a knife. His elbow digs into my back. He smashes my body against the brick building. "Now, I want your palms planted against the wall. You got me?"

I whimper against his hand in affirmation.

"Good. Make this real nice and easy, and I won't have to mark up that pretty face."

He moves back, allowing my hands to reach for the brick. The sound of his zipper lowering rebounds off the building.

"Make all the noise you want," he says around a grunt as he tears a condom wrapper open, "but if you scream, I'm going to make it hurt so much worse."

My nails dig at the brick. He plans to make it hurt regardless. This is the control he craves. Rape is never about sex. It's about stealing ownership. Dominating the victim. Asserting ones power over another.

And knowing I ultimately have the power…?

I'm humming. My excitement buzzes beneath my skin, thrilling.

He gets as far as fisting the hem of my skirt before he stills. I feel the tremble then, the hesitancy. The loss of his power.

"I'm afraid I can't allow your filthy hands to mar this beautiful creature."

Grayson's voice is deep and steady. Outside the club, with no loud music or interference, I can hear the lilt of his Irish accent and the subtle, sensual bass notes that slip over my skin like the silkiest material.

"Turn around, *baby*," Grayson says, and I spin slowly to face my attacker.

The man who threatened to punish me appears much more docile now. His arms hang limply by his sides, a crumpled condom wrapper clenched in one hand, a knife in the other. Grayson relieves the man of his weapon, then presses another blade to his neck—a switchblade. The fact that Grayson carries a weapon with him shouldn't surprise me.

By the heated look in Grayson's eyes, he's wondering if it excites me. Yes. Yes, it does.

"What are you...undercover?" the man spits. "This is entrapment."

Grayson jabs the point of the knife deeper. "Come on, you're smarter than that. Would a cop use a switchblade?" The guy says nothing. "How's our friend doing?" Grayson asks me.

I let my gaze rove downward. "A little wilted." His once-erect penis now flops flaccidly over his open jeans. Grayson has stolen his power, his control—his virility.

"I don't want any trouble," the guy claims.

Pressing closer to his back, Grayson says in a low tone,

"Neither did she. Guess trouble just knows where to look."
Then to me: "Where is the jugular? Here or here?" He
repositions the point of the blade. "Or is this the carotid?"

He winks at me, and I'm like a smitten schoolgirl.
Sharing an inside joke with her crush. It's exhilarating.

"I get them confused," Grayson continues. "How deep do
you have to cut to sever the carotid? Have to slice through
tendon and muscle. That sounds messy." He nudges the man's
shoulder. "Let's take a walk."

Squeezing his eyes closed, the guy pleads, "Please—"

"Don't." Grayson delivers one word to silence his
attempt. "You don't want to go there yet. It's far too early."

A few paces down the alley, Grayson glances at me, an
unspoken question in his eyes. He wants me to pick the kill
site.

This is too spontaneous. How many times have patients
told me that rash decisions were their downfall? I'm not sure
if this is another test, if Grayson still doubts my
transformation...

"There," I say, pointing to a darkened warehouse.

Grayson nods his agreement, and a smidgen of relief
settles over me.

"It's not that I don't like the alley you chose," Grayson
says to our captive. "It's a good location. Nice and secluded
on a dark night. It's just that I would've chosen differently."

Kill sites are Grayson's specialty. Over the years, he's
perfected his methods. Selecting places that allow him plenty
of time to torture his victims. I diagnosed Grayson with a
particular psychopathy: sadistic symphorophilia. He
experiences gratification from staging disasters.

Yet there's so much more beneath his disorder. The man
is methodical. His high intelligence alone adds layers of

complexity to his psyche...and then there's the development of a disempathetic type.

I've rebuked its claim in academia and all through my professional career, and yet I can't deny my own yearning to accept the impossible—that a psychopathic criminal has developed feelings for one woman.

Not just feelings. Love.

That all-consuming, elusive emotion the world revolves around.

It's possible I'm as delusional as the women who write to serial killers in prison. Believing they're the special one—the one who has penetrated some protective layer of their hardened heart.

No, I'm not that delusional. Not anymore. There is some unique chemistry between Grayson and I that can't be summed up with blanket terminology or compared to love. It defies reason. And as I watch him guide our victim into the abandoned warehouse, I admit, I even fear him.

For the average mentally healthy person, the emotion of love can make them do the unthinkable. What is Grayson capable of?

He pushes the man down on the concrete floor, then looks at me. That sinister spark in his eyes. It's like foreplay, the anticipation building, and I sense something in him that wasn't there before.

He fears me, too.

Grayson forces the man to remove the tacky metallic shirt and, once he has the man's wrists and ankles zip-tied behind his back, Grayson unloads the rest of the tools on his person. Another knife tucked in his boot. A sculpting wire in his back pocket. A slim roll of duct tape. A filed-down key. I raise an eyebrow.

After he tapes the man's mouth, he approaches me slowly,

stealthily. He removes my blond wig, letting it drop to the floor, then steps close to run his fingers through the escaped wisps of my brown tresses.

"There you are," he says. He trails his fingers over my shoulder and up my neck, his breathing becoming labored. "I never knew how enjoyable touching could be."

I take his hand from my neck, bringing both his arms before me. I undo the buttons of his cuffs and roll back the sleeves of his dark-gray button-up, exposing the scars and tattoos that cover his forearms.

"There you are," I whisper.

As I drag my palms along his arms, feeling every beveled and smooth scar, Grayson towers over me, a formidable force pressing against my senses. His touch, his scent, the suggestive allure in his intense eyes... I've always been his captive.

Nothing and no one could've prevented our collision. Just like now, as he closes his strong arms around me, his hand trapping the nape of my neck, and crushes his mouth to mine.

An unstoppable force.

His hands seek lower to grasp beneath my arms, then he lifts me above him. I'm a doll in his hands. Fragile and breakable. He keeps me suspended as he backs me against a shipping container. My calves hit the steel edge as I'm seated atop the unit. Grayson's hands move to my thighs, hiking up my skirt an inch, before he finally breaks the kiss.

A pained expression creases his features. He doesn't have to say a word, because I'm feeling the same constriction in my chest. The unbearable affliction of *not enough*.

This is the danger—*our* danger. Not the threat outside this warehouse; the FBI and police officials closing in on us. Not the judgmental world that would bow to hypocrisy to see us dead for our evils. No, nothing beyond these walls is powerful enough to really threaten either of us.

The danger lies in whether or not we'll survive each other.

The overbearing desire to consume and consume and consume until we're sated...but we'll never be sated. We're an endless abyss, demanding replete gratification, our disease our enemy. We're afflicted with an insatiable hunger.

"My sick matches your sick," I whisper to him.

Burning recognition ignites in the depths of his eyes. He lunges, wild and mad, seizing my wrists. He crawls over me, his knee spreading my legs, as he prowls my body like a feral animal. Every erogenous zone comes alive with the pledge of his cruel touch.

A sharp clatter draws Grayson's attention, and he releases a low growl. He nips my lower lip, a promise simmering in the dark pools beneath his contacts. Then he releases me and stands. He situates the bulge in his denim before he turns to address the rapist in our presence.

"You know, I wanted to drag this out," Grayson says as he rounds the man trying to squirm toward the roll door. He drags the guy back to the center by his ankle. "This was supposed to be a reunion present for my girl. I've been fantasizing about this moment for a while...watching her get the chance to play..."

Grayson is not a spontaneous killer. Everything he does has been planned out in meticulous detail beforehand. He rarely has any physical contact with his victims. The one thing he does know more than intuitively is if the victim is guilty of a heinous crime.

That's important to him. It means authorities won't be inspired to vindicate the victim. There are more deserving victims who warrant the time and effort—not pedophiles. Or corrupt doctors who torture their patients. Or rapists.

Is this all for me? Is his sudden shift in method a way to fuse our two techniques together? Or is it really proof he requires. I killed for him once, but it was Grayson's hand that pulled the lever. Not mine.

"But," Grayson adds, groaning as he drags a clear plastic tarp to the center. He then reaches into the man's back pocket, alleviating him of his wallet. "But, Larry Fleming—" he glances down at the man "—really? That's unfortunate. Well, Larry, I'm sure I could do a quick search on you. Find all sorts of other unfortunate things, like the fact you've probably been convicted before."

Larry stammers as he gets to his knees. He's muttering against the tape. Grayson yanks it off, his blade pressed to Larry's neck so quick the man swallows his cry of pain.

In a shaky voice, Larry says, "I was falsely accused, and I still served my time!"

Grayson rolls his shoulders back. He grabs Larry's phone he placed out of his reach from one of the crates, silent fury radiating from his body. He drops the phone to the tarp and smashes it. With a forceful yank on the guy's collar, Grayson pulls Larry upright. He drops closer to his ear. "She is beautiful, isn't she?"

Larry doesn't answer.

The *click* of the switchblade reverberates around the warehouse, then the blade is once again at Larry's throat. Larry stutters out a "Y-yes."

Grayson looks at me. "Spread your legs, London. Just like you used to in your therapy room. Nice and slow...but leave them parted."

A thrill seizes my chest. "You noticed that?"

He nods leisurely. "I noticed everything."

I uncross my ankles and make like I'm going to cross my legs, but instead, I relax back onto my hands, inching my thighs open. Grayson's gaze drops to the apex between my thighs. I can feel the heated, tangible press of his stare as he licks his lips.

"So fucking sexy," Grayson says. "Isn't she sexy?"

Larry nods.

"Touch yourself," Grayson says to me.

An immediate ache blooms in my core at his command. As I slip my hand beneath my black skirt, I see only Grayson. The man who challenged my sanity and brought me back from the brink. I'm alive—truly alive—only when I'm with him.

Grayson's chest rises and falls as he watches me, matching my own heavy breaths. The intensity in his eyes pulls at the ache in my back, the throb so deep and hot I can't help but rock my hips against the hard container.

He grabs ahold of Larry's hair and tugs his head back. "Beware," Grayson says, his voice a low threat. "She's a temptress. Seduction is one of her skills. Just look at her... Don't you want her? Don't you crave her?"

Larry remains silent. The bulge in his pants speaks to his arousal despite his lack of voice.

Grayson sighs, long and breathy. "The truth is, Larry. You're not worthy. She could snap your mind like a twig without breaking a sweat, then have you groveling at her feet, begging her to do it again, before you slit your own throat just to make the torment end."

Moonlight bleeds in from a dirty window, catching the blade as Grayson flicks it back and forth, back and forth, silver glinting.

"Maybe neither of us are worthy," Grayson continues, "but you're absolutely fucking beneath her."

26

The blade slips down to Larry's throat. Larry is shaking now. A muddle of curses and prayers fall from his mouth, melding together incoherently. And Grayson's intense stare is aimed on me.

Just as I selected a key to end a man's life before, Grayson is waiting for me to decide. Either way, Larry cannot leave here alive. He knows who we are. He knows too much. He will die by one of our hands.

Or by both.

I ease off the unit and move toward Grayson, summoned to him like light to a black hole. Only I'm a volunteer—his gravitational pull captured me willingly.

He towers above, face drawn in sharp angles and contrasting beauty, as I place myself directly opposite my lover, my fiend. With our victim between us, I lay my hand over Grayson's and, holding his unwavering gaze, drag the blade across the rapist's throat.

It's not an easy kill. It takes strength. My grip on Grayson's hand is steady and firm as I force the blade deep, slicing through cartilage. Memories of steel hitting bone assault me. The vibration ricochets through the blade as it cuts through muscle and tendon...and suddenly I'm back in that dark basement. My father's hand covering mine as he takes a life.

Understanding dawns. Grayson never does anything impulsively. The victim selection; the hasty kill; the warehouse. All my choices, but always by his design.

Where I was molded into a killer against my will, Grayson is liberating me of that experience. Reinventing it; making it ours.

I'm engrossed, drugged. There's a moment of shocked uncertainty that graces the victim's expression before blood beads in a dark-red line across his neck. It then streams

27

down his throat, a thick river coating his chest with a shiny red lacquer. His wet gurgle echoes around the enclosed space.

Warmth spreads over the back of my hand. The wet heat of blood. Copper mists the air, the scent of murder an aphrodisiac.

I'm watching our victim, but Grayson is watching me. I can feel his eyes boring through me, taking in every movement, every response.

Grayson releases the body, and it crumples to the tarp. He lets our victim fall unceremoniously without an afterthought. My gaze flicks up to meet Grayson's as a hungry pang ricochets through my body. The ache builds, ravenous, demanding to be filled. As Grayson steps around the pool of blood, his penetrating gaze drilling me, that ache pushes deeper, arching my back.

He stalks me like a hunter, like he's starving, and drops the blade before he captures my hips and hauls me up into his arms. I'm so close already. Trembling, on the brink, barely able to hold onto his shoulders as he moves us toward the container.

His movements are primal. Need dictating. He lays me down on the steel surface and pushes my skirt up, his fingers leaving a trail of red in their wake. My skirt and panties are tugged down my thighs in one swift action.

He doesn't ask—he doesn't need to; the question of whether I'm aroused by our kill is answered as he tastes me, my body giving him proof where words fail. We're beyond simple communication. Our desire only answered in raw, carnal flesh and blood.

As soon as he drops between my thighs, his mouth surrounding me, I spike with unadulterated need. A sharp pulse spears the ache deeper, a pain so pleasurable I grit my teeth as every muscle contracts, my core clenching to be fulfilled.

Grayson looks up from between my legs as he devours, watching the wave crest over me. I break with a single flick of his tongue, too stimulated to stop the crash. But I'm not sated. Far from it. The external orgasm only heightens my need to feel him inside me.

"I need you." It comes as a breathy plea, but Grayson is already in motion to claim what's his.

He braces a hand on the container as his other reaches for the closure of his jeans. I glimpse his hard length as he lowers the zipper, my sex throbbing with renewed want at the erotic sight.

"You taste like sin," he says as he hovers above. Then he hooks an arm beneath my lower back, decidedly placing me at the perfect angle.

No holding back. Grayson enters me in one forceful thrust, sealing his mouth over mine to swallow my cry. I latch on to his neck, clinging to him as he fills the void. My thighs quiver from the impact, my breasts ache to feel the abrasive rub of his chest.

He grips my hips and slams inside me again, harder, his kiss stealing oxygen from my lungs. I work at his buttons, desperate to remove all barriers between us, just as he pushes my blouse up to reveal me fully.

I yank at the collar, breaking the kiss as I finally shove the shirt over his shoulders. Then I place my palm against his bare chest. The feel of the rough, slanted scars—the number of his kills—sends an arousing tremor rocketing through my body as he buries himself deep.

That frantic desperation returns, insatiable. The frenzy consumes us—more, closer, *not enough*. Never enough. Once his shirt is stripped from his arms, I fight to get closer, my chest seeking that vital friction. His groan ricochets through me as he grabs my backside and wrenches me hard against him, lifting me off the steel.

Legs locked around his trim waist, I undulate my hips, riding him as he braces against the only solid surface to keep us from falling. It feels dirty, and raw, and like fucking perfection.

His fingers snake into my hair to gain a firm grasp as he meets each rock of my hips. "Fuck," he breathes. "You're fucking breaking me."

My body responds to his claim, clenching around his cock, my nails raking down his back. "More," I demand.

He hauls me away from the container and anchors his arm around my back, slamming inside me with hard, carnal thrusts that detonate my control. I muffle my moans against his neck, my teeth finding purchase in his skin, loving the way his pulse speeds against my tongue. The metallic trace of blood fills my mouth, and I'm not sure if it's his or mine—if I broke his skin or bit my lip—but it sends me over the edge.

We're like vampires sucking each other dry; liquid fire sears our blood as we bleed each other, draining our veins. The pain is the only answer to quench the need that pleasure can't sate.

Grayson's back flattens against a support beam, his thrusts coming wild and unrestrained. My hand goes to his neck as I search for that racing heartbeat, to get as close to him as possible. His eyes flare. "Do it," he challenges.

I wrap my fingers tighter, and he sinks to the floor, settling me atop him. I grind and fuck him with abandon as his pulse quickens against my palm.

Power.

The thrill of taking a life—of owning it—feeling it literally slip through your fingers...

His growl vibrates through my whole body as his cock hardens and pulsates along my walls. I release his throat, freeing his orgasm and mine. I ride the blissful wave of ecstasy as I rock into him.

His heavy breaths fan my face, his features creased in the most beautiful display of agony and pleasure. We're hedonists—and we're unashamed.

He's braced against the beam and cold, hard floor like he's immune to the elements—like he's used to them. Grayson spent a year in prison, but it's more...goes deeper than that.

I touch him. Starting at his fingers, the very tips of his nails. I touch his rough hands, the contrast of smooth and abraded scars, the tattoos covering his arms. I feel the muscles beneath his flesh, still contracting as his breathing evens out.

My hands slip along his shoulders and onto his chest, mapping the leanly defined muscles there, the scars carved so deep. I work my way over his body, and he lets me, a wonder in his gaze that spears me.

"Has anyone ever touched you this intimately?" I ask.

His neck muscles tighten with a hard swallow, and I feel the intensity of it under my palm as I roam up his neck. "Never," he says, his voice thick.

"I want to know every part of your body," I say, my fingers coming to rest below his mouth. I sweep my finger across his bottom lip, loving the softness, the hunger that surges within me to kiss him.

I move in slowly, capturing his mouth and tasting him lovingly, as if we're sharing a secret—sharing an insight into each other no one else can access.

As I pull back, I feel the press of his strong hand over my

chest, my heart. "It's beating faster than mine," he acknowledges. "Does that mean you're in love with me?"

"Do you need the declaration?"

"Yes," he says honestly.

"I'm in love with you, Grayson. I'm not incapable of love...I've just never been inspired before now. And I don't want to be separated from you again."

He ponders my answer for a moment, never taking his hand away. Then: "Do you still question whether I'm capable of loving you?"

I glance at the massacre we created together, and he forces my face back to him. So he can see the answer in my eyes. I take his hand in mine, removing his grip from my jaw. Our hands are still smeared with traces of blood.

"No," I say, barely above a whisper.

His gaze narrows in question. "But there's some doubt."

"Only because of my insight, Grayson. Because of what the mind dictates. But I believe you love me. In your own way. That you will try to protect me."

"Am I capable of hurting you just the same?"

I can't hesitate here. "Yes."

With a deep inhale, he accepts this. We're not like any other couples, arguing to make a point. Some things have to be accepted, especially if we're unable to change the outcome.

He catches me studying his eyes and, delicately, he removes the lenses, revealing the vibrant blue of his irises. My chest tightens.

"I don't want to hurt you," he admits.

I lay my hand over his chest, feeling the furious pulse of his beating heart. "I know that, too."

Love and obsession are so closely linked, the emotions evoked by obsession easily mistaken for love. And when obsession rules your world, you become a slave to its demands.

Grayson has no experience with emotions on the extreme spectrum. His response could be volatile. The mind and body take mercy on each other, one numbing the other when physical or mental pain becomes too much.

Grayson suddenly experiencing an extreme emotional breakthrough is akin to a burn victim suddenly regaining sensation in nerve endings. Only instead of a merciful death, the mind would shatter.

I close my eyes against the thought, and Grayson pulls me tighter to him, bringing me back. "I haven't hunted a single victim since I left you that morning."

His admission catches me off-guard. I drag his arms around me, shielding myself from the chilly air. "But the murder in Brunswick? Minneapolis? The reports said—"

"Seems I have a copycat."

He says it flippantly, but lethal agitation brims beneath his cool exterior. Most serial killers aren't flattered by an imitator. Rather, it's an insult.

"Do you know—?"

"No." He shakes his head lightly. "Not yet. But I will."

Of course, if Grayson knew who the imitator was, they'd already be eliminated.

"This could further complicate things, or..." I again look at our victim, only now in a new light. The rapist could serve a bigger purpose. "We need to dispose of the body."

"*I* need to," Grayson emphasizes. "You need to return to your life."

But I'm already thinking beyond that. My gaze snags every detail of the warehouse, and I realize it's not just a vacant building. It was once a mechanic garage. "This place has far more potential."

"I love the look on your face right now," Grayson says as he feathers my hair over my shoulder delicately. "Like someone is about to suffer."

I find his eyes, enlightened. "Is this what it feels like when you design your traps? When everything slides into place and you know it will work."

"That depends. What do you feel?" His question burns with honesty. He truly desires to know, to experience what I'm feeling.

"It feels holy—like an epiphany."

"Epiphany," he repeats, a calm expression softening the sharp lines of his features. That rare dimple carves his cheek. "You were my epiphany."

I fall into him then. Completely. Lost in the blue of his eyes, the softness of his lips, and the red staining our hands. A beautiful and brutal epiphany that could save us, or damn us further, blooms to life right here in the darkness that spawned us.

3

ORIGINATION

GRAYSON

Murder.

Is the desire to take life in our DNA? A hereditary trait passed down through generations. Or is it a malfunction of the brain? All those misfiring neurons. Or is it something more—something *other* —that which can't be assimilated in a lab?

Nature or nurture.

The age-old question of scientists and doctors the world over.

Yet it's a tired question. A boring one. And the answer doesn't affect the outcome. Just ask Dr. London Noble. The doctor who shattered my reality. The woman who wormed her way into my decaying soul and resurrected me. Like a phoenix born from ash, I'm a new man.

Because of her, the question no longer plagues me.

Because of me, she has accepted her nature.

The only surety is that once you commit the act of

murder, it's in your blood. You have a taste for the kill. You crave it like an alcoholic craves the next drink.

One is never enough.

The late-night sky over Rockland is black with a dusting of city lights casting a hazy glow across the horizon. I'm in Larry's car—the one he had parked at the Blue Clover. Larry is in the trunk.

I'm breaking one of my rules to only use public transportation while in Maine. Some of the most careful and meticulous criminals have been brought down by senseless traffic violations. Bundy. Kraft. Son of Sam. But right now, it's a necessary risk.

I don't construct a trap after the fact. It's much harder to build a story, to link pieces together and create a design, once a kill is complete. You're left with limited options. And mistakes.

It's like working backward. Designing in reverse. But London and I are fashioning something new—something messy and brilliant all at once. It will have to be formed and realized as our story unfolds.

I admit, despite my nature to be meticulous, this excites me.

The way she lit up when she spoke… How can I deny her this? Even if I know the chances for success are low. I've calculated the odds. If we fail—which we most likely will—it will still be a spectacular finale.

Her ingenious plan? Bring the copycat to us.

To do so, we need a big enough lure. A bright and shiny baited hook that he can't resist.

Larry's glittering metallic shirt is a nice touch of irony.

I pull into the densest part of a wooded park. It's too late for anyone to be around, but you never know when a group of teens or a pair of drunk lovers will decide to take advantage of the same privacy.

I have ten minutes to stage the scene.

Remove Larry from the trunk. Prop him against a bench. Wearing a pair of Latex gloves, scrawl RAPIST across his chest with his own congealed blood. Curl his hand into a claw and scrape his nails down my arm. This has to be done now, before rigger sets in. Then drive the car onto the gravel and backtrack to remove footprints and tread marks.

There is no lust in setting a scene; it's business. Heightened emotion can't be involved. There's no room for error.

I take Larry's car into downtown, where I park five blocks from the nightlife scene. It's not much of one, but even a small coastal city has a watering hole. I now have twenty minutes. I locate a bar with no cameras. Wearing Larry's obnoxious metallic shirt, I mingle with a group of women in the club, making derogatory comments they're sure to remember. Then I order a round of drinks for the women and myself, placing the order on Larry's credit card. I close out the tab and leave the card there before I exit the bar.

The moment Larry paid with cash at the Blue Clover, he made this possible.

Within thirty minutes, I've planted Larry's whereabouts. Witnesses will describe my facial features and the metallic shirt—getting the two interwoven. This is fine; eye witness accounts are often unreliable. The police will assume it's a combination of alcohol and seeing two men at the same place. They'll put two and two together, and *ta-da*. How smart they are, linking the suspect and victim together.

I typically don't return to the scene of the crime, but again, a necessary risk. I need the police to make this connection. I discard Larry's shirt into a trash bin, then I abandon the car on the other side of the park.

The police will speculate that Larry was murdered in another location and brought to the park—a body dump. That's fine, too. As long as they don't speculate he was killed anywhere near London. She's an hour and a half away from Rockland.

The police will also assume that given Larry's criminal record, he was targeting women outside of his own city, hoping to misdirect authorities of his crimes.

But the big fish we want to catch—the reason I'm going through all this trouble—is the imitator himself. The copycat needs to know I'm here.

The bus ride to Portland takes longer than I want, and the little girl sitting opposite me won't stop staring. She's tiny, with shiny black hair and dewy porcelain skin—like a small China doll. Her mother wears a grungy waitress uniform and is slouched on the seat, sleeping off a late-night shift. Needle marks dot her forearm.

"Did that hurt?"

The little girl's voice tinkles, barely audible over the roar of the bus engine.

I glance down at my hand and notice the raised white scar protruding from beneath the hoodie sleeve. I tug the cuff over my wrist. "Yes," I answer her honestly.

She tilts her head, curious. "Did your mommy make it better?"

I look at her mother, oblivious to her daughter striking up a conversation with a stranger. Then I look at the girl. She can't be more than five. "My mommy made it worse," I say, and crouch closer to her in the isle. "You shouldn't be talking to people you don't know."

She nods vehemently, like she's been told this before. "I know you. You're the man on the TV."

My mouth kicks up into a grin. She didn't say *bad* man. I glance again at her mother, and say, "Are you a good secret keeper?"

She nods, her silky hair bobbing.

"Good. You can't tell anyone but your mother this, okay?" When she agrees, I say, "Tell Mommy that the man from the TV said to stop sticking needles in her arm and drink a big coffee before she leaves work, or else he'll pay her a visit soon."

Her dark eyes widen, and she smiles. "Promise?"

I give her a wink. "Our secret, remember?" Then I stand and grab the cable, deciding to get off before the next stop. The early morning work crowd will be piling on, and I'm too drained to risk another Angel of Maine sighting.

I enter my apartment just as the sun rises. The small downtown studio is nothing like my typical haunts. It's not spacious or inviting. It's efficient, and the few essential items I need are easily stored on the inlaid shelves near the door. Ready to grab on a dash out.

I unload my pockets—knives, wire, tape—into the drawer beneath the shelving. I keep the sculpting wire on me in case a situation calls for a less messy means of removal. I cover my tools with a cloth, then tuck Larry's cash into the paper bag I keep there, too.

Cash is always a necessity while on the run. I'm not a saint, despite what the press is trying to depict me as. One needs money to survive. My victims no longer had need of their money. I do.

I had to ditch the RV. It's too conspicuous to keep a moving location along coastal towns. People remember seeing an RV; townies don't like strangers.

41

I paid the landlord cash for a short-term lease on the apartment just yesterday. Week to week. I'm Jeffery Kinsey to him. And as long as I have the cash, I'm of no more importance than his loud, nagging wife who berates him down the hall.

There's two windows: One for keeping watch, and one for escape if necessary. I keep security cameras recording at all times, from every angle of the room and outside the main door.

I shower to rid myself of Larry's stench, not because I need to remove the evidence. Criminals make mistakes all the time—even intelligent ones. Stupid, unfortunate mistakes. The taskforce will ponder it for a while; how the escaped convict they've been chasing for weeks, eluding them at every turn, suddenly makes such a grave mistake by allowing a victim to scratch him. Leaving epithelial cells beneath the vic's fingernails.

Because the MO is so different from mine, authorities will need the DNA evidence in order to link the kill to me. My gift to them.

Then the theories will start. The deviation in method spurring specialists to speculate on why my MO has suddenly shifted so drastically. According to the specialists, I'll be regressing, devolving.

There are natural stages of advancement, and one should always be evolving. My first kills, I left the bodies on display. I was a young, cocky amateur, and I wasn't above bragging back in the day.

I got smarter, of course. Pride comes before a fall and all that, so I began discarding my victims. I buried them in remote locations. The next logical progression in methodology would be to destroy the remains. Leave no evidence. No body, no crime. Fire, as we well know, is a destructive force—the earth's natural cleansing agent.

After I burned my hidden kill spot, even the taskforce could make an intelligent assumption as to my next level of progression.

This deterioration should niggle at them just enough.

But what's really going to get under their skin is the location. How close I am to London.

It's all going to happen very quickly now.

I fix a cup of coffee and sit in the worn recliner. I draped a bed sheet over it to prevent the coarse, germ-infested fabric from touching me. As the sun's rays stream through the dingy windows, creating a kaleidoscope of colors on the concrete floor, thoughts of London erect in my mind. Her satin skin. Fresh lilac scent. The key tattoo she no longer conceals along her hand.

The feel of her soft, delicate hand slipping over mine, taking a life.

It's enough to sustain me…but not for long. Since our first kill in the maze of keys, the compulsions have come on stronger, more demanding. Uniting with London has opened Pandora's box—and what I believed could be my salvation, I now fear has sparked a maddening flame that will consume me.

I push a shaky hand through my damp hair, a laugh spilling free. I'm no better than the junkie on the bus. Craving the very bad thing. Wanting her more than I want oxygen; more than I want freedom.

Why else would I be in Maine? Initiating a half-hatched plan that will get me caught if not dead.

For her.

I was designed to kill…not love.

She's destroyed me.

However, six weeks of waiting, and watching, and hiding, of feeling stagnant while I play it smart has its downside, also. But we have to give our enemies time to show themselves. We can't fight what we can't see; it's like swinging aimlessly in the dark.

That's how most criminals on the run get caught, and get caught quickly. They try to take on the whole network. The FBI is not my enemy. The local authorities in every city across the country are not my enemies. Most of these people clock in and clock out. Go home to their families and pay a mortgage. Or they're just trying to get laid on the regular.

They're people. Doing a job.

Your enemy is a little harder to spot unless you know where to look.

He's the one with an obsession.

He's the one who won't stop coming.

I stand and go to the bedroom area of the studio, where I store my map and collection hidden beneath the bed. Not the most secretive spot, but I only need to keep it out of view from a nosy landlord's wife.

I tack the board to the wall and step back, letting my gaze follow the black string on the map. The string is anchored to points denoting my locations over the past six weeks. A second string—red—aligns with the black. The timeline off by only a couple of days. Then a third string—blue—sidles up next to the first two. Four days off on the timeline.

All three have one thing in common: the dates of appearance. Both men—denoted by the red and blue string—arrived prior to the discovery of the bodies.

Both of them were present before the murders happened.

Granted, I left a pretty obvious trail of crumbs for them to follow, but only one of us staged scenes to kill off two victims—and it wasn't me.

The scenes themselves—the *traps*—should've tipped off investigators that the murders were done by someone trying to emulate my method. Again, most people do their job just good enough.

Only the perfectionists, the obsessed and the meticulous, care enough to get it right.

I cross my arms and stare at the emerging pattern. Stare at the map and strings and photos. I let it all blur together, becoming a collage. A labyrinth.

The FBI and police officials have all been asking the same questions, trying to make sense of it, trying to make the connection that will answer the why and, ultimately, the *where*—that will lead them to me.

Why did I let Dr. London Noble go?

Using a red pen, I circle the image of London. Over and over. She takes up residency in the middle of my board. For me, she's the answer to every question. And to two fanatical men, she might just hold the key.

The circumstance surrounding my escape has spurred certain individuals to look more closely at her. Their interest in the good doctor is alarming, and dangerous.

London is insightful and clever. She might even be a better manipulator than I am. With intuition comes power. The power to do damn near anything we want. But because we were not born naturally to this world, we're set apart, we're *other*—that which gives us insight also serves as a weakness.

We're a target for those trained in deception.

Enter Special Agent Randall Nelson of the FBI.

He rescued London, storming the blazing scene like a white knight. This agent has a real hard-on for me. It's almost cliché, but then, everything's been done before, hasn't it? Every career criminal needs his counterpart. The white knight cop pursuing the chaotic-evil bad guy. The great cat and mouse chase.

Agent Nelson has declared himself the yin to my yang.

And he's using London to get to me.

He can become an obstacle, or a means to an end.

Agent Nelson is only one phase of the elimination process, though. There's a second element in the form of an obsessed detective who has sworn my demise by his own hands. We can't leave out Detective Foster. He's been on Nelson's tail the whole way, always coming up in the rear. He just won't go away.

Foster may be less of a threat, but he's still another obstacle to hurdle. I made the mistake of underestimating him before. I learn from my mistakes.

I've been feeding them crumbs for weeks; they've got to be starved by now. Ready for a big, juicy meal. Larry should have them chewing for a while. I can't give either of them the answers all at once. That would overstimulate them. Like children, they need to be fed little by little. Bite-sized answers they can swallow without choking.

We don't want them to choke. Not yet.

London's trap needs to be realized first.

I could've taken her with me on the run. Settled in Canada. She could've even opened a new practice under an assumed name. We could've moved around, never staying in one place too long, never getting caught.

But what kind of life would that be for her?

No, with London's talents, she deserves better. Bigger. Brighter.

What's more, why remove a perfectly positioned chess piece?

Now the image is coming into focus. She's right in the

center of the investigation. She can reach out and physically touch our enemies. She plays the most pivotal role of all.

Process of elimination.

Once you've eliminated your obstacles, you're free. The FBI manhunt can't use tax dollars forever. Resources run out. Cases go cold. And eventually, criminals at large are assumed dead when leads die off.

Now that the big picture is revealed, it's time to break down the details. Cut them up into tiny, chewable pieces.

I tack a marker to the newest location. Rockland—the crime scene that will tip the first domino. I string the black thread to the marker. Maine is my final destination. It has to begin and end here.

Agent Nelson in the red and Detective Foster looking so blue, trail behind. Who will be the first to reach the Rockland crime scene?

4

MALICIOUS INTENT

LONDON

Press conferences have a distinct aroma. A mix of stale coffee and aftershave, with an undercurrent of breath mints and leather. The way church smells. Even the man standing at the podium wears a gravely serious expression like a pastor, delivering his practiced speech for the masses.

I've learned to stare at the center of the podium. This way I don't mimic the speaker's facial expressions as I zone out. People have a tendency to take facial cues from others. An inherent trait we all learn early on to convey empathy.

And with so many eyes and cameras directed on me, it's important that I don't frown or smile, giving the media a thread to twist and tangle.

"Having gone over what remains of the evidence, I've concluded there was a gross negligence in the handling of victims' cases." States Attorney Kyle Sandow addresses the press with a stern glare into the cameras. "Therefore, the Mize Sheriff Department has been instructed to relinquish all pertinent evidence pertaining to the deceased Sheriff Malcolm Noble and the victims to the Federal Bureau of Investigation."

I'm seated in the front row, flanked by Agent Nelson and Detective Foster, who has become my shadow this past week. Every prominent member of law enforcement is here. Even the head of the FBI taskforce conducting the manhunt.

No one is interested in the Mize investigation. That's so five weeks ago. The assembled congregation is waiting to hear the update that will confirm the Angel of Maine's return.

The news stations are already capitalizing on the murder in Rockland, jumping ahead of authorities to declare that either their very own avenging angel has come home, or there is a new player in town, hope alive in their assertions. The people embrace Grayson as their vigilante, and the media adores the ratings he provides.

I'm here against my lawyer's advice in order to study the crowd. A copycat killer isn't unlike any other serial killer— he feeds off his celebrity, requiring recognition of his acts. He would insert himself close to the investigation, but not close enough to get caught.

After the murder of Larry Fleming was revealed to the public, with the media's help, Bangor has once again become the hub—a prime feeding ground for a narcissistic imitator. A collection of all the major players gathered in one place would be impossible for him to resist.

Sandow's face tightens into a solemn expression. "The FBI are now heading up this investigation as the search for Grayson Sullivan continues. We have no updates on his whereabouts at this time." Sandow collects his notes. "Thank you."

A collective barrage of questions rises in the room. One reporter stands and demands to know why Malcolm Noble, the confirmed Hollows Reaper, is being honored as a deceased sheriff, instead of the killer he was. Another pushes for a response to a recent article claiming the FBI's focus on me has hindered their efforts to apprehend the Angel of Maine Killer. More shouts inquire about the murder in Rockland and its "alleged" connection to Grayson Sullivan.

Sandow quickly exits the stage, leaving the journalists' questions unanswered.

I take my cue and flee the room before the vultures descend on me. Secured near the green room, I find a good spot to observe the departing crowd. Sandow's refusal to talk about the murder will most likely irritate the copycat. He needs information—facts about the case. Not theories and hyped sensationalism from the media.

On a professional standpoint, I'm more than curious to observe the copycat's response to the murder—his reaction and retaliation; how he'll progress. I've never had the opportunity to interview a copycat killer before. I admit, ever since Grayson told me, my excitement to conduct research on the subject has manifested in an unhealthy obsession to reveal his identity.

A press reporter spots me, eagerness lighting his face. Before he can corner me, I push past the gathered bodies in the green room and through the back exit door.

An overcast sky greets me outside. The muggy humidity sinks right into my skin. There's a charge in the air, a summer storm brewing. The alley darkens as looming, rain-bloated clouds cross the sun.

I fill my lungs with a deep breath, still astonished at how fast I moved to reach the outside. Not a stitch of pain to hinder my getaway. I arch my back and suck in another fresh breath, just to test my lumbar.

The mind never ceases to amaze. One moment I'm

suffering acute back pain that has plagued me since the accident, the next it's as if I can't recall what that pain ever felt like.

Am I free, or is this sweet glimpse of liberty a prelude to my end? Like the brief reprieve you're given before death, when all pain receptors shut down.

"They're not getting any easier, are they?"

I close my eyes at the sound of Agent Nelson's gruff voice. "No," I answer simply, honestly.

"I wish I could say this was the last press conference," he says. "But the public is intrigued with your story. They're curious."

A sardonic laugh slips free. "Appalled is more like it." The number of enraged emails and letters I've received since my initial press conference announcing the buried dead girls that I—*suddenly*—recalled in my childhood home backyard has garnered me a lot of negative attention.

I'm accustomed to being despised for what I do; my career isn't a glamorous one. But I've never before been loathed with such vitriol on a national level. The narcissist in me wants to set the record straight, but my lawyer has smartly kept me from engaging in any more conferences myself.

I turn and face the agent. "Has there really been no updates on Sullivan's whereabouts?"

His expression shutters. That expert close-off agents are so skilled at. "You're not in danger."

"That's not what I asked."

He drives a hand through his shaggy, dirty-blond hair. His slight rebellious act against the FBI. And it's his tell. Whenever he means to misdirect me, he goes for the hair. A clear sign that it's worked for him on other women in the past.

"What about the murder in Rockland?" I hedge. "The

press seem to believe there's a connection. Sandow didn't even dance around it—he deliberately ignored it. To me, a blatant omission like that is very revealing."

"Always analyzing," he mutters.

"Occupational hazard."

His nostrils flare. "You shouldn't be following the news, London. You, above all, know how reporters distort the truth."

It's risky, my own methods of misdirection. Nelson is intelligent, and the more time we spend together, the more he's learning *my* tells. But I need some shred of information from him. A hint as to whether or not he's looking into the murder of one Larry Fleming in connection to Grayson.

When the stakes are high enough, you go all in.

As Grayson doesn't do anything halfway, I'm sure he left his calling card with Larry. His DNA, or another decisive marker the FBI will uncover soon, if they haven't already.

Why else would Agent Nelson be here?

"There's some speculation that Sullivan has left the country," Nelson says, stuffing his hands into his suit pockets. "But I'm not giving you those details. It's not confirmed, and anything I might tell you could put you in danger. The less you know—"

"The better," I finish for him. He's lying. I cross my arms. "You do understand what my specialty is. There's no one else that can help you get inside Sullivan's mind like I can. I'm an asset, agent. Not a victim."

"I couldn't agree more," Detective Foster interrupts. "Does that mean you're ready to confess your part?"

My attention shifts to the bulky detective exiting the back door. Detective Foster has been the loudest conspirator against me, citing publicly that I was Grayson's accomplice in helping him escape.

The fact that certain unfavorable details from my past have come to light only adds fuel to his fire.

I push my glasses up, getting a better look at him. He's gained a considerable amount of weight since the trial. "Detective Foster, should I schedule a session soon in regards to stress eating? You know it's not healthy to eat your weight in disappointment."

A mock smile stretches his ruddy face. "Thanks for the offer, doc. But truth be told, I'm a little terrified to be under your care. Or should I say, influence?"

Agent Nelson huffs his frustration. He's not a particular fan of the New Castle detective, either. "You're not required to attend the press meetings, Foster. Why are you here?"

The detective adjusts the dipping waist of his cheap slacks. "I like to stay in the loop firsthand. It's interesting that Sandow didn't state anything about Rockland." He reaches into his inseam for a pack of cigarettes. "Don't you find that interesting, Agent Nelson? With Sullivan's DNA having been found on the vic…it's like the FBI are trying to conceal the evidence. Why is that?"

Disbelief snatches my breath. My shocked gaze swings to Nelson. "Is this true?"

When Nelson didn't return right away after the summit in Mize, I believed he remained there to press forensics on my sister's remains. Like he claimed. The fact that he had a lead on Grayson and didn't tell me proves I've made very little progress with him.

Nelson steps to Foster aggressively. "I want you out of my crime scenes, Foster. I'll take out a restraining order if I have to."

Foster chuckles. "You Feds don't threaten me."

"If you leak one word of this to the press—"

"If you'll excuse me, gentlemen," I say, glancing between

the two men. "This is my testosterone limit for the day. I need to get back to my patients."

"I was hoping you could give me a statement on your whereabouts the night of the vic's murder," Foster says, stopping my retreat short. "There's a station right around the corner." He nods past the three-story building. "I'm sure the boys in blue wouldn't mind loaning me an interrogation room."

"You have no jurisdiction here, detective. My lawyer and I agree that your obsessive interest in me is now bordering on harassment." Every chance I get, I bring my lawyer up to Foster. It makes him flinch, being reminded of the way Allen Young belittled him on the witness stand during Grayson's trial.

"Let me call an officer detail to escort you," Nelson says to me in a low tone.

I shake my head. "No. I'm fine. I'm only a few blocks away."

"Then I'll take you myself," he counters.

Defeated, I nod my acceptance. Constant monitoring has become the new norm for my life. The closer they watch me, the further from Grayson I feel.

And now Nelson is keeping the investigation from me. I have to remedy that.

I lift my chin toward Foster. "Call my lawyer if you need a statement. You know who he is." Then I start out of the alley.

Foster steps into my path. "Some things just don't line up."

He's like a mutt with a bone. I sigh my frustration and check my phone notifications, denying him my full attention.

He taps an unlit cigarette against his hand. "You had contusions around your neck that couldn't have been from the car wreck. Your father"—he pauses with a snide smile—"I'm sorry, *Malcolm* sustained a lethal injury to the external jugular vein that was documented incorrectly, as a laceration due to the broken window shield of the vehicle."

I relax my facial muscles, my expression unreadable. I've been up against smarter, tougher opponents before—some of which I faced more recently as I gave my official statement to the FBI. If Foster thinks I'm going to come undone for him in an alley, he's undeserving of the little respect I hold for him.

"Lawyer," I pronounce slowly.

He nods his head, then steps aside. "I'll have my answers, Dr. Noble. Soon."

"Ignore him," Nelson says as he guides me past the detective. "His powerlessness on the case is just getting to him."

I glance over, surprised by his insight. "I know."

Agent Nelson is mostly quiet as we walk toward my building. The morning noises of the city are a comfort in spite of his relentless hovering. Ever since the day he discovered me cuffed to one of Grayson's death traps, the FBI agent has inserted himself into my life, keeping a constant vigil over me. When he can't be present, he makes sure I have a detail. As my friend, I suspect he wants me to believe, or even as a romantic interest. Someone who I can trust.

But the truth of his intentions lie in the guarded looks he gives me when he assumes I'm not paying attention. I'm a person of interest. A possible connection to Grayson. Nelson is quite skilled in the art of duplicity, as he should be in order to carry his badge.

I'm better, though.

My training exceeds the years I devoted to studying human behavior. I've been a student of deception from the moment Malcolm Noble swiped me and my sister from our parents.

Humans use each other. I don't fault the agent for his tactics. I'm using him just the same. He's my only means to discover any new leads the authorities uncover on Grayson. He's my only way to know whether or not the FBI will turn on me.

I need him to trust me.

Although there's nothing damning that Foster can say to tarnish my reputation further, I'm not conceited enough to think I'm above the law. My statement to Agent Nelson and the FBI referenced the accusations the detective leveled against me in detail. Hence why the agent at my side had no reaction to Foster.

I divulged the story as I can recall it:

The man I believed to be my father attempted to strangle me after I discovered the dead girl in our basement. He locked me in the cell while he disposed of her body, then he forced me to drive us away from our home with the awareness that I was driving toward my own death... Weary and distraught, I wrecked the car into a giant oak.

When I awoke, I had no memory of Malcolm's victims or his attack on me. The accident masked my injuries as well as his, and the officials documented the entire incident as a tragic accident.

I left Mize, Mississippi shortly afterward to pursue a grant for a college education. Sixteen was young, yes—but as I homeschooled myself and graduated early, I had nothing—no family, no friends—to tether me to that life.

The rest, as they say, was history.

Clear. Concise. Easy to recite. No holes in my story unless you know where to look.

I was analyzed by an FBI psychologist who deemed the

trauma of both the attack and the wreck had repressed the truth of the horrific events. I even underwent a brain scan that revealed lesions on my right and left frontal lobes may have developed due to moderate-to-dramatic brain injury during the accident, further backing my story of repression and exonerating me of any malicious connections to Malcolm or Grayson.

Frontal lobe damage. The areas of the brain that control behavior, judgment, and impulse control. Not to mention sexual conduct. A neurologist would have a field day dissecting me.

Yet, had the Mize investigating officers done their due diligence and questioned the evidence to confront me, I might have recovered my memories sooner. Rather, I had to suffer through another horrific event for the truth to be revealed.

This is what's documented in my file. The report stamped and sealed in an FBI manila folder. The electronic data protected by a government security system.

With the discovery of the missing dead girls, and the small population of Mize traumatized by their late, beloved Sheriff Noble becoming a grotesque fiend, Agent Nelson and his superiors felt there was no need to enlighten the press with details that won't 1) hinder the investigation, and 2) turn the media into more of a circus than it already is.

They have their hands full with analyzing the remains of nine young women and the manhunt for an escaped serial killer. As long as all the pieces connect neatly, their puzzle of me is complete.

Grayson saw to it that my puzzle connected neatly.

"You should've told me," I say, breaking the prolonged silence.

Nelson tucks his hands into the pockets of his slacks. "You're right. I apologize. You should've been made aware of Sullivan's vicinity to you." He glances my way. "I made that call. I felt you were under enough stress."

Chivalry was not his motive. Being unaware of Grayson made me a sitting target the FBI could use. How many agents are watching me right now?

"You handled that well...back there," Nelson says as we near the steps of my building. "Once the dust settles, maybe you could write a book. Tell your whole story."

I bow my head, give it a slight shake. "No. I've relived my story enough already. Whatever is still buried there—" I tap my temple "—I'd rather not provoke it."

When I look up, the creases around his eyes are softer. His gaze understanding. "And when you get the call about your sister?"

My chest rises as I force air into my lungs. "If...*when* you discover her identity, I'll honor her memory properly. I'll bury her remains."

But that's not what he's asking. Once her identity is revealed, so is mine. I'll know who I was before Malcolm stole me, and who my parents were. The question of whether or not they're still alive was answered after the first week.

There were plenty of claims made by attention seekers. People stepping forward to declare me as their long-lost child. Or those who maintained they knew my parents.

None of those leads resulted in any truth. Whoever my parents were, wherever they are, they're no longer alive. I feel sure of this. The false claims just muddied the investigation and pushed me further down the rabbit hole.

I've been steadily climbing out of that hole.

I am London Grace Noble.

My dead sister...my deceased parents... They hold no bearing over who I am. The mind does not accept an alternate reality; two lives cannot exist in one form. The life I've lived will not suddenly upend the moment I discover the name given to me by my biological parents.

I was raised by a man that I knew as my father, who—for all intents and purposes—was good to me until the moment I uncovered his evil secret. Though looking back now, I can clearly discern discrepancies my adolescent mind found no fault with, at the time, it was a normal life.

No one knows the absolute truth about anyone.

As we age, we become more and more limited with the degree in which we can change. At my current age, my personality and mindset are firmly in place. The discovery of my roots will do little to alter my existence.

With a hesitant hand, Nelson swipes loose strands from my eyes. "That's too bad. You'd write a riveting story. Full of big words and psych terms no one could follow."

I allow a small laugh to bubble up. This is what's expected of a woman attracted to a man. She flatters him by indulging his sense of humor.

"I admit, I'd love to read it, if only to answer some of my own…" He trails off.

My defenses go on alert. It's also expected of me to ask this man to finish his sentence. Securing my interest in him and his thoughts. But the psychologist reads the change in his breathing. The dilation of his pupils. His adrenaline just spiked. He's practiced this question, the moment rehearsed. If it was impulse, his demeanor wouldn't change.

He's preparing his lie.

I lick my lips, drawing his attention to my mouth. "What do you want to know, agent?"

He leaves his hand fixed to my neck, a touch of dominance. "The key," he says. "What happened to the key?"

The key Malcolm Noble wore around his neck. The one I drove into his jugular to end his life.

The murder weapon.

No one except Grayson knows the complete truth of that night. That my "father" forced me to help take a girl's life. That I in turn killed him during his attack on me. That I wrecked into a tree with the intent to end my own life…

So much darker than the story I told the FBI.

I step closer to him and put my hand on his chest. My point of contact serves two purposes. To distract him from the acceleration of my heartbeat that occurs when telling a lie, and to divert his focus to the sexual tension between us.

He may be a federal agent, but he's still a man. Simple in his desires. Sex is a tried-and-true method of control.

I inhale deeply, allowing my breasts to graze his chest. "I don't remember," I say, a tremor causing my voice to crack. "It must've gotten lost at some point during his attack on me…or the accident. I don't know, and I'm not sure I want to remember…"

He cups the back of my neck, brings me into an embrace. His arm locks around my waist as he releases a heavy exhale. His reaction is either one of disappointment, or relief. Deep down, I don't believe Agent Nelson wants me to be a villain.

He wants to be the hero of my story. He wants to fuck me without any guilt.

That could never happen. I need an antihero to complete me. A man that looks beneath my surface into the black abyss of my soul and licks his lips, ravenous to devour me.

All one has to do is look at my brain scan to see that.

As he pulls away, his eyes crease in a squint, gaze narrowed on where his thumb rests on my neck. I used foundation to try to conceal the bruise left behind by Grayson's rough touch. Nelson glimpses that mark, and I wonder if it arouses him, the thought of me fucking—roughly —away my worries.

"Call me if you need anything." He steps back without having acted on his attraction.

I nod, demurely pushing a hank of hair behind my ear. "I will. Thank you."

I reach the top step and turn to watch him walk away. He's satisfied with my answers for now, but once the dust settles—as he put it—he'll have more questions. Those trifling little inconsistencies that drive men like him to do the job they do and excel at it.

He has more in common with the men he hunts than he realizes. How else could he work these types of cases, get inside deviants' heads to bring them to justice? If Agent Nelson had suffered one or two horrific events in his own life, he may have even ended up the villain himself.

Just like Grayson, Nelson needs the pieces to snap together neatly. He won't be satisfied until he has all the answers.

5

THE PAWN

GRAYSON

Every killer has a signature. Even a copycat trying to emulate another murderer leaves behind a telltale calling card. Like a fingerprint, his signature makes the crime distinctly his.

Unlike a killer's motive, the method to conduct the kill, the signature is deeply imprinted on his psyche. It's a fixation that was already developed before he ever took his first life. And just like a compulsion, the killer wouldn't be able to deny his carnal desire to commit this action.

He's driven to do it.

My signature is pretty simple in design: torture. London uncovered this easily enough, citing I achieved gratification from staging scenes where my victims ultimately suffered.

Not everything I do has to be an elaborate design. For me, essentially, the simplest things are the most beautiful.

But this one aspect gives us very sharp insight into the copycat killer.

If we look closely, we might even see where the lines

overlap and where they don't, creating a new pattern: his signature.

Today's newspaper has an interesting cover feature: *Officials Confirm Two Homicides Linked to Same Perpetrator.*

A second murder victim was discovered in another park in Rockland. Same MO—throat slashed; body dump—but the press isn't giving away any further details. There's no mention of whether or not there was a word written in blood across the victim's chest.

I need this information.

It's only been a week since Larry was discovered and Agent Nelson and Detective Foster raced each other to the crime scene. Seven days between victims.

I wonder what London thinks. How she's evaluating our little imitator's escalation. Is he angered over the lack of news coverage; the refusal from authorities to announce my presence in Maine?

I'm so curious over her thoughts that I'm looking for clues in the papers. Online. News broadcasts. Only the Feds are keeping London safely tucked away. No statements from the good doctor.

Ultimately, what this proves is that the copycat has inside knowledge. The DNA discovery was never revealed to the public. I can't be sure, but I believe a purest—as the copycat has proven to be so far—wouldn't act on theory alone. Especially a hyped one from the media.

Our copycat has access to the crime scenes.

Nelson arrived in Rockland first, staking the FBI's claim on the scene, despite the local police objecting and pissing all over their territory.

Foster followed closely behind, always coming up in the rear. He has no official authority in Rockland, but he's not working on the clock—he's feeding his obsession. He's been chasing me since the New Castle murders, and he's not about to let some FBI hot-shot swoop in and steal his glory.

We can't get too close to either of these characters; they're too aware, too volatile. So we need a third party perspective. A way inside the crime scenes without physically entering them ourselves.

I look up from the paper, marking our objective right on time.

Forensic technician Michael Lawson works for the Rockland Police CSU Department. He's twenty-five, just had a baby with his wife of a few months, and buried beneath a mortgage his salary can't really afford. He's perfectly preoccupied with life.

An ideal candidate.

What do you fear?

It's the question I ask of all my victims. It's my first move on the chessboard—our first interaction. The answer is the precursor to the design. The exchange doesn't need to happen in person. We give our answers away freely. One only needs to pay attention.

We can break anyone down to their most basic attributes by simply uncovering their fears. Every choice we make or will make is rooted in what frightens us. Those fears direct our course.

Take our target, for instance. Let's break him down.

Right now he's seated on a bench. The afternoon sun to his back as he thumbs through his phone. He's not really interested in what he's looking at; he's avoiding staring at the woman in the elegant suit standing two feet before him.

She's beautiful. Shiny blond hair rolls over her shoulders in bouncy waves. Her gray pencil skirt hugs her curves; not too revealing, but leaving little to the imagination. She's classy, and sensual.

The other pedestrians standing around the bus stop notice her, too. One man has no qualms in ogling her outright.

Lawson lifts the bill of his ball cap just enough to get a glimpse of the woman. Then he returns his gaze to his phone. This is the second time he's checked her out since his arrival.

Because humans are governed by fear, we are exposed.

The ogling, confident man approaches her from the side. There's a brief exchange between them. She tilts her head, her expression apologetic, then he nods before returning to his original post.

We don't have to be behavioral specialists to understand what occurred.

In the background, our target has followed along as we have. His conduct has shifted slightly. He thumbs his phone more emphatically. Touches his forehead repeatedly. His leg bounces with a nervous, jittery tic. The alpha male was rejected, so what hope does he have in winning her affections?

Rejection: it's one of our fundamental fears.

According to the late Dr. Albrecht, this fear falls under the basic fear hierarchy of ego-death. Fear of humiliation and the collapse of one's worthiness. I learned this from London.

Lawson fears this failure so deeply that it's triggered a physical response within him. He's becoming agitated, angry. And what is anger but the natural reaction to fear? It's our mind processing the information so we can make decisions.

It's that simple.

What's more, how do we use his fear to manipulate the outcome we want?

I mark the date and time on my newspaper as the bus

pulls to a stop. Lawson is carried away to his evening destination, and I follow.

The bus ride doesn't take long before we're in the heart of the port district. I continue to follow Lawson as he exits the bus and heads in the opposite direction of his home.

I round a corner, and that's when it happens.

A man in a business suit recognizes me.

It's a slow realization at first. He glances up from his phone, then back down, and then his eyes snap to my face and widen in recognition. It's unmistakable, that moment when all the senses heighten, adrenaline rushing.

There's no sense in trying to run or hide, or to deny who I am. My only option is to discover his next move.

His mouth twitches, a natural, nervous reaction, as he says, "Good job." He gives me a thumbs-up.

I tilt my head as I gauge his body language, his facial expression. He's not a threat.

He won't call the police. This man believes I'm a vigilante. The Angel of Maine. A hero. Taking out the trash.

I've read all the articles online and in the paper. Reporters citing citizens that claim I'm doing what the police fail to do.

Let's clarify something: I'm not a fucking hero.

My victim selection is not based on any obligation to rid the world of filth. My victim selection is purely self-serving —an intelligent formula devised not to arouse suspicion.

Over the years, serial killers targeted prostitutes not because of their contempt for women—though some did suffer this defect—but mostly, because prostitutes wouldn't be missed.

Of course, the police have wised up to this method, and so picking off hookers is no longer a viable option.

As such, my victims are scum. Sex offenders and the

dregs of society loathed with such vitriol that authorities won't waste resources to investigate their murders.

It doesn't make me a good person. It just makes me smarter than the rest.

But, whatever helps people sleep at night. Trusting the big bad boogie man is out here hunting the evil of the world. Truthfully, I only see it as another means of cover. One more way to hide and secure my objective.

I give the man a curt nod before I pass him, saying none of this.

The interruption costs me nearly a minute before I can recover Lawson. I catch up to him as he's heading farther into the port district. I tail him to the same bar he's gone to for the past two nights. It's his pattern, his routine—to unwind from his hectic day with two beers and then go home to his family.

I don't go inside. Instead, I take up the corner of the building, jotting down the time on my paper, then start toward Portland.

For a year, I fantasized about how London and I would work in tandem. Partners. Accomplices. Lovers. There are obstacles, there always are, but her incredible talents have given us a way to overcome them, turn them into opportunities.

A carefully staged chessboard, where all players are pieces. Even London is purposely positioned to be moved on our board—she's my favorite piece.

We need a pawn.

Building a trap is like courting a lover. It doesn't have to be all hard frames and mechanics. You have to finesse the design. Nurture it into animation. Romance it with delicate strokes, and graceful strategy. Dance with your lover and she'll fuck you good and hard.

Because that's always the outcome we want.

Before London, I was too forceful. I was a brute. All physical strength and conceit in my knowledge, trapping my victims by coercing them to make a choice.

Choice.

A key element.

London's time in the cage taught me a lot. People are willing to take the blame; they're susceptible to their guilt. The human mind is a web of shame just waiting to be exploited.

Manipulation.

If used correctly, it's a powerful tool.

While on the bus, I unfold the newspaper and transfer the dates and times to my book.

A list of names. A list of sins.

Some men keep little black books of their conquests. I keep a list of people and their offenses. Detailing them down to their rotten marrow.

One of these players has been a busy bee.

I arrive home in time for the evening news. I let it play in the background as I tack the map on the wall. I've added pictures to coincide with the string, creating a grid formation listing the murders, whereabouts, dates, and times.

Local authorities have not confirmed the theory that the recent, horrific murders of two Rockland men are linked to the elusive Angel of Maine, who is still at large. The FBI taskforce conducting the nationwide manhunt have made no statements connecting the crimes to the escaped convict, despite having at least one commonality: The perpetrator appears to be targeting victims based on their criminal records. Just like the Angel of Maine, Grayson Pierce Sullivan.

At least the media is on the right page. I'm sure the copycat is following the coverage just as closely, as are

Nelson and Foster. Notably, these two players both have access to inside knowledge, and criminal records.

They're also the most obsessed with catching *me*.

I stand and stare at the grid. My eyes see the details—the structure of the crude diagram—but my mind sees beyond. I stare at the images and details, not focusing on any one thing. Instead, I let my gaze blur. My mind moves ahead of the basic outline. Three-dimensional in construct, the design lifts off the wall and assembles into lines and patterns. A mental picture of the complete module.

Daydreaming got me beaten regularly as a kid. My mother had no patience for my easily distracted nature as a child. I often spent time in her closet, learning how to pick the door lock. But now I openly allow the trap to manifest and take shape.

London has decided the end game—but there are many moves to be played before we reach game over.

This is the rush. When the pieces align, and every part of the working model snaps together effortlessly. I feel it in my blood. Euphoria.

6

FALLING UNDER

LONDON

When the call comes, I'm in the middle of a therapy session with a one of my longtime patients.

"And how does that make you feel about your boss?" I ask Cynthia, then try not to glance at my phone for the time.

"Well…" she begins, her hands already wringing in her lap.

My thoughts wander as soon as she slips into a monotonous account of her female boss and their issues. At least she's one of my easy patients. Cynthia can drone on for an hour with little input from me.

I thought I could transition into full-time general psychology easily enough, but my patients are always dealing with their "feelings". So many fucking feelings. Grayson wasn't wrong when he said I channeled my sickness through my patients, but it's more than that, why I chose to work with killers.

Psychopaths only imitate emotions.

Listening to patients talk and talk and talk—endless, mindless, self-involved chatter about feelings and their problems—most of them melodramatic—makes me ill. I get home in the evenings and heave. Get sick before I barely cross the threshold, to purge it from my system.

I'm not sure how much longer I can employ the charade.

There has been another murder, presumably by the copycat killer, although certain, vital details of the murder have been omitted, making it difficult to know for sure. And I admit, in the back of my thoughts, there's a question of whether the kill was Grayson's...

I fail and look down at my phone, and my heart knocks. A missed call from Agent Nelson with a follow up text: *I have information on your sister.*

The world implodes.

Nothing will be the same after this. It's a moment of vibrant awareness.

We get stuck—a swirling vortex of the same thoughts, centered on the same routine. A well-worn track of comfort. We're bored, but too busy to notice the boredom slowly killing us.

Until something inspiring interrupts our course, and we skip the rails onto a new track.

Inspiration is the food of life.

We're so hungry for it, so ravenous...that once we realize we're starving, and that first taste hits our tongue, we're capable of genius.

A song, a movie, a novel—a single phrase or moment— we recognize it in an instant. We're motionless in the dark, then we're thrust into the light. Clear and focused.

Grayson was my fresh taste. He's my interruption. I was starving for his promise of genius, and that genius shattered my world to bring me a sister I never knew existed before now.

"Cynthia," I interrupt. "I'm sorry, but I just received a text. It's an emergency. We need to reschedule."

She's jolted for a second before she graciously recovers. "Of course, Dr. Noble. I understand."

I usher her from my office with another apology, then shut and lock the door. I let the solid brace of the door support me as I collect myself. Then I make the call.

Agent Nelson answers on the second ring. "You got my message."

"Yes."

Time seems to suspend as I wait to hear the news.

Then: "Mia Prescott."

I close my eyes, blocking all other distractions so I can focus on his voice.

"Forensics places her remains between sixteen- and eighteen-years-old. The state of decomposition suggests she died somewhere within twenty years ago. But all this you knew."

I did. I recovered enough of my memory to believe I had a sister. The fact that she's real...that she—that we—have a name, makes it a certainty.

"I have a team concentrating on the victims' families," Nelson continues. "I've pulled together a couple of agents to focus primarily on Mia."

I appreciate that he uses her name. "Thank you. Do you know anything yet?"

He clears his throat. "A quick search on the name pulled up a report. But—"

"Nelson, please," I say. "You know that I'm able to handle it, and I have similar access to uncover this information..."

"I know," he says. "I wanted to do this in person, but I respect your quest for answers. Okay. Mia Prescott was reported deceased with the discovery of Jacqueline and Phillip Prescott. Their bodies washed ashore the Ohio River just outside Cincinnati. It was assumed their two children, Mia and Lydia, had also drowned, but their bodies were never discovered."

The name detonates on impact.

Lydia.

"Jacqueline's sister persisted with the search for the children until she fell ill with ovarian cancer and died five years after her sister."

I had an aunt.

"London," he breathes my name. "Why don't we meet soon. I can give you a copy of the reports. We shouldn't have to do this over the phone."

"All right," I answer simply.

"Okay. Good. Give me a couple of hours."

I end the call, slipping the phone into my jacket pocket.

London Noble.

Lydia Prescott.

Two worlds collide, and suddenly, every certainty I ever knew feels unstable. As if the cover sheet of my existence has been yanked away, and I'm not sure what awaits the unveiling.

I walk to my desk. Stand over it, my gaze lingering on papers and folders and coffee cups. I swipe my arms across the desktop. Contents crash to the floor with a satisfying clatter.

A knock sounds at the door. "Dr. Noble, is everything okay?"

Bracing my palms against the desk's edge, I ground myself. "Everything's fine, Lacy."

A hesitant moment of silence, then her footsteps retreat.

I close my eyes. I've been asking Agent Nelson for updates for weeks, with no follow up on his end. Then, a second murder is announced in Rockland—just hours away—and answers materialize.

Answers that will take me to Hollows and away from here.

How convenient.

It's possible Nelson and the FBI feel I'm in danger. Or they think I'm a complication to the manhunt. Either way, I should stay here—to procure the trap Grayson and I set for the copycat. That is, if the imitator is in fact in Maine.

I glance at the Dali hanging on the office wall. Beneath the piece of art is hours of extensive research and personal thoughts and findings. All my research into Grayson. I've been keeping a diary of sorts; insight into the man as well as the killer.

My notes serve a larger purpose, but the discernment it's given me has also caused a thread of doubt. Even without a counterpart, Grayson should be evolving. With his IQ and the years he's been an active killer, his methodology should be progressing.

Not devolving.

I hate doubt. I try to push it away, but I can't help thinking I'm an upset to his pattern. What's more, I'm treading in unknown waters myself. We're embarking into uncharted territory, and I have to continue to question the process or I could sink.

One of us has to remain in control.

I hit the intercom and tell Lacy to book my flight to Mississippi.

7

UNDERBELLY

GRAYSON

The scent of alcohol and cigarettes infuses the evening air. This part of town harbor reminds me of The Burrows. Dirty and dank and crawling with filth. Every beautiful town has an underbelly.

Snugly nestled in a pocket of Rush, the coastal hood where I grew up houses rows and rows of greenhouses. Not every evil happens in a basement. You can dig pretty far down before hitting water. Just the right depth to enclose a special room, where screams are muffled, and the sun of the massive greenhouse can't reach you.

The smell of dirt and fertilizer always triggers fond memories of my second home. My wardens had a lot of children over the years. As many as five kids shared the dank, dark room at one time. Probably why I didn't mind solitary confinement. I don't like being in crowds; near people. We were the evil Brady Bunch. We had a mother and a father, and rules.

The rules were utmost important.

The rules were enforced by fear.

The rules were ingrained so deeply, chiseled into my marrow, that after the first year in captivity, my young mind believed they governed the world. It was how it worked; the reason why life existed in the first place. To serve these rules and my rulers.

Every child had a purpose. And no one broke the rules. My abductors weren't unintelligent *culchie*—or rednecks, for a close American comparison. They were smart and cunning, and master manipulators.

I suppose that's where I picked up my training.

Manipulation comes second nature to me. London figured this out easily enough. I remember that first glimpse of fear in her eyes—the moment she questioned who was in control.

She's the one with the power, yet she still harbors fear of losing that control. Her fear of *loss*.

Fear. Fear. Fear. It makes the world go round.

As I head farther into downtown, where the reflective glare of the setting sun bounces off buildings and the noise shrouds my presence, I move along the shadowed city lines. Those dark pockets every city has. They keep me invisible. I'm just another man walking the streets.

I pull the hoodie of my jacket over my head. Look down at the sidewalk as I progress toward the entrance of the bar, my pulse careening chaotically against my veins. This feeling is more powerful than the lust for the hunt.

Every day I emerge, could be the day he finds me.

Special Agent Nelson has announced his presence, renewed in his faith to apprehend the Angel of Maine. Or so the brief news clip claims. After a leak in the local department revealed the DNA evidence, authorities had to make an official statement.

Detective Foster follows in Nelson's footsteps, popping

up like a whack-a-mole everywhere the agent appears. Foster's a bit harder to track, as he doesn't have a media presence like the FBI.

I push through the doors of the Refuge, the bar Lawson frequents. It's hard not to feel invincible when every law official in the state of Maine is looking you. Here I am, boys. *Come and get me.*

Only there are no cops here. Only a group of rowdy college kids, two homely prostitutes, a few bikers in leather and beards, and one lonely bartender. A few other strays crowd the bar top, seeking release from their mundane lives, too.

An eclectic mix of the broken, downtrodden, and bored. An easy crowd to go unnoticed in. This is where our target losses himself nightly, sloughing off his tiring days like the dead skin he works around.

I find a seat in the far corner booth. From here, I can view the entrance, the bar, the crowd, and the bathrooms. I order a beer from the only waitress on duty.

"Sure thing, baby," she says in hopes of scoring a decent tip before she saunters off. But her glazed-over, vacant eyes reveal she has no sexual interest in me.

The rowdy college boys aren't as perceptive to her disinterest, though, and one slaps her ass as she passes their table, earning boisterous laughs from the rest of his friends.

She ignores them with the practiced apathy of a woman who's lived too hard, too fast, for her years. I know the type. Her life coated in nicotine. Every accomplishment stained with the yellow tinge of disappointment.

The scene stirs a memory of my mother.

Her empty blue eyes, glassy and distant. My stepfather's thick hand striking her pale cheek. It's not a bad memory. Just a memory. Could be any memory from my childhood. They were all much the same.

I recall the moment with the same kind of practiced apathy as the waitress. Easily swatting the thought aside like an annoying gnat. Forgotten.

She returns with my drink, and this time, I give her a nod of commiseration. I'm sure we have a few things in common from our past. By the darkened skin beneath her eye that's poorly concealed with caked makeup, I say she's got more than a few things in common with my mother.

I sip the beer. I'm not much of a drinker—I don't like the feeling of being out of control. But what kind of guise would this be if I didn't have a drink in my hand?

Now my father, he was a drinker. My old man could put down two bottles of Paddy whiskey a night. It's ultimately what sent him to his grave. Liver disease. The sour stench of whisky still turns my stomach. The only recollection of my childhood that had a direct and profound impact on me. Though I suspect London would strongly disagree.

A smile twists my lips as I glance at the door, expecting her to walk in. As if I can make her materialize with just a thought. I take another sip just to feel the burn. It matches the sting of disappointment.

London has been whisked back to her hometown, where she fights the state to release her sister's remains. I've followed the story closely as she and my former lawyer appeared on TV; interviews exposing the dark secrets of her life. Spinoff clips of psychologists attempting to explain the conundrum of her circumstance. Even a few disbelievers shouting doubts and trying to defame her.

There's also been an investigation opened into the whereabouts of her parents' estranged family. Like one big fucking soap opera. It makes for good daytime television.

Who is Dr. London Noble really? one reporter asked the nation during a breaking news broadcast.

Apparently, she's come to be known as Lydia Prescott.

I scrub a hand over my head and push back the hood. Doubt is a festering sore. It starts out small, barely noticeable, but you know it's there. The more you touch it, probe it, worry it, the bigger it gets, until it's a black, gaping wound.

London plays her part well in front of an audience. Maybe too well. She's actively seeking information about her former life, and helping officials comb the state for the madman who abducted and tortured her.

All she has to do is drive an hour toward the coast.

Here I am, baby.

The front door swings open, and in walks our crime-scene tech. Lawson is running late today, a weary expression on his face as he heads directly to the bar to order his beer. He's had a hectic day.

Two grisly murders within a week and the pressure is on.

I drop my head and stare into my tumbler. The locals in this bar could give two shits about who I am, but Lawson works within the system. He's been made aware of my description. He's working the crime scenes that the FBI know are linked to me.

So we wait. And watch.

With every gulp of his beer, Lawson eases into his comfort zone. He's already on his third drink—one more than he usually downs before he goes home.

Every once in a while, he glances over to the two women working the back of the room. He comes in here often enough to know what they do for a living. With his fear of rejection, soliciting a prostitute is a natural step for him. But his fear is too great—even by the time he's on his fourth beer, he can't drum up the courage to approach them.

I wonder how he met his wife?

He signals the bartender to cash out.

I drain the glass and toss a healthy tip on the table. Not too healthy—I don't want the waitress to observe me any closer than she needs to. Her disinterest keeps this bar a safe haven for us. Lawson and me.

With that thought comes a fresh lance to the wound. London is my haven. Like cancer, that festering doubt spreads wider.

If I want to speed this up, I need answers. Now.

The drunken college boys get into an altercation with the bikers, and I use the ruckus to sidle up next to one of the working girls. She's claimed her john for the night, getting ready to meet him at the entrance so they can covertly leave together.

"You gotta offer more than three-hundred, sugar," she says to me as she drapes her jacket on. "Otherwise, I've got my date for the night."

I slip a wad of cash into her pocket. "Five-hundred. Count it if you want."

She finally turns toward me, giving me a perusing once over. "You don't look like you're desperate for a date."

"It's for my friend." I nod toward the bar top where Lawson is closing out his tab. "He's shy."

She nods slowly. "Ah. That guy." She looks me over again curiously. She works this bar. She's never seen me before. I'm not Lawson's friend.

I slip another roll of cash into her pocket. "Two-hundred more not to mention me. He's really shy. Tell him it's a freebie." I glance around the bar. "Make sure he has a beer first." I give her a bottle. "Will help loosen him up."

She's a perceptive girl. She has to be in her line of work. She takes the bottle, pocketing it beneath her jacket quickly.

"Will it kill him?" She holds up a hand. "You know what, baby. I don't want to know. Just don't show yourself around here again."

"Done." I give her a nod of gratitude, then head toward the exit.

As I linger in the alley outside the bar, waiting to follow Lawson, I find I'm buzzing. Wishing London was here for this next part. No one can break a mind the way she can. I know, because I've seen her process. Studied her technique on the tapes. Looking for ways to combine our methods.

Larry was just a small taste of what we're capable of together.

I spot Lawson and the prostitute leaving the bar, and I wait a few beats before picking up my stashed duffle bag and falling into step behind them. They're walking arm-in-arm, laughing. Lawson's inebriated state mollifies his fears.

I know how to bring them roaring back.

Unlike London, I was able to release my former life with the ease of letting go of a helium balloon. It floated up, up, gone. Blotted out by the sun. I severed all connections to the boy born in Hells Kells.

Maybe London has found a thread in the life that was stolen from her—some string to tether her. She loves her string. Her dead sister, perhaps. Or wealthy, respectable parents she can now be proud of, unlike the man she murdered to escape his deviant legacy.

Well, if my lovely lilac is falling victim to her poisonous delusions again, there's really only one answer: pluck off the offending petals.

Time to remind Dr. London Noble of who she is.

8

DISSOCIATION

LONDON

Two months ago, I watched officials dig up the bodies.

Nine decomposed young women were exhumed from the lifeless garden and surrounding corn field behind my house.

I watched the machinery roll in, the metal claw tear into the earth. My backyard became mounds of dry dirt; the land having died long ago. I remember coughing, choking on the dusty air. There was some part of me that felt shame, wondering if I was breathing in particles of dead girls.

Then I led Agent Nelson and the forensics crew into the basement, where I secretly discovered a plucked clover. And the shame evaporated.

I knew that Grayson had been there to remove any incriminating evidence of me from the basement. What little they might discover would only corroborate my story. My father's blood still stained the concrete. The story that cellar told matched my own.

I realized that's why Grayson wanted the details of my crime. Having me go over and over what transpired back then. I presumed it was for his own gratification—but he also needed to know what to remove from the scene so I wouldn't be implicated.

Grayson and I…we were apart, but we were working in tandem. Our moves choreographed and calculated, the rest of the world unable to follow our lead. We were above them. We were apart, but it was the closest I ever felt to another person.

I stare at the house. Rotten and decaying. The windows shuttered with planks nailed to chipped siding. I cross my arms, deciding my childhood home looks far more abandoned than when I was last here. Then, the yard was crawling with forensic techs and law enforcement. Federal agents infested the tiny farmhouse like the termites I see fluttering around the exterior.

Yellow crime scene tape marks off the front yard, stretching the perimeter. In the back, empty graves scatter the field. No one will fill them in.

Lydia Prescott doesn't belong here. Not the way London Noble does.

I fought the connection so hard, for so long, but the blood soaking this earth stains my bones. Swims in my marrow. It's a part of me just as much as Grayson.

We're connected.

I feel Agent Nelson's presence before he's close enough to speak.

"You always know where to find me," I say, keeping my gaze on the house.

"There's no reason to stay here," he says, expertly dodging my accusation. "The state isn't releasing Mia. Not yet."

I wrap my arms tighter around my midsection. The tall pines cast a dark, looming shadow across the house, their branches stretching across the sky like spindly spider legs. Just like when I was a child.

"What are you looking for, London?"

Nelson still refers to me by that name. It's similar enough, isn't it? Lydia/London. I can see how Malcolm might've chosen it. He always told me that my mother named me after her favorite soap opera before she died.

For the first time, I wonder who's buried in the unmarked grave in the Mize cemetery that I used to visit.

I never had a mother.

"Nothing," I finally respond as I turn away from the house. I meet Nelson's squinted gaze. "Let's go."

We make a slow progression toward our vehicles. His standard FBI-issued SUV, and my rental sedan. What was I looking for? An answer? A clue? Another piece of the puzzle?

Grayson won't return here.

He's a master puzzler, and he's already figured out every secret kept at this place. There's nothing more to tell, or uncover.

"I had blond hair as a kid," I say suddenly.

The agent sends me a guarded look. "I think everyone does. Don't they?"

I think back on my dyed-blond hair. Platinum blond. I had believed that I wanted it—that I begged my father for it. But like most of my memories, this one is skewed. "Yes, but mine was very blond. He dyed my hair up until I was twelve. I guess by that point, he figured no one would recognize me."

Thirteen is the age of accountability. I don't recall Malcolm ever having been religious, but this has also become an abstract belief by society in general. Simply meaning a person becomes of age to grasp right and wrong.

Like the tree of knowledge that bore the forbidden fruit, the man who raised me was preparing to offer me an awareness that would transform me from a child into a woman in his eyes. He'd grown too attached to the little girl with blond hair. It wasn't an emotional attachment; Malcolm wasn't capable of forming a parental bond. It was an association of familiarity. A psychopath can learn this behavior in order to employ it.

Especially on their victims.

Lydia is forming this familiarity—this bond—with a sister she never knew. Lydia could love Mia. Lydia would've been capable of the deepest love.

She doesn't belong here.

Nelson walks me to the rental and braces his hand on the roof over the driver-side door. "It's not your fault."

I look up at him. Moving into his shadow to block the setting sun, I lean against the car door. "Why do you assume I think it is?"

"I've worked more cases than I know how to count, London. And almost always, in this type of circumstance, the victim believes they should've known. They go over the details of their past, trying to understand how they could've been so blind, when the horrid truth is suddenly so clear."

I shake my head. "That's not what I'm doing." Not entirely. On some level, I knew—I had to have known. What I'm trying to understand is why I waited so long to do anything about it.

Could I have saved Lydia before it was too late?

Nelson brushes my hair over my shoulder. He uses this move often. Then he usually leaves, but not today. Maybe it's being isolated so far away from civilization, or the fact that we're so near the place of my turmoil, but he grasps my neck. Runs his thumb across my bottom lip, his gaze following the slow perusal over my mouth.

Then he leans in.

"Agent," I say, my tone severe as I call him by title to trigger his professionalism.

I turn my head just as he makes an attempt to kiss me, and I glimpse the flash of hurt on his face before I'm again staring at the house.

He exhales audibly as he releases me and steps away. "That was inappropriate." He acknowledges his action, but doesn't apologize for it.

"Yes, it was," I agree. This charade can only go so far.

I'm supposed to be gathering information from him, using his resources to discover the identity of the copycat killer. Instead, I've gotten derailed, lost. Wrapped up in my own side story and pain.

If Nelson proves to be of no use for my objective, then it's time to foster a new connection with someone more valuable.

His eyes nail me with an incensed glare. Nelson—like most men—doesn't take rejection well. Within seconds, hurt morphs into anger. I've wounded him.

"I should go," I say, but he doesn't move. He continues to barricade me from the car.

"So I've been imagining it," he says. He works open his suit button, mounting his hands on his hips. "I'm perceptive, being it's part of my job. And I've perceived your interest, London. Or is that just your way of diverting me?"

When his adrenaline drops, and he's had time to reflect, he'll feel remorse for his actions—or at least he should. That remorse will transform into guilt, and guilt will further cloud his observations of me. Saying or doing anything in this moment to further provoke him will only make him feel justified later.

I say nothing and dig out my keys from my pocket. I try to move around him. His hands form steely bands around my biceps, holding me in place.

Alarm flares within me. "Let me go."

After a brief standoff, he removes his hands. He turns around and pushes a hand into his hair. "I'm sorry. I thought... I don't know."

I loosen my grip on the keys. I had fisted the key ring, three keys braced between the slats of my fingers to form a weapon. If Nelson noticed, he doesn't let on. I insert the one for the car and open the door. "This has been a strenuous case," I say. "With the recent murders in Maine, I can't imagine the pressure you're under. I apologize if I've misled you in any way."

His light chuckle forces my spine straight.

"Don't shrink me." He refastens his suit jacket. "I'm a man, too. Not just a federal agent."

I get inside the car, safely removing myself from his proximity. "Your fixation with me is a direct result of your obsession to catch Grayson."

I start to pull the door shut, but he catches it before it latches. "What did you say?"

My pulse thunders in my ears. "Your perceived feelings for me are a correlation of—"

"You called him Grayson."

I did, and there's no backpedalling. I stare into Agent Nelson's sharp gaze and wonder whom has been deceiving whom. Was his advance a moment ago true desire, or a rehearsed method to lower my defenses? Either way, the damage is done.

"He was my patient," I clarify. "And I was shaken…just now." The explanation is weak, resorting to demure, skittish female versus oppressive male. But it seems to work.

Nelson's expression softens. "I'm sorry," he says again, then sighs heavily. "You're right. It's the case. And that fucking Foster." He frowns. "Sorry."

"No need," I say, allowing him to use the excuse I provided to restore his ego.

"He's constantly getting in the way. I think it was Foster who leaked the DNA evidence to the press." He scrubs a hand down his face. "From your observations, do you consider him unhinged? Your assessment could help secure a restraining order to get Foster off my crime scenes."

Truthfully, in this moment, I find both men to be bordering obsession and possibly unhinged in their pursuit of Grayson. But I say, "It's difficult to evaluate someone properly with only sporadic encounters, agent."

He nods, but he's not finished. "And Sullivan is escalating. The murders have been spaced out until now, similar in nature. If he's devolving so close…" He trails off, then looks at me. "He's too close to you."

"I thought you said I wasn't in danger."

He measures his response. "Let me take you back."

This is the first time he's spoken to me extensively about the killings in Rockland. The agent could be concerned for me, worried that Grayson will make an attempt to see me…or worse. Or he's getting anxious. Knowing I'm his only real link to Grayson and not wanting me out of his sight for precisely that reason.

I grip the steering wheel with one hand, my other clamped around the door handle. "My plane leaves in less than an hour. I think it's best for our professional relationship if I get on that plane."

His gaze goes to the spot where he glimpsed the bruise on my neck before. "Has Sullivan tried to make contact with you?"

My features purse in bewilderment. "If he had, you'd have been the first to know."

He studies me for a moment and then nods. "I'll make sure your detail is at the airport for your arrival."

"Thank you, Agent Nelson."

He shuts the car door, watches me drive away. I glance in the rearview mirror to see him standing with his arms crossed, a formidable silhouette against the grim backdrop of my past.

I could've lied to him. I could've spouted my typical excuse, using my patients as the reason I need to get back to my practice quickly. I probably should have, allowing his ego to mend further.

But it's time Agent Nelson and I stop all pretense.

He never asked me directly about the rape examination after I was taken to the hospital. The results were put in my file, and I'm sure he read those results.

The test was inconclusive. Proving that I'd neither been coerced by Grayson during my abduction, nor that I hadn't.

At the time, I thought the agent simply deduced that, based on Grayson's MO, a violation against a victim like that was extremely outside his methods. It was highly unlikely, and so the exam therefor gave credence to my statement where I affirmed my abductor had not sexually violated me.

But then, there are times like now, where I wonder if Nelson questions the results—wondering if my slip of the tongue in saying Grayson's name with such familiarity reveals a shared intimacy with my patient. Not coerced in the least.

I turn onto the airport exit off the highway.

The truth is, I'm a doctor. That exam was botched right from the start. It's not difficult to do if you know how. Unfortunately, Agent Nelson is intelligent enough to come to this conclusion.

9

DEVOLVING

GRAYSON

"He's all yours." Charity slips her arms inside her leather jacket and starts toward the motel room door.

I've been waiting inside the room for five minutes while Charity—which I'm sure isn't her real name—got dressed in the bathroom. Lawson is asleep on the bed, his wrists bound together behind his back.

Most motels stopped using open-frame headboards a while back. Less risk that you'll walk in to find a person tied or cuffed to the bed. I'll have to improvise.

"He drank it all?" I ask before she opens the door.

"Yeah. He did," she says. "Room's in his name. Good luck, sugar." She leaves, and I lock and chain the door behind her.

I push back my hoodie. Draw the second row of curtains over the window. I lay my burner cell on the table, glancing at the time. Lawson got in a good half hour before he passed out.

Opening the small duffle bag, I dig out Duct tape, zip ties, and the rest of my supplies. I slip on a pair of gloves before pulling a black ski mask over his face, the eye and mouth slats open to the back of his head.

He starts to rouse as I cut away the necktie Charity used to bind his wrists. I roll him over and zip tie his wrists together, then make quick work of the rest.

"What's going on?" Lawson asks, groggy.

He's not drugged. Still just bleary from a night of drinking. The beer I paid Charity to give him contained a very important component for this next act. And by the tent he's sporting in the sheets, she kept her word.

"Be still," I tell him. "Your wrists are tied for your own protection. If you move, try to escape, the cable tie around your dick will cinch tight. The more you move or struggle, the tighter it will get." I back up a few paces. "You get the idea."

It's in our nature to rebel. Lawson panics, tries to free his wrists, and cries out when the plastic tie around his dick does just as I said it would.

"You can slip out in a few hours," I say. "When the Viagra wears off." I toss the beer bottle in the trash. "Until then, I need some answers."

He begins to shout, and I press the tip of the blade to his throat. "There's another way this can end even quicker." I insert the tip just enough to draw blood so he knows I'm serious.

"What kind of sick fuck...?" Lawson is still panicking, but he's at least stopped testing the restraints. Progress.

I wait for him to calm down. Then I take a seat across from the bed.

"What do you want from me?" he asks.

That's the right question. It's not my finest trap, but

sometimes simple and concise is what's needed. A modest trap that fits the crime. I'm sure his wife sitting at home with their newborn would agree.

What Lawson can't know is who I am. The information I need can give that away. Even an oblivious crime-scene tech can put it together. I could just kill him once I'm done, but that would leave a body. Another messy murder to handle.

Besides, I try to save the real fun for bigger fish.

"A friend of mine has gone missing," I start. "The police aren't giving up any information on the most recent murder. I need to know if the victim is my friend." I pause here. "He owes me money."

Lawson breathes heavily through the mask. "That's it?"

"It's a lot of money," I add.

"The vic's name is Christian Zinkowski. Now let me go."

"That's unfortunate," I say, standing. "That just happens to be my friend." I hover near the foot of the bed. "I need to know who killed him."

He hesitates before he says, "I don't have that info."

"I think you do." I kick the bed, making the box spring bounce. Lawson curses as the movement causes him to flinch.

"You're going to tell me everything you know about Christian Zinkowski and the crime scene. I know you are, because despite your actions tonight, you don't want your family to be hurt. Charity likes to keep a photo gallery of her johns. Her memory's not that good. She likes having a log of names and fetishes. What they like. What they don't." I get close to his ear. "And sometimes, when a john fucks up real bad, she likes to send copies to his family. To his work. Technology is a crazy thing—how so many people can be reached with the click of a button. Like setting off a bomb; lives explode on detonation."

Michael Lawson tells me everything he knows.

I record the conversation on my phone, and when he's done, I pack up my supplies, leaving him bound on the bed with his face covered.

"You're just leaving me here like this?" he asks, panic lacing his voice.

I pause at the door, wondering again if I should simply kill him. I don't like leaving loose ends. It's sloppy. I glance at the bed, where he's still in the same position. Back propped against the headboard. Wrists tied to his dick.

On the other hand, who the fuck is he going to tell?

"You can scream for help now," I say, cracking the door open. "Or you can wait a few hours for your limp dick to slip out of the zip tie. Your choice."

I wait in the open doorway to see what he'll decide. His decision is more important than he knows. One shout will end his life.

He doesn't stir or say a word. Maybe he is smarter than the average tech.

"Think about Grandma and baseball," I say, then close the door.

I hover outside the room for a moment longer, just to make sure. At Lawson's silence, I take off through the parking lot.

Maybe I'm going soft. Before London, I wouldn't have left Lawson alive.

I understand what love is; the emotion, the feeling. Chemicals in the brain—the same chemicals that make up personalities and disorders. At a certain age, it's nearly impossible to change who we are and how we behave.

But if something significant occurs—chemical-altering emotions felt for the first time—would that impact the chemistry of the brain? Would that change the person, the disorder?

People wake from comas. People who have never been violent suddenly commit murder. And psychopaths feel love for the first time.

What the fuck is the world coming to.

I suppose these are questions for a psychologist.

I just happen to know one. Intimately.

DEPENDENCE

LONDON

The hum of the fish tank fills my office. The lack of noise from the waiting room makes the typically undetected sound loud in the too-quiet room. I recline in my chair, close my eyes, letting the drone soothe my mind. The patients are gone. The day through.

After an intense afternoon, I've successfully escaped the officer detail Agent Nelson sent to receive me at the airport. The two FBI agents he has escort me on occasion. The ones I know are always watching. They have gone from trying to be politely inconspicuous, to downright unavoidable. Hovering in the building lobby, near the reception desk. One even tried to camp out inside my office today.

Thankfully, the agents were called to Rockland for a more urgent matter than protecting me. Apparently, the FBI's budget doesn't allow for babysitting. They're also too economical to spring for plane tickets, leaving Agent Nelson on a slow commute back to Maine. Which could be my only chance to make contact with Grayson.

Maybe that was Agent Nelson's intention. After what transpired between us in Hollows, I have little faith that he harbors any trust for me. So there's a chance that his patsy agents are still skulking around, watching.

I could go now. Right now. Don my disguise to the Blue Clover. Hope that Grayson senses my need…

Or I could be patient. Trust that Grayson and I are still working in tandem.

But are we?

Ever since I learned of Lydia, a sort of disconnect has descended over me like a gauzy veil, a feeling of detachment from Grayson that's frightening. The more I wonder about the girl—the *woman*—who could've been, the more I allow myself to see and experience through her.

I'm fascinated, and I'm terrified.

I tighten the string around my index finger to the point of pain. It relieves some of the pressure wrapping my head as I swivel my chair back and forth, gaze cast out the window overlooking downtown.

Before I can proceed with my plan, I need reassurance. That's reasonable. I'm not some lovesick teen fretting over her boyfriend's lack of communication; I'm suffering the pangs of withdrawal. Like any drug, lust-sex-love pumps endorphins into the brain. And when depleted of those endorphins, the cravings can be as strong as the yearning for a hit of heroin.

I'm addicted to Grayson, and the way he makes me feel.

And yet I fear him just as powerfully.

It's unhealthy, but there's no such thing as a "healthy relationship". Any interaction with another person that alters chemicals in the brain is going to be risky. Our behavior changes when in a romantic relationship. That's just the science of it.

Love—that all-consuming love artists pen sonnets about —is a short-lived emotion.

That kind of love can't be sustained. It's wild and passionate and consumes you like a wildfire tears through a forest, burning hotter and raging rampant until its only option is to die out. That's what Grayson and I are: a wildfire. We'll burn through each other until our resources are expired.

That kind of love also makes you blind.

Before Grayson, *trust* was a figurative idea. Only obtained if one was blinded by their emotions. You can't question what you can't see—what you don't know exists.

I pocket the string and spin my chair around to my desk, decision made. I pick up the office phone to return the call from the message Lacy gave me hours ago.

Trust.

That's what comes next, Grayson said. I move, he moves. We're a shadow of each other, fused to one another through pain and pleasure and a hedonistic illness that rivals even the greatest serial killer teams.

We're a duet—we belong together. One cannot exist without the other.

I can accept this, but I want to accept it with my eyes wide open.

The operator on the line transfers me to the forensics' department, and before I can hang up, second-guessing myself, Calvin's sure voice booms across the line.

"Hello, London. You send me the most interesting things, you know that?"

I do. Like pig's blood when I'm doused with it after a trial. Calvin is my trusted contact in the local forensics' lab. He works for money under the table. They barely pay him enough to make rent.

"Someone has to keep you busy," I say, opening my desk

drawer. I pull out the vial I keep locked up. "This city is pretty boring, otherwise."

"Well, you're making sure to see to that, aren't you?"

After a moment of trivial conversation, Calvin jumps in. "Genealogy isn't my specialty, but I was able to scratch up a healthy report for you on the sample you sent over last week. Are you in front of your computer?"

I flip open my laptop. "Is it safe to send?"

"From the everyday hacker, yes. If that's what you're wary about. From the FBI? Probably not."

A second of hesitation, then: "Send it."

My apartment is under surveillance. The only safe and secure place for me to keep my research on Grayson is my practice. These walls are protected under patient-doctor confidentiality. In turn, the FBI may be able to trace and access my data, but they can't use it. Not against me, or Grayson.

I hold up the vial. A few dark-brown hairs line the glass. I close my eyes and flash back to the moment Grayson thrust inside me and I gripped his hair, coming away with the strands.

I wrapped them around my finger—woven along my string—for safekeeping.

Pushing the memory away, I click open the report. "What am I looking at?"

Calvin goes over the basics: blood type, heritage, immediate family. Then he says, "But I figured you were looking for something a little more interesting. Considering the heritage, I ran the DNA through the international database and got a hit. A relative with a pretty lengthy record citing crimes against children came up."

I locate the name on the report. "Shane Sullivan." As I read, my stomach knots.

"Apparently, he was wanted in connection to a child sex trafficking ring. But when authorities finally caught up to him, he and his wife were found dead. Brutally murdered. Cut up into pieces. Pretty gruesome, huh?"

The police report attached to the document states their deaths were unnatural. A crude pendulum contraption was used to "dice" their bodies. Reading over the description, I realize it might've been more than an instrument to kill and mutilate; it's possible it was designed to get answers. To work out a puzzle...and their failure resulted in their dismemberment.

A handmade puzzle constructed from woodchips was found at the scene in one of the large greenhouses. Images and words scrawled on the jigsaw pieces garnered no resolution for authorities to the murderer. The duo having many unsavory connections, the local police concluded it was a trade gone wrong. The case was closed with no further investigation.

What were you trying to puzzle out, Grayson?

"Thank you, Calvin. This is good information. Oh, one more thing. Does it say how his mother died? I don't see a death cert in the docs."

"That's because there isn't one," he says. "She's still alive."

A cold dread whispers over my skin. "Okay. Thank you," I manage, then hang up the receiver.

Before I lose my nerve, I cross my office and unlock the filing cabinet where I keep confidential patient folders not stored on my computer. I pull out Grayson's file and bring it to the desk.

Having a computer do the search would be easier, but not wise. Technically, the transcribed sessions in the folder are off the record. I had shut the camera off—but I left the audio recording. I'm unethical. I've established that. I scroll down the dates, seeking one session in particular.

My mother liked to watch. But we're not talking about that. You're not ready.

A statement Grayson made when I questioned him about his mother. But which mother was he referencing? His birth mother, or the woman who held him prisoner?

As I read through the report, making comparisons to Grayson's sessions, I come away with a terrible conclusion. All the children were sold to the couple by relatives.

Grayson was not kidnapped by his abductors. Someone sold him to them.

The only likely suspect would be his own mother.

A sinking feeling pulls at my stomach.

He murdered his blood relatives to escape a hell that no child should suffer. And yet, he didn't return to his mother once he was free. He fled Ireland, leaving her alive. She didn't undergo his vengeance.

Why?

I print out the report, highlighting and sectioning off the areas of interest for further research, and then tack the new material to my private corkboard embedded beneath my Dali painting. Grayson studied me for nearly a year before our official introduction. It's only fair that I gather insight into his past, as well.

There's a reason why he refuses to give me answers.

I want it.

For more than just my own curiosity. It's keeping the status quo.

Grayson set me free, and liberated me of my past at the same time. I'm unsure if he believes I'm able to do the same for him…or whether or not he's decided I already have.

His compulsions haven't changed. How he channels

them has changed. His disorder has progressed into one of a team dynamic, and that takes trust. Something that was stripped away from him at an early age. By the person who he should've been able to trust the most in his world.

His own mother sold him into hell.

I replace the painting along the wall, then unlock the bottom drawer of my filing cabinet. Tapes of my patient sessions are organized by name, year/date, and diagnosis.

When I first arrived home after the excavation of my father's victims, my office was my immediate destination. To this drawer. To where the videos of my deceased patients awaited confirmation of my malpractice.

I plugged in the video of my last session with Thom Mercer and waited, breath bated, for what I knew was about to unfold. The alternate memories I created had been eradicated while I was caged in Grayson's cell. But that wasn't enough. I had to see it with my own eyes. Hear it with my ears. Experience the sessions—this time—with no hindrance of a deluded state.

Some kind of morbid awakening, I suppose.

Only the evidence—the only tangible proof of my misconduct—had been erased.

The tapes were blank.

At the time, I reasoned I did so myself, a form of counter forensics—a measure taken to protect myself. I still had holes in my memory. Gaps. Not everything recovered. It made sense that I would hide the evidence of my crime even from myself.

I check the tapes once a week. Just to be sure. It's a frightening thing not to trust your own mind.

Static flickers over the TV screen.

I eject the tape and return it to the filing cabinet, the

pressure at my temples easing, but only marginally. There's still a record in existence.

Trust.

Grayson has a recording of my confession. It's captured under duress, and it's unlikely authorities would consider it authentic. It could've been enhanced, manipulated. My lawyer could work up a strong defense. And yet, just the existence of that confession disturbs me.

Every serial killer partnership suffered one common flaw: complacency. One or both became too secure in the relationship. This security wasn't established with trust; it was established through power.

One dominated the other. Their trust exploited.

It always comes down to power and control.

Grayson having something over me places him in a position of power—and I'm not reluctant to admit I'm struggling with the trust part of our relationship.

Lydia would never belong in a relationship such as this.

I press my palms to the cool surface of my desk, letting the temperature bleed from my body. My hand imprints mark the wood when I move away. It's been an exhausting week.

I lock up my desk, making sure everything is secure, before I start out.

A sound startles me as I near the door, and I stop. My breathing sounds too loud in the enclosed space. Then the door opens.

11

WHERE I WANT YOU

GRAYSON

The expression on her face is worth the risk. I step into London's office and quietly shut the door behind me. The muted *click* echoes around us, sealing us inside. "Hi, doc."

Her fists unclench. "Jesus, Grayson. What are you doing here? Are you—?"

"Crazy?" I supply.

She drops her purse on the desk. "I'm being watched. Your actions are reckless. If you were my patient—"

"I still am—"

"—I would suggest you were devolving. Becoming unbalanced. And yes, maybe a touch crazy." She bites her bottom lip. "And you are not my patient."

"What am I, then?" I cross the room, coming up close enough to smell her lilac body lotion. The lavender notes in her hair.

She visibly shivers as she looks up at me. "Dangerous."

Her hair is down, falling in a loose tumble over her

shoulders. The way I love it; like she knew I was coming. I push the strands behind her ear, leaning in to whisper, "And you're a paradox."

A current snaps between us, and she physically reacts to my nearness, my touch. The air is electrified. I feel the hitch in her breath as it pulses across my skin. Slowly, I remove her glasses and lay them on the desk, revealing her eyes.

"Besides," I say as I step back, taking her hand in mine. "By all accounts, this is the safest place to be." I lead her to the adjoining hall, and she allows me. I swipe a finger along the fish tank, giving her a wink. "Good memories."

Before she can react, I push her up against the glass, grip her waist. The rooms are dark, but she's lit by the glow of the tank. I draw close to her mouth, watching the way her face twists as if she's in pain. That same fiery ache scorches my body. Just the threat of touching her skin burns.

The best kind of anticipation.

"A paradox isn't exactly a compliment," she says, her voice a low rasp.

Mouth hovering near hers, I find her gaze. "It is if one enjoys puzzles." I brush my lips across hers, the softest tease. "You're my favorite puzzle, London."

Her hands seek my arms, nails digging into the material of my shirt. As if she's just as desperate for the fire to singe her. "This isn't a game."

I slide my hands up her slim waist, grazing the sides of her breasts, until I reach her neck, where I fasten my fingers to her nape and tip her head back, thumbs imprinting her jawline. She's such a perfect fit.

"Sometimes I forget you like your patients easy to control," I say. "I suppose that goes for your men, too."

Heat flushes her face. "Thrill-seeking behavior isn't like you. It will get you caught." Her eyes flare. "Again."

My mouth curls into a smile. "How do you know that I didn't get caught on purpose last time?"

Her gaze flicks over my face as she tries to decipher the truth. "Did you?"

I shake my head slowly. "I've been off the clock for a long time, doc."

"Grayson—" She attempts to push me away, but it's halfhearted. "The FBI can show up here at any time. *I'm* not safe."

I stare down at her strained features. She's serious. She's afraid for me. With a tender touch, I caress her cheek. "Then let's give them a show."

Defiance sparks in her eyes. Dr. London doesn't back down from a dare.

"I see you," I whisper against her lips. "I could feel your pain from fucking miles away. I know what you need." I capture her mouth, crushing our lips together. I drown out the world and its threats—the fear, the pain—with one kiss.

She's the only thing that makes the compulsions quiet. A still reed in my storm.

London kisses me back with a hard demand that bruises my mouth. Pleasure courses my system, and I crave more. There's no give; only take. We're feeding off each other.

I bracket her wrists to the glass, stealing her control. She hates and loves the loss of her willpower. The same way she hates to love me—but I'm her own sick compulsion, the need driving her actions in spite of her judgment.

She bites into the kiss and draws blood. The action stirs my desire, pouring liquid fire into my veins. Pain and pleasure receptors fight for dominance. Seeking air, she turns away to break the kiss.

"Stop," she says with a pant. "You have to go."

Anger ignites in a flash, searing as hot as my want for her. "Is this London talking or Lydia?"

Her heated gaze matches my fire, but her body planks, hard as ice. She wrenches her wrists free and shoves me aside. Agony is the loss of her touch.

She enters the dark therapy room, crosses her arms over her chest. "Where did you acquire the uniform?"

Ironic. The good doctor using avoidance.

I lean against the wall at the end of the gallery, tracking her movements as she switches on a lamp. "The guards leave them in their lockers overnight," I say, and begin to unbutton the shirt. "Figured no one would question a security officer roaming the building." I tug off the uniform shirt and toss it on the slender writing desk, then I untuck the white T-shirt from my slacks. "But that's not what you're asking."

She faces me, features cast in stern assessment. "Considering the last time you stole a uniform? No, it's not. I want to know if anyone in my building was harmed."

"Are you truly concerned? Or are you worried about an investigation that could connect you?"

She inhales a deep breath. "You know that would be unwise."

She's right, of course. My behavior is borderline Neanderthal. I could whip my dick out and start marking my territory and it wouldn't shock her. She's assessing me right now, anticipating my next move.

I start toward her. "I didn't harm anyone." That's not a lie. Lawson is still alive and intact.

She nods. "You have to find a way to alert me. Let me know…" She trails off with a huff of frustration. "It's not fair that you know where I am at any given moment, and I have no idea where you are."

I stop short of reaching her. There it is, the root of her

anger. It brings a crooked smile to my face. "Being on the run gets tedious. Makes for a dull romance." I push the patient chair aside and kick the rug away, revealing the floor manacle. "Do you want me to take a seat? So you can dig around in my mind. Get your doctor rocks off."

She's not amused. "I just want a head's up, Grayson. I don't like surprises."

I crane an eyebrow. "Like our agent friend gives you? He's so well behaved, isn't he?"

I can almost feel her hackles raise. "You're being hostile," she accuses.

"I'm bored, London. There's a difference." I sit in the chair. "I bet you have some extra chains and cuffs around here."

She moves closer. "You trust me that much? To shackle you…to take away your ability to escape?"

"I trust your reasoning to do so, if it came to that."

The room grows quiet with the heavy pause. London runs her palms down her skirt, working out imaginary creases. "You'd pick the lock, regardless," she says. "Where did you learn that talent, anyway?"

I gift her a smile, avoiding her question just the same. "You felt more in control when I was locked up. Maybe that's the spark that's missing. Don't you feel it lately? Like something is amiss?"

"Are you jealous of Agent Nelson?" she asks outright, shifting the topic. No dancing around a matter when her professional mask is in place.

"He's a man obsessed," I say. "I can't be jealous. I empathize… No, that's wrong. I *pity* him."

Nothing compares to the ecstasy I feel with London. If I'm being honest, this is a poor attempt to fill the well. Once you ascend so high, the plummet afterward leaves a gaping hole, the addiction that much harder to feed.

I understand Nelson's urges all too well. The driving need to see her…hear her voice…plot the moment they'll meet. I really do pity him.

The seething look London sends me ignites my skin.

"His mind is probably a chew toy by now." I rub my palms along the leather arms of the chair, enjoying the freedom I never experienced here before.

"I wouldn't know," she says, drawing my attention up to her. "I'm not evaluating him."

My brows crease. "You're such a fucking paradox."

"I'm not playing mind games with you, Grayson."

"And yet, you're dying to know."

A battle of wills arcs between us. She yields first. "All right. Tell me why, then."

"Because of your desire to embrace Lydia." I can be pointblank, too. "To be this better version that you believe was stolen away. Don't deny it. You forget that I know you."

Her walls erect. She's shielding Lydia from London's world, which means hiding this part of herself from me.

Dangerous.

Her word. I pose a threat to this fragile part of her that she desperately wants to protect. The way she couldn't protect her or her sister. Psychology is a nasty little twist.

"I'm not embracing anything," she finally says. "Lydia Prescott would not be here right now. She wouldn't be with you. Clearly, I am."

I study her closely. How much of a threat does Lydia pose to us? "I think I could seduce Lydia," I say.

"How very cocky of you." London shakes her head. "Is that a challenge?"

"You know how much I enjoy a challenge."

She searches her suit pocket for her string. "I won't let you turn this into a sordid game," she says, wrapping the black thread around her finger.

"It's not a game to me." I sit forward. "Who else are you going to confide in?"

Something sparks in her eyes as she looks at me. "You want to...what? Analyze me? Work through my *feelings*?"

I nod to the chair across from me. Her chair.

She releases a lengthy breath. "You're intelligent, Grayson. You've probably memorized every disorder in the book, but you're hardly qualified."

"And you don't trust me," I clarify for her. "Not with your mind."

She shrugs. "One could argue it's not so much distrust in you, rather than the fact that I manipulated my own patients, resulting in my distrust of everyone."

"That's a start." I nod again to her chair.

"We don't have time for this." She rubs at her forehead.

"If it's affecting you, we make time."

Seconds pass where she considers her options, then she brings the chair up to the yellow line. I'm not shackled, nor am I a physical danger to her. She's mentally distancing herself from me in her safe zone.

"Tell me about Lydia." It's the easiest place to start.

Her gaze settles on me. "Lydia would never betray her patients."

I smile slightly, urging her on.

"Lydia would never forget her parents. She would never lie to the authorities, or aid and abet a criminal. Especially a killer." A beat. "Lydia would never be aroused right now."

Her words bridge the expanse between us and grip me. I dig my fingers into the armrest, maintaining control. London is the master when it comes to psychological

121

warfare. She knows how to distract me, but I'm not her doctor.

I'm her conduit.

"What *would* Lydia do?" I prompt.

She huffs a derisive breath. "That, I don't know."

"When thoughts of Lydia arise, how do you feel?"

"Distanced. Outside myself. I believe I'm experiencing a mild form of depersonalization induced by high-anxiety." She clings to the thread in her hand. "Some form of disassociation."

"How do you deal with anxiety?"

Her breath stutters. "I immerse myself in work. In my patients."

"A distraction?"

She shakes her head. "No…a form of therapy. A way to retain control." Her string is wound so tightly around her finger the tip turns white.

I scrutinize her, letting my gaze travel leisurely over her demurely crossed ankles, her legs, body. She's tense; able to feel my perusal like an invasive touch. "Who feels more out of control?" I ask. "Lydia or London?"

Her eyes meet mine. "Right now, Lydia. She wouldn't open herself up like this."

"Not to me," I complete her thought. I sit back, run my hand over my forearm, drawing her attention to the ink and scars. I even allow my accent to bleed through. "How do I make Lydia feel?"

"Grayson…" She touches her forehead again to create a barrier. "I know what you're trying to do."

"Answer."

Her gaze locks on to mine. "If I never became the person I became, then I'd feel intimidated. Scared. Anxious. But more than anything…curious."

A smile slants my mouth. "I do make good girls curious. It's the lure. That indefinable characteristic we both have. What attracts prey to predator."

Her breathing intensifies. "Lydia would only be prey to you."

"You're not giving her enough credit. She's stronger than you think. Spread your legs."

Caught off guard, she directs a lethal glare my way. "That's unethical."

I slide my chair forward and, sitting back down, kick her ankles apart. "Wide."

Her chest rises and falls quickly, her breathing labored. With more reserve than I feel, London casually inches her skirt up and parts her knees.

"Wider," I say, voice thick.

She spreads her thighs until her knees nearly touch the armrests.

I lick my lips as I take in every inch of her exposed skin, feeling no shame. "I want to talk to Lydia only."

A tense tremor of lust crackles the air. Just her exposed position makes every word I say suggestive, erotic. Evoking the emotions London is trying to suppress.

"Recently," I say, "I conducted an important meeting with a man who's working the crime scenes in Rockland."

Her eyes widen. "Grayson, what—?"

"Listen," I cut her off. "I'm talking to Lydia right now. She would never interrupt me, would she?"

I like this *would never* game. It's useful.

The column of her throat drags upward in a hard swallow. "No manipulation," she says.

"I would never harm you." I admire London's intelligence too much to try to twist her in that way. "I just want to get to know Lydia. Understand this side of you. It's important to me."

She concedes with a nod.

"Take off your suit jacket."

This time, she complies without resistance. She removes her jacket and drapes it across the back of her chair.

"The second murder in Rockland has helped narrow the suspect pool," I say.

She blinks rapidly. "How did you select the victim?"

"I didn't. The copycat did."

She narrows her gaze, uncertain.

"You thought it was me," I say, reverent. Her guarded behavior makes sense now.

London lifts her chin. "I wasn't sure, to be honest. The time between murders seemed too quick. The method was easily enough mimicked, more simplistic—" she licks her lips "—but it was also more impulsive, personalized. I thought the copycat would need more time to be sure it was you before making a move."

I tilt my head. "If you thought it was me, then you must've been worried. Nervous that I'd give us away."

"Your compulsion to torture and take life will always dominate you," she says coldly.

"Regardless of us," I add.

"Regardless of anyone or anything, but yes."

I study her closer. Look for her tells. "And if I was devolving, what lengths would you go to in order to protect yourself? To protect Lydia?"

"That's an unfair question," she says. "Since you clearly kept me in the dark about the suspect that you'd already discovered beforehand, I have to assume you did so on purpose to test me."

I smile. "We're a team, London. You already passed my tests."

She closes her legs. "This is not a team dynamic. I don't know what this is but…it's not anything I can classify."

"There's no alpha," I say, agreeing with her assessment. "There always has to be a dominant in a duo."

"Precisely."

"But whose rule is that?"

She reflexively rubs at the inked key along her hand. "Doesn't matter. We've already proven that it's important. We'll unravel, otherwise. Trust doesn't come easily between two people who have suffered an early life trauma." She sucks in a breath. "Someone has to take charge."

Having a partner is a new experience for me, and for London. It's like dancing, figuring out who will lead.

"It should be you," I decide.

She looks up from toying with her string. "Why?"

"Because you're able to reside in public. You have a reputable career. You're above reproach. And, because I do trust you, London. As long as Lydia doesn't call the shots."

She considers this a moment, then: "A submissive partner typically employs manipulative tactics to sway and control the dominant. I suppose that describes us quite accurately." Her light laugh dances over my skin.

"Let's consider it foreplay," I say.

"Wait—" Her amused expression drops. "Who is the suspect? I need to know so I can get an understanding of their motive. A copycat isn't that different from a typical serial offender, but there are marked variances. They have a reason as to why they're motivated to kill. Is it an obsessed fan? No." She dismisses that right away. "Not all the details were revealed to the public. That means—"

"The copycat has inside knowledge." Had she not been

sidetracked with the Mize investigation, London would've figured this out sooner. Makes me wonder if the derailment was done to her on purpose.

After a moment of thought, she shakes her head. "No. That is a huge reach, Grayson. You're trying to take the game to a level that—besides risking you, me, everything—will end badly."

"This isn't a theory, London. It's a fact. Only two men fit the copycat profile. Which means either Detective Foster or Agent Nelson has been moonlighting as the Angel of Maine."

"That's ridiculous." She swipes her bangs from her forehead, dismissing the theory. "How do the Rockland crime scenes confirm this?"

"This person has done his own study on me, adopting my MO. He's good. Good enough to fool most, but as you know, method is ritual. Signature excites. The compulsion to experience the kill...the temptation to make it his own... Every man falls victim to pride. We're simple beasts." I shrug, indifferent. "It's where we fail."

"How did you collect this information?"

"I took a chance," I admit. "Which I may regret later, but we needed the intel." She raises an eyebrow, not impressed. "One of the CSU techs has a weakness for call girls."

She sighs heavily. "You left him alive."

"My affections for you apparently make me soft." I smile. "How would Lydia feel about this topic of conversation?"

She inches her legs open as she relaxes into the chair. "Intrigued."

Good. "I gathered enough to know that my suspicion on the signature is accurate. He mimics everything, like a perfect echo, except for one flaw: He indulges himself at the end. My kills are about technique, the design. He enjoys feeling the life he's taking leave the body. He can't help himself.

"Every trap he crafted allowed for contusions around the victims' necks. Easily disguised behind the design itself, but if you look closely, you understand why he rigged it this way. So he—not the trap—could kill them." Disgust roils through me. "It's an insult to my craft, really."

London slips her fingers over her thigh. This part always excited her—the details.

"That's why Larry's death had to be different; a shift in MO," I continue. "Allowing the killer to get closer to the victim, delivering a more personalized death. We had to test the theory."

Her hand stills. "We? I wasn't a part of your scheme. You kept me in the dark."

I push my hands along the armrests. "You were too close to both Foster and Nelson. Any indication that you were aware of either one of them could put you in danger."

"I don't buy that, Grayson. I think it comes back to trust. You're still operating solo. I have the perfect position to evaluate their behavior."

My reflexive instinct is to deny her allegation, but I stop myself. We're governed by our fears, and I've feared losing London since the moment I found her. Despite my intelligence level, I'm no different than the average man, fearing rejection, loss.

"You're right," I admit. Her eyebrows hike at my admission. "There was a giant, unknown variable around your past and how you'd respond to all the emerging details."

She touches her tattoo key again, thoughtful. "As you can see, it's been difficult."

Something akin to guilt slices through me. "I'm here now," I say. "You don't have to work through your dissociation alone." I plan to work Lydia right out of her system.

Her gaze narrows; always assessing. "I don't like the distance I've felt between us for the past two weeks. Even while you were in prison, even with the weeks of separation after you escaped, I didn't feel the disconnect the way I do now." She releases a breath. "Partly my doing, I admit. Outside pressures are causing us both strain."

"You're risking everything," I tell her.

Her eyes find and hold mine. "It's my choice."

I believe her. I bury the doubt. "I won't let it happen again."

And like that, London and I are in sync, an effortless team.

"Agreed." She gifts me a sultry smile. "So let's think about this logically and logistically. No matter who the copycat is, we're still ending it here."

"That's an inevitability. The chase and running becomes tiring. Neither side can go on forever. Better to end it on our terms."

She considers this a while, and adds, "We need both of them."

I nod. "They each have a distinct role."

"Detective Foster is a brute. He'd be capable, and he hardly exhibits enough patience in his own investigations. There's a lot of similarity."

My skin hums as she breaks it down. Her mind excites me. "I've been considering as much. But Agent Nelson suffered a setback at work over the past year. That's a...what is it called?"

"Stressor," she supplies.

"Stressor. His FBI career is his life. Something threatening that, like not closing enough cases, could send a perfectionist like him over the edge."

Her fingers halt their ascent along her leg, and the sudden

dimness covering her expression dampens my libido. "Nelson had another setback recently," she says. "I rejected his advances."

A slow curling fire licks the back of my neck. "Interesting," I say, my voice grinding out like gravel. The primal Neanderthal inside me rears up, London in danger of a brutal fucking where I stake my claim like the carnal animal she makes me.

"Do you think he suspects us?" she asks.

It's an intelligent estimate. If Nelson believes, like Foster, that London is in fact my accomplice, then pushing his way into my territory is the natural order for beasts like us.

"You're beautiful," I tell her. "Regardless of his motivations, I have no doubt that he wants you." And that realization sears what's left of my control.

As if she senses my waning restraint, London arches her back, slipping her hand higher and dragging her fitted skirt up her thighs.

"It would be even more interesting if there was a partnership at hand. Two unlikely allies, teaming up to hunt killers. Who in turn become killers themselves." *What are the odds?*

But something has shifted in her demeanor. This discussion is over. "How did you work the information from the tech?" Her voice is breathy.

"Who wants to know? London or Lydia?"

"Both."

Finding a way to unify the conflicting shores at war within her is key. I can't have any part of London as my enemy.

"I zip-tied his cock to his wrists and rigged it so if he moved, even a millimeter, the tie would cinch closed. I can only imagine how painful it was for him every time he struggled. How does that make Lydia feel?"

"Aroused."

I sink my teeth into my lip, fingers gripping the armrest.

"And you think he won't report this?" she asks.

"I think that he doesn't want anyone to know how he ended up in such a compromising—not to mention humiliating—situation. Especially his wife."

"Still, you took a risk."

I stand and, reaching behind my head, tug off my shirt. I walk forward to stand before her. She's trembling. Lust glazes her eyes.

I palm the arms of the chair and lean over her. "Everything I do, every single day, is a risk for you." Then I kneel, cupping the back of her knee. With a forceful tug, I bring her farther down, her ass positioned at the edge of the seat.

Her sharp inhale sends a thrill right to my cock as I plant a tender kiss to her inner thigh. I travel up her skin, tongue dragging across the rising gooseflesh, kissing and sucking with gentle touches.

"Is this a new form of torture?" she says, chest heaving against her blouse.

I smile against her leg, and reach up to start working the bottom button of her top. I guide my hand beneath her skirt, settling at the apex between her thighs, as I drop a heated kiss to her exposed belly.

"I can be romantic," I say, hooking a finger beneath the seat of her panties. She's hot, wet, drenching them. "I can make love to Lydia and fuck London at the same time." I haul the thin material down to her knees, causing her to quake with a hard shiver.

Her hands go to my hair, fingers, nails seeking purchase.

Then I'm undoing each button, reverently opening her up to me as I kiss a path toward her chest. Her light-pink satin bra is trimmed in black lace. That does something to me—the sight so innocent and sexy all at once.

A heavy groan tears free. I'm straining against the zipper of my pants. Every roll of her hips and arch of her back drives me wild; Lydia doesn't stand a chance. I sink both hands under her ass and prop her pelvis up, getting unfettered access as I bury my head between her thighs.

I suck her soft lips into my mouth, eliciting the sweetest moan as a tremor riots through her body.

Pulling back just enough, I say, "Whenever Lydia fights for control, think of me touching you. Just like this."

"God, if we start, we'll never stop. You have to let me go."

"Never. I got you right where I want you."

A ringtone sounds from the office. London's cellphone. She opens her eyes, the spell broken. "It's him."

12

DUET

LONDON

The ringing chime crashes into our sacred space, and I tense, reality seeping in through the cracks. I let the call go to voicemail, but the ringing starts again.

"Ignore it," Grayson says, and he's doing everything in his power to convince me to do just that. He licks the seam of my lips, fondles my clit, deepening the ache in my core.

"I can't. I know it's him." I don't have to say his name. The sudden rigidness coiling Grayson's shoulders denotes he knows that I'm referring to Agent Nelson. "If I don't answer, he'll send agents to my apartment and here, or he'll come himself."

With a grunt, Grayson releases me and moves back.

This is difficult for him. Grayson doesn't yield to intimidation, but he's intelligent; he knows when to rein in his defiant nature.

I stand and hurriedly situate my clothes before I pad to the office. My purse is on the desk where I left it. I dig out my phone. Nelson's contact flashes on the screen.

I brace myself. "Agent Nelson," I address him formally. No need for pretense at this point. We've moved past the games.

"London, how are you?" His voice sounds edgy, strained.

"Fine." I'm as tempered as bulletproof glass—unbreakable. Until I feel the current of Grayson's nearness from behind. "Has there been a development?"

"What? No. Nothing like that. I hadn't heard from you since you got back to Bangor." An expectant pause hangs between us, what he's leaving unsaid. "I wanted to make sure you're all right. I had to pull Silks and Mahoney from your detail due to low funding at the crime scenes in Rockland."

"That's all right. I understand. I really am okay. There's no need to waste agency resources on me." Grayson's chest presses against my back, his hands tentatively settle at my hips. His deliberate eavesdropping is distracting.

"You are not a waste of resources. I want you to know that I'm dedicated to your safety—that it doesn't come second to the agency, despite the politics." When I don't respond immediately, he adds, "Are you at home?"

"No," Grayson whispers in my ear as his hands rove to the backside clasp of my skirt.

"I'm not," I say, talking over the sound of Grayson lowering the zipper. The rough pads of his fingers trail in its cool wake, nearly stealing my voice. "I've stayed late at the office. I have a lot of things to catch up on."

When telling a convincing lie, make sure that it's partly the truth. I glance at the Dali painting and, while my skirt slithers down my legs, feel more than exposed. My research into Grayson's past preoccupies more than my daytime career.

Nelson assembles my statement into his own understanding. "You'll bring your sister home," he assures me. "You've sacrificed too much time fighting the system. Let it run its course."

I close my eyes against the onslaught of emotions and the feel of Grayson sweeping my hair over my shoulder. He lowers himself to press his lips to the nape of my neck as his hand snakes around to my belly, fingers dipping beneath the lace trim of my panties.

"Thank you," I manage. "I do appreciate all your help in this matter, Agent Nelson."

A lengthy beat, where I'm hyper-aware of Grayson's mouth, his heated skin, his touch, then: "About what happened in—"

"It was nothing," I say, startled back into the conversation.

"No, it was inappropriate. My ego was too bruised at the time to admit it, but…London, this isn't my MO. I want you to know that. This never happens, especially on the job." I hear his weighted sigh. "I'm sorry."

Grayson pushes closer, his mouth at my ear. "Tomorrow."

"It's fine," I say. "I understand. In fact, it's my job to understand. I think we should meet tomorrow. If you're available."

"I'd like that." The relief in his voice is palpable. "When I get back, I have a number of things to wrap up in Rockland, then I'll call you."

"Perfect. Talk to you then." I end the call before Grayson maneuvers me right into the crime scenes. I set my phone on the desk. "Why am I meeting him?"

I grip the edge of the desk as he sinks to the floor, his hands mapping my body along his descent. The abrasive rub of his callused fingers over the silk of my bra and panties snags the fine material. "Because he's your target," he says, his hand sliding back up the curve of my thigh. "And because the agent is obsessed with you. He'll find a way to see you, regardless. Better to make it on your terms."

"He's not obsessed with me." My nails dig at the wood as his fingers slip under the edge of my underwear, finding the erogenous spot that makes my voice quaver. "He's obsessed with *you*."

He nips my flesh before he takes the elastic trim between his teeth, tugging my panties away from my body and slowly dragging them down. This time, he doesn't stop until they're snuggly around my ankles.

"One and the same," Grayson says, getting to his feet. He flattens his palm over my pelvis, his other hand clears a space on my desk. "We're a package deal." Then, with sure, swift movements, he turns me around and hoists me onto the desk.

I plant my hands behind my back, bracing for balance, as Grayson hovers above. A predator looming over his prey. My gaze sweeps the diagonal scars on his sculpted chest. The tattoo sleeves reaching up his defined arms. I had fantasies that consisted of a scenario much like this during our sessions…and the realization that I'm here, in my office with Grayson, sends a thrill racing through me.

"You like pinning me to desks," I say, a taunt in my voice.

That slight dimple carves his cheek, his rare, devilish smile making an appearance. "I love pinning you. Period." He palms my face delicately and tilts my head back as he kisses my lips, savoring me. The coarseness of the starchy uniform slacks rubs against my clit, increasing the throbbing ache between my legs to a sharp pain.

I latch on to his neck to bring him closer, craving all of him at once.

My needy response steals over him with a hard shiver of

restraint, then he's grabbing my ass, fusing our bodies together. He lifts me off the desk with hardly any effort, only breaking the kiss to say, "I want you in that fucking chair."

The guttural rasp of his voice grates along my skin like his brusque touch, his Irish accent bleeding through. I wrap my legs around his waist, locked to him the way his inked puzzle pieces link together. Uninhibited. Shameless. I grind against the hardness trapped in coarse pants that ignites my senses. Loving the feel of his strained muscles as he carries me to the therapy room to make good on his claim.

He collapses in the patient chair with me on top of him. This is a sacrilege to my profession. I'm spitting in the face of my practice.

And it feels cathartic.

I clutch the headrest, my hair an unruly veil shielding us, as Grayson works my bra off to bare my breasts. He's not gentle, nearly shredding the flimsy material with unfettered need. The pressure isn't enough, we're too far apart still, and he grips the fleshy curves of my hips and forces me harder against his erection. Like starved and depraved savages, we tear at each other. *Never enough.*

We communicate without words. On a carnal level. Whether we're fighting or connecting. Challenging each other or submitting to our weaknesses. Conversing or fucking. None of it matters on a topical level—we delve deeper, exploring the cavernous abyss of our psyche, what some might call the soul.

For people with limited emotional range, this is a frenzy.

In a fit of emotive overload, Grayson could profess his love or kill me with an equal measure of indifference. Both would satisfy his overstimulated state, and return him to his comfort zone.

I could fear what I know he's capable of, but I don't. His

intelligence dictates that he'd never chance a risk like he did today, by coming here. He went against the grain of his nature in doing so. He's here to reconnect, to feed the hunger that drives both of us toward an unknown destination.

It's thrilling.

Frightening.

And neither one of us are capable of derailing this course now.

Once I jumped the tracks, I belonged to him, the same way exposing his innermost thoughts makes him mine. It's more than trust—it's dependence. We can no longer survive without each other.

Even in the face of discovery. Even with the threat of death.

Lydia would never survive this.

He'd devour her just as he's devouring me now.

As Grayson ravishes my body, exposing his primal male nature, craving my flesh—I feel powerful. He's reduced the smartest people to idiots with his mind, and the feel of him losing control beneath me nearly makes me orgasm.

His fingers drive into my hair, gripping at the roots to bare my neck so he can taste me. His stomach muscles flex under my touch as I feel my way down to the closure of his slacks. A sharp hiss lets me know that he's just as wild with need as I am.

My heart thunders as I pull the clasp apart and yank his pants open. His unguarded thrusts work him free of his boxers, and I wrap my hand around his hard length, loving the way that one action twists his expression. Creased in a mix of pleasure and pain, his eyes flare with a silent challenge.

Lifting up, I slide my sex over his shaft...all the way up to the tip, slicking the smooth skin with my wetness. His dark groan encases us, the agony unbearable as my muscles clench to offset the achy need to feel him inside me.

He bears the torturously slow tease only a few seconds more before he meets the roll of my hips with an eager slam of his, stealing my breath and carving a blistering path right up the middle of my body.

A pleasurable shiver skitters down my back, replacing the spike of pain, and I'm lost—giving in completely as he guides my body to his brutal rhythm.

"God, fuck…" He's streaming unintelligible profanities, breaking off only to thrust deeper, grip me harder to him, become one.

When the need becomes too much, Grayson kisses me passionately, and his arms anchor around my lower back. He hoists us off the chair and moves to the floor, spreading me out so he can drive inside me once more, eliciting a throaty moan.

My nails sink into his shoulders as he hooks an arm beneath my knee, positioning me where he can fuck me as hard and as deep as he wants with no obstruction. Every time he pulls out, my body rebels, a fiery spasm rolling through my muscles, my veins liquefying with the pulse of adrenaline pumping through my heart.

"Don't stop," I say, my breaths ragged around my shaky voice.

The impending climax grips me, the pain all-consuming until he fills me again. Every single thrust sends me spiraling. I arch off the floor, my body tensing, and the feel of him hard against my flesh, following in my wake, detonates a resounding orgasm.

All sounds mute as the tightness pulls everywhere, then the rush. My skin prickles, and still he drives in, one last time, rock-hard and throbbing against my walls. So fucking hot—I wrap myself around him as he groans into my neck.

Our breaths are heavy, merging together in the sudden stillness. The cool air is a relief to my flushed skin. The weight of his body resting on top of mine feels solid. Comforting. Then I feel the wetness trickle from the corners of my eyes. Shock snatches the air from my lungs.

I dab my temple, coming away with a trace of tears.

Grayson pushes onto his elbows, his gaze fierce.

"Adrenaline," I say in explanation.

But the deep groove between his brows reveals his disbelief. He feathers my dampened hair away from my eyes, his finger tracing the tear track. I hold his gaze, trying to glimpse his thoughts. He says nothing as he presses his lips tenderly to my temple.

The action is so vulnerable, baring his wonder at my emotional state, that I'm awed by his perception. I desperately try to bank my introspective anxieties and place my palm to his cheek, questioning whether this sudden insight is true connection, or curated sentiment.

"What do you feel?" I ask.

His glacier blue eyes flick over my face. "Fascinated."

It's an honest answer. Most men would either downplay the moment, terrified, or overblow it, seeped in insecurities. Grayson cannot experience the emotional pull, but he's aware of it—he knows it exists between us.

I let my hand drift to his back, run my fingers over the tattooed keyhole between his shoulder blades, outlining the patterns and numbers. I'm fascinated by him, too. I was the first moment I saw him.

I skim my nails through his hair, feeling the scars that are now hidden. "How did it happen?" The question slips out, thoughtless.

And just as quickly, Grayson's open expression shutters. I read the pain behind his eyes before he shifts his gaze to the wall clock. "That's another session, doc."

Then his comforting weight is gone. He grabs the T-shirt off the floor and offers it to me. I use it to drape myself as I head to the office bathroom, snatching my blouse along the way. When I reemerge, Grayson is again dressed in the security uniform and standing in front of the filing cabinet.

A thought flickers through my mind; a question of whether this is the first time Grayson sneaked into my office.

Doubt is a terrible affliction.

"Is there something you need?" I ask as I gather my skirt and underwear from their discarded location. I finish dressing, forcefully pushing doubts aside.

"Yes. I need you inside Nelson's head," he says, turning to face me. "You're already close to him. I can handle Foster."

"Fine. But I should go." I check my phone. "If agents are watching, anything longer than two hours is questionable."

Grayson inclines his head, watching me closely. He stalks toward me, the darkened office concealing his features until he's right before me. "Stay close to him, but if he gives you any proof that he's the copycat and that he's becoming unhinged, leave. Get far away."

"I can handle myself."

"I know you can." He takes the phone from me and sets it aside on the desk. "I'm not worried about your actions. I'm worried about what I'll do."

I squint up at him. I hadn't considered Grayson's reaction to a threat against me personally. He's never before had to confront an emotional overload. If Nelson hurt me…what would Grayson be capable of? What would that do to him?

"I understand," I say.

He grasps my neck, his thumb searching out the pulse of my heartbeat. "Sometimes the past is just the past, London. It doesn't have any bearing on us now."

This is in response to my question earlier, and my distant behavior now. Grayson may only be able to impersonate feelings, to blend into society, but that intense study into it makes him a master at deciphering others' emotions.

I've invested countless hours into the study, also. I know that what I glimpsed in the therapy room signifies importance —some tie to his past that he's desperate to sever.

For now, I nod against his hand, then move into his arms, savoring the last seconds I have with him.

We all have secrets, and I can't judge too harshly. I'm keeping certain truths from him. Some variations on our trap, and my research into his past. I've made a decision that could crumble our already unstable foundation. As his significant other, my actions are considered a betrayal. As his psychologist, that betrayal is far more offensive. This could do irrevocable damage not only to him—but also to *us*.

But if he won't give me the answers, I now know where I need to go to find them.

To his homeland. To the one woman who gave Grayson this dark life.

His mother.

13

RUSSIAN ROULETTE

GRAYSON

To avoid suspicion, I use the facilities at a nearby park to change into my regular street clothes. Then I discard the stolen uniform into a trash bin. I've missed the scheduled bus to Portland by less than fifteen minutes. It's a greater risk, but instead of waiting half an hour in the city where my face is best known for the next bus, I hail a cab.

The clear partition between the driver and me feels foreboding. Reminiscent of the day the police stormed my apartment with a search warrant and hauled me into a squad car. Good times.

Out of habit, I pick up on little details of the driver's life that's sporadically placed around the taxi.

His ID states he's twenty-three. He has a picture of a young woman in the visor. His cell lights up with an image of the same girl. He's missed three calls from Skylar already, and he promptly sends her to voicemail. I glance in the rearview mirror and note the dark circles under his eyes. He's too young to carry so much stress.

On closer inspection, I catch a glimpse of an appointment card as he tucks it into the console. The emblazoned letters on the card read: OB-GYN.

The driver is about to embark on a new beginning in his life, and like most of us, he's fighting the change.

As stolen children, London and I never knew our beginning. It was ripped away by monsters in the night. Thieves of innocence. Our precious first moments in this world tainted, erased.

Unlike London, I have a select number of memories of my life before. I suppose that makes me different in some way—not unique, but rather, conditioned. Less born to this world and more like I've adapted.

We were not born the day we took our first breath. We were born the moment we stole it.

I said these words to London, and the truth of that statement still haunts me as much as her darkly golden eyes.

London has been digging into my past.

In the same way that I'm prone to gather details of the driver's life, London's office harbors clues to her furtive dealings. Message logs to a forensics' lab. Searches on her computer on my hometown. A genealogy report.

I could argue that, as a psychologist, London needs to examine and understand my beginning in a professional sense, but she's mostly just curious. The scars on my body read like a roadmap to her—and she needs to follow those roads to my start. Discover the inciting incident that created the monster.

We were both casualties in a sense. The loss we suffered not mortal but a death of self. Our identities traumatized.

Forced to rebuild our psyche with chipped and flawed fragments.

But we were gifted something else in the process.

Insight.

Have you ever received a present only to be disappointed once the shiny wrapping paper was torn away to reveal the contents? What if you never had to feel that disappointment again. Always having an understanding of the inner nature of how things work, of what to expect from others.

Sounds alluring. There's a tradeoff, though. With this perception comes not just the prospect to never again be disappointed, but to never be surprised, either. That brief moment of astonishment when you get the unexpected.

People live for that shit.

My whole life, London has been my only surprise.

I tore off the wrapping paper and dove in with only a veiled idea of the contents…and she was so much more than I expected.

She's the glossy present I never dreamed I'd receive.

I desperately want not to break her.

London needs to stop digging.

Muscles tense, I stare into the head beams reflected in the taxi's side-view mirror. The same blue sedan has been tailing the cab since we left downtown.

"Let me out here," I tell the driver.

He sends me a confused look in the mirror. "I can't stop here."

"Pull onto the median," I say, growing impatient. I slide fifty dollars through the slat in the divider.

"All right, man. You got it."

Parked on the side of the highway, I watch the blue sedan pass us. I get out of the cab and motion for the driver to roll the window down. "Marry the girl and get a better job. The choice between being a father and a cab driver should be a no-brainer."

His eyes widen in alarm, but I pat the taxi's rooftop and walk off before he finds the words to confront me. What can I say? Deep down, I'm a rather nice guy.

Eastbound, I head across the next highway over. I stop and wait along the side of the median. When I spot the sedan taking the exit up ahead, I curse.

I could run, evade the mystery man—but I'm curious. There's no line of flashing blue and red lights barreling down the highway. If I'd been reported by someone, the cops would have shown up by now.

The mystery man doesn't keep me waiting long. The sedan heads this way, coming right at me. I step into the brush along the highway to conceal myself, but I make sure he spots me first. The car slows to a crawl as it pulls onto the shoulder.

Cars rush past on the highway, and I use the distraction of a blaring horn to dip farther into the buffer of trees. If this guy has been on my tail since Bangor, he's not giving up now.

He wants me badly. And he wants me to himself.

I clear the trees and enter the back parking lot of a large super-center. This space is too open, too public. I do a quick scan from the incline and notice a church steeple in the near distance.

I smile. Perfect. Destination decided, I round the lot toward the side of the building. I don't move too quickly, so as not to lose him. This guy isn't stealthy, despite what he probably thinks. I can hear his heavy footfalls on the gravel as I ease alongside the building.

The town is a one-shot stop. Its main purpose to serve travelers passing through. Which means the road is practically vacant once I cut across Main Street. One street lamp sits in front of the otherwise darkened church.

Behind the small brick structure is a graveyard. It's a little cliché, giving chase in a cemetery, but open gravesites make great conversational pieces.

His footsteps near, and I locate a decent-sized headstone to dip behind. From here, I can make out his wide profile. He's winded and bends over to catch his breath. Then, as he rights himself, he cups his hand over his mouth and sparks a lighter. A hazy orange flare blooms against the night. Smoke wafts up, a thin tendril slithering toward the streetlight.

He starts in the opposite direction, so I toe up a rock and kick it. The stone smacks a headstone. The man jerks to a stop, then pulls a gun from his holster as he heads into the cemetery. The adrenaline of the hunt surges through my veins like molten lava. It's intoxicating. Nearly my favorite drug.

I stand behind a tree, camouflaged by the dark, as he flicks the cherry off the cigarette and pockets the butt. Very considerate of him.

When I fear he's about to give up the chase, I make myself known. I walk right up behind him and, as he's invested in lighting another cigarette, wrap my sculpting wire around his neck.

His folds of fat prevent me from getting a good hold. I choke up on the wire, muscles straining. A couple shocked seconds, then he lashes out, fighting as he tries to pry the wire loose. He backs into me, struggling, before I'm able to lower him to the ground.

During the scuffle, he dropped his gun. When he's close to blacking out, I relax the wire and allow him to pull in a wheezing breath. I pick up the gun and slip it into my waistband.

"You must be the bravest cop, or the stupidest," I say, moving into a blade of moonlight so he can see my face.

Detective Foster coughs, his eyes bulging against the pressure. It's a few more seconds before he's able to talk. "Sullivan..." He sputters, inhales a rattling breath.

"Smoking is a killer." I kneel beside him and flick my switchblade out.

Hand to his throat, Foster eyes the blade. "Fuck you."

Foster is a surprise. One of those rare gifts. I wasn't expecting this kind of boldness from the cumbersome detective. The pressure of his job must be getting to him to make such a rash move.

"I knew you couldn't keep away from her," he says, finally catching his breath. "And I knew she was in on it. Just had to keep watching and waiting. I knew you'd show."

He gets points for persistence. I've been focused on Nelson as more of a threat over Foster. But there's something to be said for his shear obstinacy. I rotate the knife, catching the light. "There's a flaw in your plan, detective. Where's your backup?"

His jaw sets, gaze narrowed. Stubborn.

I nod once. Then I flip open his trench coat. "I noticed that you're missing your badge. Did you lose it? Aren't cops reprimanded for that?"

"Are you going to kill me?" he says, evading my question.

I look him over. "Answer me, and I'll make it quick and painless."

The hard dip of his Adam's apple dispels some of his bravado. "I lost it," he says. "Mandatory suspension disguised as vacation without pay."

That's how Foster's been able to follow me around the country. There was no mention of his suspension in the news, but then, the headlines have been fixated on the worthy stories. London and the dead girls. The manhunt for a serial killer. FBI investigations. No one particularly cares for an aging, overweight detective from New Castle.

Pursuing me—the one that got away right in his own city —has cost Detective Foster his career. For an obstinate man like him, that's a giant stressor.

Is it enough to make a cop of twenty-plus years snap and start torturing and killing?

I'm not sure, but he has been stalking London. Camped out near her building, and probably close to her home. If he believes London is my accomplice, he's a danger to her. An unhinged cop who feels vindicated in breaking the law to get to me.

"I can't let you go, Foster. I've taken too many risks lately." I raise the blade to his chin. "You've proven that tonight."

I give him a few seconds to absorb the reality of his situation. What will he do? He's surprised me once—maybe he's capable of more.

He lunges for the weapon.

His beefy grip on the knife results in a slash to his palm. Red spreads to the cuff of his coat. He manages to knock me off balance, taking me to the dewy earth. Spittle flies from his mouth as he grunts from above, still trying to wrangle the knife from my grasp.

"You cost me everything, you fucker." Enraged, Foster throws a blow toward my head. He strikes my ear, and I release my grip on the weapon.

I'm able to nudge my booted foot under his ample stomach and shove him off. He lands on his back, knife in hand. I get to my feet and stand over him. "Dr. Noble is above you. Skulking around her like a prick with a hard-on reveals your incompetency."

He wheezes in a breath. "I'm not the only one with a hard-on for the doc," he says. His hand shoots out quicker than I predict. The razor-sharp edge of the blade slices into my shin. The pain is delayed; my adrenaline too ramped. I stomp on Foster's wrist, pinning his hand, and extract the switchblade from his meaty digits.

"Besides," I say as I wipe the blade clean on his collar. "You're wrong about her. Your preoccupation with the good doctor is giving you tunnel vision. You need to cast your net wider." Hands on knees, I get close to his face. "Unless that's your plan. To frame London."

Debilitating fear clouds his expression, hindering my assessment. I'm unable to get a clear read on him. Foster trembles with a combination of rage and anxiety, masking any hint of shock on his part.

"What are you talking about, you psycho?"

His response is disappointing. Since I can't have him getting in the way any further...

"We should make this look good," I say. "It would be too much of an embarrassment on your part if I got away too easy, don't you think?" I plant my foot on his forearm and grab his wrist.

Confusion draws his eyebrows together, until the sickening crunch of bone snapping reverberates off the tombstones. Finally, real emotion displays on his face. I feel the crack of Foster's radial bone beneath my boot.

A litany of foul words imbue the night as Foster moves through the stages of shock, pain, fear. And finally, rage.

"You motherfucker—" His tirade persists, spittle flying, as he draws his broken arm to his chest. Sprawled on his back, the detective resembles a flipped turtle, limbs striking the ground with no ability to right himself.

"A broken wing won't stop you for long." I prod beneath his waist and unclip the set of handcuffs. Then I drag Foster toward the staked headstone where I kicked up the stone. It's not an open grave, but it will do. Besides, I can't have the detective traumatized. We still need him.

His feet kick out at me, but he's too preoccupied with his pain to put up much of a fight. I fasten one cuff to his chubby ankle, the other to the exposed rebar of the cheap headstone. He cries out as the steel cuff bites into his flesh.

"You should think about a diet, old man." I pocket the handcuff keys, thinking they'd look beautiful strung around London's neck.

After a useless attempt to work the cuff free of the rebar, Foster relents. Breathless, he glares up at me. "I don't care what the media says, you're a killer. Just a fucking killer like any other homicidal criminal locked up in prison."

I squat next to him and—I give him credit—he doesn't flinch. "Do you really think now is the time to have me come to God?" My tone is brutally serious.

Real fear flashes in his eyes. For the first time, the detective who's looked death in the eyes every day of his career realizes that today might be his last.

I reach into the inseam of his coat and take out his phone. "You have two choices," I say, setting the cell next to his head. "Get yourself out of the handcuffs, or call for help."

His gaze narrows. "You're giving me options?"

I shrug a shoulder. "Not much of an option. You can chew through your ankle rather than face the degradation of your department and every other official…not to mention the media you so loathe. But I just don't think you have the stomach for it."

Cradling his wounded arm, Foster glances between me and the phone. I stand. "Good luck."

As I start off, he says, "Just tell me she's in on it."

My eyes close. "You just can't leave it alone. Even for your own good."

"I'm a detective," he says around a grunt. "If the doc was a conspirator in your escape, I'll figure it out."

No, he won't.

I turn around and collect Foster's phone. Scrolling through the messages and recent calls, I shake my head. "You haven't contacted anyone since yesterday." I push the phone into my pocket. "That's unfortunate. No one knows where you are, and you're the only one who can place me inside London's office building. You're the only one who can warn her."

Through the haze of pain, it takes a moment for him to decipher my meaning. "What do you want with her?"

I untuck the Glock from my pants. "You wasted my mercy. I'm not an endless well of sympathy." I release the magazine and, one by one, spit the bullets to the ground with a flick of my thumb.

"What are you doing?" Foster asks.

I insert the empty mag and pull the slide back. Tilting the gun toward Foster, I show him the chamber. "Pick a bullet," I say.

Still gripping his broken arm to his chest, Foster glances at the bronze bullets splayed around his head, refusing to play the game.

"Stubborn as ever," I mutter, and select one myself. I hold it up, then chamber the round and drop the slide. The resounding *click* makes Foster squeeze his eyes closed.

"Ever play Russian Roulette, Foster?"

His eyes snap open. "You're crazy. You can't play Roulette with a fucking Glock—"

"Sure you can." I cock the gun and press the muzzle to his temple. "Rules are real simple. Answer the question honestly, and I don't shoot you."

He tries to squirm away and releases a strangled cry as the cuff jerks his leg back.

I reposition the gun to his head. "Done?" He sends me a lethal glare but doesn't move this time.

"What the fuck do you want to know?" he grits out through clenched teeth.

"Have you ever harmed an animal?" I ask.

"The fuck—?"

"Honesty, Foster. It's very important right now. I'll know if you're lying."

He blows out a harsh breath, pain mounting despite his adrenaline. "No. Never."

I tilt my head, studying him. Deciding he's telling the truth, I pull back the gun and yank the slide open, popping out the bullet. "One down," I say, and toss the bullet over my shoulder.

Foster's head smacks the ground as he relaxes, breathing hard. "Is this some sick psych evaluation?"

"Something like that." I load another round into the chamber and cock the gun. "Thirteen bullets to go. Bet you wish you didn't load a full mag today."

"Christ."

"Have you ever fired your gun on the job?"

Foster doesn't blink. "No."

We go on like this, working our way through bullets, him giving me the answers I want to know. Until we're down to the final round.

At this point, Foster has stopped sweating. He's slipping

into shock. I still haven't gotten the answer I need, however. Whether or not it's his signature on the vics.

I load the bullet.

"It's not Russian Roulette unless you point the damn thing at yourself once in a while," he says between wheezes. His eyes fluttered closed.

I nudge his head with the barrel, rousing him. "Fair enough. Now pay attention." I stretch his arm out and he bites off a scream. I place the Glock in his shaky hand, helping him secure his finger to the trigger. "Don't break the rules."

His gaze holds me in a disbelieving stare. He blinks rapidly, trying to clear the sting of dried sweat from his eyes, then maneuvers himself onto his elbow and aims at my head. I lower myself to make it easier for him. I put my forehead right up to the muzzle.

Unsteady, he can barely keep the gun raised. I give Foster credit, though, his sheer stubborn determination won't let him drop that gun.

"Ask," I say.

The cool steel trembles against my forehead. Foster smiles. "Fuck you." His finger twitches, he pulls the trigger, and the slide jams home with a resounding *click*. Foster's eyes widen. He tries to pull the trigger again, and I pry the gun away.

I show him the bullet in my hand. "No one ever passes their test," I say as I chamber the bullet, this time without first dropping it into my hand. "Sorry. That's not right. London passed hers."

"Is that why you left her alive?"

I check the gun, making sure it's ready, and get to my feet. "You're the detective," I say, pointing the weapon at him. "Figure it out."

"Wait!" Foster holds up his hand, as if he'll stop the bullet. "You can't do this…"

I really can. "I don't like guns. Unimaginative. But our game has inspired me." I slip my finger around the trigger and take aim.

The passing cars are too far away to hear the gunshot.

14

NUANCE

LONDON

The entrance to the hospital is teeming with reporters and news crews. Agent Nelson swears and steers his SUV toward the backside of the building.

"I still say you shouldn't be here," he says.

When the announcement aired that Detective Foster was hospitalized early this morning, Nelson and a team of agents showed up at my apartment shortly afterward.

Foster gave a brief statement to the press that cited Grayson Sullivan as his attacker. Authorities are still awaiting DNA analysis from his person to confirm this, but it's already become an accepted truth by the media. And when Foster publicly stated that he spotted Grayson inside my building, chaos ensued. The alarms went off across the city, the nationwide manhunt now zeroing in on Bangor.

A protective detail was assigned to me immediately. I underwent questioning from the FBI, touting repeatedly that I had not had any interaction with the escaped convict. Once I was cleared, I had to contact my lawyer to prevent the FBI from searching my office floor. Allen Young won't prevail—all he can do is postpone the search. Until the search warrant is presented, he's working to get my patient files protected.

I had to persistently rant to leave my own home in order to visit Foster in the hospital.

I haven't yet processed what this means, or if it's a part of Grayson's overall scheme.

I'll handle Foster.

Grayson's words before he left me, but this level of impulsiveness is extremely out of character for him. I cannot believe that, after last night, Grayson intended for this madness to happen. Rather, we allowed Foster to interfere, and this is the fallout from our colossal neglect.

Foster has been a thorn in my side since before the trial. And now his amateur detecting and brash, tactless behavior for the media has turned my life into a circus once again.

Agent Nelson makes a call to another agent already inside the ER unit, and then swivels to address me. "Ten minutes. Then I have to get you out of here."

Stunned, I stare back at him. "Am I a suspect?"

His features crease in confusion. "No," he says hesitantly.

"Am I under arrest?" I press.

"Of course not. London—"

"Then I'm a free citizen, agent. And while I appreciate everything the FBI has done to protect me, quite frankly, I'm tired of taking orders. I'm going to speak to Foster now."

Nelson drives a hand through his hair, releasing a terse breath. "I haven't protected you." He glances away, and I open my mouth to reassure him, but he continues. "I was wrong to remove your detail. Foster is a disgrace, but he was there when I wasn't. You could've been harmed...or worse.

Sullivan was inside your building while you were there." He looks at me then. "It frightens me...what his motive was. What could've happened."

I hold his gaze, stricken at how believable his guilt appears. "If Sullivan wanted me dead, then he would've killed me before."

His stare intensifies. "There are things worse than death."

The air of the SUV thickens, the silence stretching between us. Nelson believes, as he has since he first discovered me at the crime scene, that Grayson's unhealthy obsession with his psychologist is what's kept me alive, and also puts me in the greatest danger.

Yes. There are things worse than death. Grayson tortured me and left me alive. To Nelson, that has been the most confounding part of all.

This time, we leave that argument unstated, and I clasp the door handle. "Dangerous serial offenders are my specialty, Agent Nelson." I open the door. "Thank you for your efforts, but I can look after myself from now on."

I hop out of the SUV and shut the door before he can reiterate his feelings. Right now, I'm not able to deal with my level of anxiousness over the search of my office and the possibility that he has been masquerading as the serial killer he's hunting.

Both Foster and Nelson have been in my presence for months, and I didn't suspect either of them. Doubt in my abilities festers deeply—but I have to regain the upper hand.

I have to *be* Dr. London Noble.

I rush toward the side entrance of the hospital, dodging a couple stray reporters. I'm too volatile; I can't face the media. The automatic doors *whoosh* open, and the distinct antiseptic scent of the hospital overpowers me as the cool air fans my face. The sterile chill prickles my skin as I make my way to reception.

I have no doubt that I'll have to throw my clout around to get visiting rights. I'm working myself up for the battle when the receptionist looks directly at me, her bright green eyes widening.

"I'm Dr. London Noble and—"

"Dr. Noble?" she repeats.

"Yes?" I say, cautiously.

She turns to her monitor and types. "You're on Marshall Foster's approved visitor's list." She looks up at me. "Actually, you're the only name listed."

Surprise gathers my features tight. "Is he receiving visitors?"

"He is," she says, clicking a button on her keyboard. The door to my right buzzes open. "Turn left and he's the second room on the right."

"Thank you."

Before I enter the ER wing, I notice Agent Nelson coming in. There's a brief moment where we lock eyes, then I go through the door.

I know the fact that Grayson used me to escape custody in a hospital is at the top of his thoughts. I pass a number of agents in the hallway, their gazes trained on me. Maybe Nelson's protective rant was a ruse. Maybe he's counting on Grayson making an appearance.

Maybe I'm paranoid. Or even hopeful.

I find Foster's room and knock once before entering.

His casted arm is in a sling, and purple colors beneath his worn eyes. I stop counting the number of contusions as I draw closer. His bloodshot gaze focuses on me.

"He did this to you." It's not a question, but for some reason, I need confirmation.

162

Foster grunts his affirmation. He then nods to the plastic cup with a straw on the tray next to the gurney.

I roll my eyes and grab the water. "I'm not your nurse." But I let him take a couple of sips before I place the cup back on the tray. "What were you doing stalking my building? Stalking *me*?"

Foster clears his throat. "I knew he'd come back for you. It was just a matter of time."

I fist my hands on my hips. "Well, you certainly proved it. To the whole world. Have you read the latest press release?"

"I don't care what those assholes say."

I dig out my phone and open a webpage. "*Small Town Cop Takes on Serial Killer and Lives*." The headline reads like a war hero piece, but the article itself is a mockery of Foster. A Barney Fife type representation of his solo efforts to pursue one of the most dangerous criminals outside the law.

"Detective Marshall Foster of the New Castle Police Department was discovered early this morning near an unmarked grave inside a cemetery off highway ninety-five," I read aloud. Unmarked grave—sounds like Grayson already. "The Delaware detective had been relieved of his weapon and cellphone, his arm broken and suffering multiple injuries. He was found handcuffed to the rebar of a headstone, suffering shock by the time officials were notified and arrived at the scene. Foster was dehydrated and delirious, ranting about the Angel of Maine and his next victim."

I look up from my phone. "What next victim?"

His weathered gaze spears me. "You."

I pocket my phone, cross my arms. I'm unsure if his declaration is out of concern, or a threat. The article also stated that Foster had been suspended, operating on his own as he tracked Grayson across the country. He suffered a major stressor and has no family ties to ground him. If he was my patient, I'd declare him delusional, unhinged from reality.

A temporary break in his psyche could make him capable of more than just stalking—he could be dangerous. To himself and others. Is it a leap to say that a man who has devoted majority of his life to upholding the law suddenly—like a switch—begins killing?

Maybe I'm biased, but from a personal standpoint, I've discovered that the very people put in charge to honor the law and protect us are the ones we should fear the most.

"You shouldn't worry about me," I say, offering him another sip from the cup. "I'm well protected, detective."

He shakes his head at my offer. "You weren't last night, London. When Sullivan was inside your building. He didn't approach you, which leads me to believe that whatever he's up to is something sinister."

I set the cup down. Foster has never addressed me so informally. We're not on a first name basis. I study him, looking for any sign of Machiavellian tactics. The detective is far more cunning than what he demonstrates publicly, but he's not shrewd enough to be a master manipulator.

And he's serious.

Whatever happened between Grayson and Foster has the detective believing in my innocence.

"I would think that you'd be shouting the loudest that I was in cohorts with Grayson. Having some clandestine reunion with him. Plotting..." I wave my hand aimlessly. "Everyone's demise."

He scoffs. "That's just a tactic. To get you riled in hopes you'll spill something that you hadn't to the Feds."

I nod slowly. *Right.* Grayson must have *riled* him up pretty good last night. I inspect his cast. "How did you break your arm?"

"He broke it." His unrestricted hand clenches into a fist. "I don't know why Sullivan was there, but I knew he would be. He's not finished with you yet. You're in danger. You need to leave, London. Get away until he's caught or dead."

I quirk an eyebrow. "How heavy is your pain meds?"

"I'm serious," he says with a huff. "He tried to kill me."

"If Grayson wanted you dead, Foster, you'd be dead." I lean in close to his ear. "Which means he still has a purpose for you, too."

As I pull away, he watches me closely.

"I appreciate your concern," I say, "but you should be more concerned for yourself. You're not safe from him in a hospital, as you well know. You're not safe anywhere."

The truth of my statement registers in his swollen eyes. "You're right. He didn't kill me. He could've, but he left me alive. Fired my own gun at me and missed."

I stay quiet, waiting for him to make the connection to whatever he's sorting out.

"The things he said…that he asked me…" He shakes his head and winces. "It was like he's looking for something in particular. And when he didn't find it, he just…left."

Still, I say nothing. But Foster's statement reveals more than he could possibly know.

"You've gotten inside his demented head," he says to me. "Explain it to me."

I raise my eyebrows, shake my head. "His disorder is complicated. There are many different reasons for what he did, possible theories…and I can't know for sure unless I evaluate him now."

Foster's gaze narrows. "Why are you here?"

"To ask you not to speak to the press again." And to see for myself if by looking into Foster's eyes, I will recognize a killer.

I sigh, exasperated. On all accounts. "The media doesn't report the truth, Foster," I say. "They'll spin whatever you give them into the worst tale for the both of us." I lay my hand on his arm, then I reach into my purse and pull out a card. I tuck it into his cast. "Here's my lawyer's direct line. I've made him aware of the situation. Please call him before you make anymore speeches to the press."

I turn to go, and he says, "Allen Young? Are you serious?"

"You recall how fierce he was. That's exactly why I retained his services. You're welcome."

He frowns. "Thanks, doc. Try to stay out of trouble."

I let a slight smile break through before I leave the ER room.

Agent Nelson is waiting in the hall.

"Eavesdropping?" I say as I pass him.

He catches up to me easily with his long strides. "Doing my job doesn't make me the bad guy."

I give him a sideways glance, but say nothing.

"Believe it or not," he says, "I agree with Foster. It's not safe for you to stay in Bangor."

My immediate, reflexive response is to continue arguing my points with the agent. But I take a moment to consider my options. "Maybe Foster is finally right about something. I'll leave by this afternoon." I sign out at reception, then head toward the double doors.

Agent Nelson stops me before I cross over into the media craze. "Let me secure a place for you."

I put distance between us. "No, thank you. Please. I don't want to go to some FBI safe house." I swipe my bangs from my face. "I have a place to stay. A friend's. I'll be safe there."

"Can I have this friend's information?"

"You're the FBI," I say as I walk through the parting doors. "I have no doubt you'll figure it out before the end of the day."

Actually, I'm counting on it.

15

POWER OF SUGGESTION

GRAYSON

The vultures have landed.

From Portland to Bangor, a swarm of hungry, greedy scavengers have infiltrated every city and town. News crews, journalists, law enforcement, serial killer fanatics. Those hoping to get their fifteen minutes are infesting the area and squeezing me out, pushing me farther into the shadows.

Gaze trained on the laptop screen, I complete a rep. I lower my body, muscles strung tight, then pull myself up again. My chin meets the edge of the wooden beam, and suddenly I'm thrust back into an eight-by-five cell. White walls. Bars. The footfalls of guards. I release the beam with a groan, chest heaving.

The reporter on the monitor mentions Foster, and I crank the volume.

The New Castle detective is reported as recovering well, where he's being kept in the ICU under heavy guard. No further updates…

He'll recover enough before long. He's only hindered, not broken.

Despite Foster's interference and his brainless interviews with the press, I remain in the very state I once hunted in. Where I was apprehended and served a year of a life sentence behind bars at the Cotsworth Correctional Facility.

Daring or reckless?

I heard the safest place to hide is right beneath your enemy in plain sight.

I'm not sure if this statement merits any truth, as I can't recall who first uttered such ludicrous words, but it serves my cause, my purpose, and so here I am.

Foster forced my hand, so now my choices are limited. Either I initiate the final phase, or I run.

Only one option aligns with my objective.

London.

The thread tethered between us is too strong to be broken by the simple threat of captivity or death. Black or not, dead or not...my heart beats because of her.

That's a bit melodramatic—but this is all relatively new. It's like I'm lovesick, belting ballads at her window. Or burying her alive... Which for us, is a clear affirmation of devotion. Not many possess that kind of dedication, that level of commitment, to their significant other.

Love is pain.

Real love—the one not spewed in poetry—is agony.

It tears at your soul, strips you bare, drives you mad and demands the veracity of our existence.

Love is madness.

I wipe my face and pull on a T-shirt. Adrenaline rushes my system. I pump my hands a couple times, then shake them out.

It's time.

Foster's meddling heroics is forcing me to initiate the next stage earlier than planned. I have to take a step back, rethink and realign the dominos. Detective Foster is not the copycat. Our little game proved as much. No matter the reason behind the killer's motive, an imitator still has respect —admiration—for the object of their study. Meticulous analysis and recreation of a murder takes esteem on the copycat's part, and Foster still loathes me just as much now as he did the first day he questioned me.

With Foster out of commission, I can focus my efforts on Nelson. He's the most likely suspect.

And he's with London.

My jaw sets. I think I've made a grave error on that end.

But with the FBI keeping vigilant watch over London, it can work.

A scene on the monitor captures my attention. A reporter stands in front of London's building, giving the latest update. It's not live. From earlier this morning.

London had only recently reopened her practice. Due to her sudden celebrity, the demand to be treated by Dr. Noble had boomed. The clinically insane and deviant arrived from all over the country. That frenzy settled once I was no longer front-page worthy.

According to the report, she's again closed her practice. The shot clearly shows circus media freaks circling in front of her building. Then Agent Nelson emerges. My interest piques.

I watch curiously as Nelson and a couple of his proxies scatter the mob, clearing away the unwanted hindrance.

Sources report that Dr. Noble has temporarily closed her renowned practice. As you can see here, FBI agents have barricaded the downtown Bangor building, the location of the latest Angel of Maine sighting.

171

The scene switches, and a short glimpse of London exiting the hospital where Foster is being treated appears. A rare emotion clogs my throat. The beat of my pulse heavy and thick. My chest tightens.

I think this feeling is something akin to nostalgia. It's difficult to feel homesick when the only places you've ever called home were ones you worked to escape from. But it's the closest thing I can compare this emotion to.

She's my home. And she's my sickness.

I don't push the ill feeling away; I latch on to it. Craving any feeling that I can relate to her. Then I get to work. I use the fiery ache in my chest to propel me forward.

I sit before my laptop, using the program I compiled to bounce my signal off proxies around the world. I'm not tech savvy—but the Internet is designed like any system. You just have to understand the mechanics.

You can be intelligent, a genius even, and still be fucking stupid. Using the Internet to target Agent Nelson isn't the wisest when the FBI is hunting for my online activity.

One could describe that as stupidity. Arrogance. Conceit.

Or desperation.

But the deepening ache in my chest argues against logic. I've never understood the concept of sacrifice until now.

Nelson's activities are pretty well masked. His use of the FBI's equipment and channels makes him virtually invisible on the Net. But everyone leaves a trail. A distinct online footprint.

I've been shadowing his real life footprints, too. During my late-night strolls, I've set up checkpoints. Staging the board. The first in a series of suggestive images to trigger his compulsions.

See, regardless of his copycat nature, he's still a deviant. He's just simply an unoriginal one.

There's a lot of unknown variables surrounding him. The biggest unknown: the *why*. He has the inside knowledge in order to get away with murder. He even has a couple stressors kicking around for us to ultimately decide the *when*. We don't need his motive to trap him, but it would be beneficial to the design.

We do, however, need Agent Nelson to act on his compulsions sooner. We're accelerating the timeline. If I'm devolving, my counterpart must devolve with me.

I pull up a map and mark off the checkpoints. The locations along his routes to the Rockland crime scenes.

To anyone else, the strategically placed posters of domestic abuse hotlines for women are inconsequential. To Nelson, the pictures entice deviant cravings. The farther along he gets, the more explicit the images become. Erotic images. Right in his line of sight.

The power of suggestion.

As Nelson moves through his day in pursuit of his target, he'll become agitated. Off kilter. His subconscious primed.

If someone wants to fuck with you in today's age, it's not a difficult feat. It doesn't take much technical skill to uncover an account password. Fill an inbox with spam of violent pornography. Target a user's social media accounts to receive allusive content. Activate Web ads during Internet searches to recommend discrete call girls for those seeking release.

Keywords like "release" are trigger words.

The evocative images will arouse him, push him to act on his compulsions sooner.

A smart man once told me the wait for something to happen can drive a sane man mad. His wisdom got me through a year at Cotsworth. This man was my biological father, what little I recall of him. He also stated that when the madness started to creep in, there was nothing wrong with giving fate a push.

Take the initiative.

If people didn't want to be manipulated, they wouldn't make it so damn easy.

One final preparation secures that when the agent acts on his compulsion, it will be where I want him. In a controlled environment. That's important. That's key.

Every lock has a key.

16

ALLY

LONDON

The Virginia skyline is seamed in shades of gold and pink as my plane touches down in DC. The last time I was in the capital, I was speaking at a conference on criminal behavior. I barely saw the city.

Despite what Agent Nelson believes, I won't be seeing it now, either.

I de-board the plane, and Sadie greets me at the gate. She's wearing her usual jeans and T-shirt, a gun snuggly holstered at her hip. I smile as I take her in, comforted by her consistency.

"I finally got you back on my turf," she says. "Where's your bags? I'll grab them then we can—" Sadie breaks off as she searches my face. Not a minute into our meeting and the behavioral analyst has already detected my hesitancy.

"I know this isn't a social visit," she says, lowering her voice. "I've been following the news. So tell me why you're really here, and how I can help."

TRISHA WOLFE

"God, Sadie. You've already helped me so much..." I look at the tarmac through the glass. I'm a terrible liar when it comes to her, and she deserves my honesty.

"London. What is it?"

I meet her vibrant green eyes. "I need you to purchase a plane ticket for me."

But that's not all, and she further scrutinizes me. My dressed-down appearance. The jeans and T-shirt I changed into on the plane. The green contacts concealing my brown irises. Realization opens her pursed expression.

"Christ," she mutters.

"I need this, Sadie. I can't ask anyone else."

"Are you in trouble?"

I shake my head. "I just need two days. Two days where no one knows where I am."

"Like that FBI agent who's attached himself to your hip?"

I smile. She doesn't miss anything. "Exactly."

She silently thinks it over. I can practically hear the gears turning in her head. "Are you meeting him there?"

"No," I say honestly. I know she's referring to Grayson. He was the center of my last session with her. "My patient is not in Ireland, but I am going there for him. It's the only way I'll get the answers I need."

After a moment of critical observation, she nods toward a more private area of the busy airport. We find a bank of vacant chairs near the massive, domed windows that line the whole level. The high vaulted ceiling is painted in creams and pale yellows. The ambient light makes the interior look as if it's leafed in gold.

"What made you decide to return to the DC area?" I ask, taking the heat off myself for a second. "Are you working Arlington again?"

Sadie sighs. "Not really. I'm here as a consultant. Helping my old partner out on a case. That's all."

I raise an eyebrow. "So you secure a long-term rental in DC just for a consultant gig." She told me before I arrived that she'd rented an apartment, and I was welcome to stay with her for as long as I needed.

"Also, my mother..." She trails off. Sadie has never been one to go into detail about her person life. "I need to keep a place close by to her. But on the job front, let's just say that I'm leaving the option to return open." She directs her focus out the window. "It was the only place that actually felt like...home."

This is a deep profession from Sadie. My college friend has never harbored a connection to any one place, or person. Her previous career had her traveling around Virginia state, profiling criminals. For her to even consider settling in one place means she's found more than a significant other; she's formed familial bonds with other people.

A near impossibility for my friend.

"I'm happy for you," I say, and I mean it.

Her fleeting smile confirms my conclusion. "When we last spoke, you were struggling with countertransference with your patient." And like that, Sadie is all business. "With all that has happened, tell me why—truthfully—you're making this trip."

All that has happened. Inferring to my abduction. Psychological torture. Discovery of my kidnapper and biological parents and sister... All at the hands of Grayson—my patient.

If I was in Sadie's place, I would seriously consider having myself committed rather than allowing me to leave the country.

I look into her eyes, holding nothing back. "I need the last piece of the puzzle."

I'm not seeking to uncover lies—Grayson has been truthful. I believe that. But it's what's been omitted from his story that will reveal the whole truth.

I'm seeking to discover why Grayson chose me from the start.

"I feel like I'm teetering on a pendulum," I confess further. "Swinging back and forth between two counterparts. Both equally vital, and equally damaged. The pendulum can't swing forever, and when it stops, I need to make sure the right person prevails."

She assesses me closely, that penetrative gaze peels back layer after layer. For once, I'm not afraid of what she'll find. Sadie is the one person I can trust with my secrets.

She nods solemnly. "When is your departure?"

I check my phone. "Less than an hour," I say, reassured. "Nine hours to Dublin with the layover in Boston. Quickest and most *expensive* flight I could find."

"All right." She stands.

"Where are you going?"

She swivels around briefly. "To get my passport."

I hold back a smile as relief crashes over me. While Sadie's gone, I make quick work of gathering my bag and checking online for updates. Foster is out of critical care but remains hospitalized. Agent Nelson's presence has been documented from Bangor to Portland. My brow furrows as I fact check the Portland report. What's in Portland?

Sadie returns as I'm starting to feel anxious. "I'm not sure this is any reassurance," she says as she places an envelope in my hand. "But it's unbelievably fortunate that our descriptions match. Hair color. Height. The only marked difference is eye color, and you've taken care of that with contacts."

I consider just how fortunate it is. "I had the contacts already," I admit. "My doctor offered them to me and I accepted, regardless that I never planned to use them." I smile and shake my head. "Grayson would say that it's not a coincidence or luck. That we design our life on purpose. Set things into motion long before we understand that purpose."

Her eyebrow quirks. "A believer in fate?"

"It's more like we gravitated to each other early on because our subconscious determined we'd be of value to one another at some point in our life."

She laughs. "I've missed you, London, but not the brain cramps that come with having you as a friend."

I offer her a sincere smile. "Touché."

She moves in close and lowers her voice. "I put my driver's license in the documents, as well as a burner phone and credit card. Ten-thousand limit. Do what you need to do, and we'll worry about everything else later. Now give me your phone." At the confused draw of my eyebrows, she says, "So you're not traced."

I hand her my cell. "Thank you." Her trust in me secures my decision. This is the right path. I unearth my wallet and hand her a credit card. She tries to wave it away. "It's to plant my whereabouts. No limit. Go crazy."

As she accepts the card, she says, "Well then. Maybe I'll get my hair done. And a new wardrobe. So I can prance around the city as the distinguished Dr. Noble." She shakes her hair back, nose in the air.

"Are you mocking me?"

She places her finger an inch apart from her thumb. "Only a little." Then a serious expression settles over her face. "Be careful."

I bring her into a hug. I'm surprised when Sadie hugs me back. "I will," I promise.

I leave then, with my new identity, and only a vague starting point once I arrive in Dublin. Trusting that Grayson and I—that our design—is merely an inevitability and not ill-fated.

My swinging pendulum might be metaphoric to his literal design—but both were set in motion long ago.

17

DEVINE MONSTERS

GRAYSON

Over the past twenty-four hours, Foster's attack has gone viral. The once-peaceful fanatics and protesters have clashed and began to war with each other. Fights, riots. Hysteria. Cops in riot gear clog the streets. The news is saturated with reports of this brewing insanity. Law officials from across the state are being called in to help reinforce order.

I haven't slept in as many hours.

The chaos has become a shelter of sorts, helping to keep me hidden while the taskforce focuses their efforts on Bangor. London remains on the reporters' tongues, but she's disappeared from the spotlight.

Uneasiness rattles me. Not knowing where she is—where Nelson is—keeps me from sleep. Restlessness is creeping in. I crave a release. The compulsions never stay checked for long.

As I walk the streets, I'm starting to wonder if I'm a

contagion, spreading psychosis, infecting minds. It could all be in my head. What I'm witnessing might be a warped sense of the world, and I'm seated in London's therapy room right now wearing a straightjacket.

I scrub my hands over my face, disoriented, craving caffeine. Sleep deprivation. It's a fucking killer.

I pull my hoodie down low and head into the daytime work crowd as they navigate Rockland. It's the same path Nelson takes to the crimes scenes. He passes right by the Refuge.

I duck into the heaving cluster, like little worker ants migrating down the sidewalk. The large wooden sign is a beacon for the bar. Agent Nelson has seen the sign before. Random ads popping out at him online, beckoning him to the bar with a promise of easy targets. Relief.

I take up my post across the street at a coffee shop. Two birds. One stone. I order a large coffee from a hungover barista, then seat myself near the window, where I can keep watch.

By the time I've drained the mug, Nelson still hasn't shown.

I leave a few dollars on the table and then head out. I can't risk staying in one place for too long. Maybe Nelson can't risk temptation during the day. As I reemerge into the daylight, pain slices through my skull. Black spots fill my vision.

I move into an alley and press my back to the brick. Breathe through the discomfort. The lingering scent of lilac that still clings to my jacket diffuses some of the pain. I use the reprieve to make it to the bus stop.

I need sleep. Even the greatest minds can't function without it.

On the ride to Bangor, I think about the little China doll

girl and her mother. How her situation seemed so easy to fix. Take her mother out of the equation, and she might have a chance at a better life.

Or maybe not.

She could wind up in a terrible foster home with terrible people.

I know all too well about the monsters who prey on the system.

I blink the dark spots from my vision, eyelids heavy. My thoughts are getting muddled. If not for London, I probably would've already killed Nelson. It seems the most logical solution.

But if he dies, the proof of his secret persona dies with him.

No one would believe there was a copycat killer. Especially if the finger points to a federal agent.

London's right. We still need him. *Patience.*

I keep on the move, circling back to Rockland, sitting on the Refuge in preparation for Nelson. He'll show up there eventually. But first, I just want a glimpse of London's building. Just one peek—like a small hit for a junkie. Feeding the cravings. The buss passes her building, and I take in the scene.

A group of protestors circle before the steps. A smile twitches at my mouth when I realize they're chanting about London.

The protesters are enraged, angered with the system that lets animals like the Angel of Maine free.

I suppose clueing them in to the fact that psychologists have very little to do with government probably wouldn't help. These people can't be swayed; they don't want to be. They're righteous in their beliefs—no matter how ridiculous.

Demanding peace by enforcing the death penalty for convicted murderers.

How ironic.

Their singsong chant gets stuck in my head. I rather like it.

The truth is, we are a violent species. We will never be peaceful. Earth itself was conceived in a womb of violence. She didn't sneak into the void of space with a whisper to be populated. She burst into existence with a bang—a violent explosion. We are predisposed to violence because it exists in the very atoms we're made of.

Murder.

War.

Hitler. Genghis Khan. Alexander the Great. They killed in the thousands, *millions*. They killed for power. They wielded fear and mercy as a weapon. Evil in its purest form. Civilizations were built on the blood they shed.

I've heard scholars argue that these men were mad—but what is genius if not madness? Mental illness is a common euphemism for evil.

Very few sadistic killers are actually insane. Quite the opposite. They have to be in control of all their faculties to get away with murder. And to profit from it.

The cheering fanatics worship me and they worship London. Bowing at the foot of her office building, praising her as a goddess, while the protesters spit in their face.

We might as well be gods.

Through the ages, gods have been banished as much as worshiped. The masses loathing their failure, and yet they were always feared. Fear is more powerful than love. Gods have no compassion. That's how they're able to slaughter the multitudes.

Someone has to wield that fear, that power. And those

who are too weak to stomach the natural order can only hide and judge from their safe corners. We are gods, and we must be feared.

I laugh to myself.

Or, I'm probably just insane.

18

OCEANS APART

LONDON

There's a reason why I don't drive.

I curse and try to downshift the gears of the tiny, foreign rental car, grinding as I steer one-handed. I swerve into the wrong lane and quickly right the car. "Dammit."

I'm a horrible driver.

I landed in Dublin an hour ago, was making good time, until I discovered there were no early morning trains or busses to Kells. With time already against me, my only option was to swallow my fear and rent a car. I used Sadie's credit card, and here I am, grinding my way down a winding two-lane highway in the wee hours of the morning.

The heavy blackness that blankets the sky isn't helping, the headlights fogged and barely lighting the road ahead.

I have to be crazy.

Other than the sheer lunacy that got me on a plane to Ireland, I have to be certifiable for trying to track down Grayson's mother. What do I expect to find?

I check the time on the burner phone. It's nearing 5:00 a.m. A last-minute search into Rebecca Sullivan gave me her last known address. I can only hope she's still there, and that knocking on her door at this hour won't get a door slammed in my face.

I've come too far.

Literally.

I spot a small street sign ahead and slow to a rolling crawl before I make the turn. Street lamps illuminate the way through a string of identical brick townhomes. I locate the unit that was Rebecca's most recent address and park alongside the driveway.

Taking measured breaths, I keep ahold of the wheel. Then I pry my fingers free and leave the warmth of the car. The slam of the car door bounces around the quaint neighborhood. I shake out my hands, thinking of the string in my jacket pocket, as I move up the driveway.

I'm almost to the door when a dog bark makes me flinch, and the porch light flicks on. "Shit."

I stay right where I am, frozen. Unsure of what happens now, or of my next move.

The front door opens. "Who are you?"

The female voice is rough, like the woman has smoked most of her life. She has a thick Northern Ireland accent, reminding me of the lilt I occasionally hear in Grayson's deep voice. A pang ricochets through me.

I take a step forward, lift my chin. "Hi. My name is—" I stop myself short of giving her my name out of habit. "Sadie Bonds. I'm with American law enforcement—"

She scoffs. "Aye, I can see that. What do you want this bloody early?"

In the dim light, I can barely make out her face, but she's dressed in a pale-pink robe, her gray-streaked hair pulled into a messy bun. She aggressively tries to quiet the black lab at her side, and finally claps her hands to send the whining dog back inside.

I stuff my hands into my jacket, the cold morning and my nerves causing me to shiver. "Are you Rebecca Sullivan?"

"For Christ's sake," she mutters, shutting the door. When she looks up, I can clearly discern a white scar running the length of her cheek. She quickly brushes a loose hank of hair forward to cover her face. "I thought you people were done with all that. He's not here. Hasn't had anything to do with his mother in ages." She scoffs again. "A damn sight longer than that."

My shoulders drop, tension deflating from my body. This is not Grayson's mother. "I'm sorry to have bothered you, ma'am."

"Now wait." She tugs her robe together, cinching the belt tight. "Just what do you want with Becky, anyhow?"

She's not his mother, but she does know where she is. "I have questions. Things only she knows that could help authorities—"

"You won't be getting any answers from Becky, I tell ya. Might as well go on back to Merica. The boy won't be coming here again. Not after what was done to him."

I squint, trying to follow along with her quick, accented words. "Do you know where I can find Rebecca?"

She waves a hand through the air. "That slag is gone in the head." When I raise an eyebrow, she clarifies. "Becky's in the madhouse. Good riddance."

As it turns out, the woman currently living in Rebecca's townhome is her only living relative, who cared for her up until the disability checks stopped. From what I could gather, Becky became a burden, and her sister let the hospital have her. *Good riddance* was her final avow before she slammed the door in my face.

Another hour of braving the roadways, and I pull into Meadow Health Services, a psychiatric institute seated on the outskirts of Dublin. I drive around the parking lot until I find a spot, then I try to pull up the ward's information on my phone.

According to the website, the facility isn't open yet. I release a breathy curse, frustrated. I slept on the plane, so I'm too wired, too out of my element, to rest. "What the hell am I doing here..."

I spend the next hour reading updates online, and as I'm browsing my local news station, my heart cinches. The FBI procured a search warrant for my office. The report states that Agent Nelson is heading up the search.

Of course he is.

I left you a surprise, Nelson.

I now wonder if by asking me to leave Maine, his apparent concern for my safety was more for his benefit—to get me out of the way.

I send a text to both Lacy and Young to ensure at least one of them was present during the search. An alarmed feeling jolts me when neither reply, but then I remember the time difference. Shit. I send another text asking them to please make sure the FBI don't weasel into my patient files.

I drag a breath into my constricted lungs.

The tapes are blank.

Still, the relief is minimal. It wouldn't be the first time I deluded myself into believing a false sense of security. My only real concern should be if Agent Nelson isn't the one to discover what I left behind the Dali. But other than the FBI's own personal distaste for my evident obsessive affection for my patient, there's nothing much they can do with that in the way of evidence.

I was careful to stage it just right.

A car door slams, snagging my attention. I look up to find a man walking toward the facility. I quickly pocket the phone and grab the keys. I trail the man toward the front of the building.

"Excuse me," I say, jogging to catch up.

He turns around, his thin white hair catching the chilly breeze. "Yes? How can I help you?"

"You're American." It comes out like an accusation, and the man smiles.

"I am in fact. Are you lost?"

"No, sorry," I say, regrouping my thoughts. "I'm here to visit a patient."

His smile thins. "Visiting hours aren't until nine."

He turns to go, and I try again. "I apologize, but I'm only here for a very short time…and it's extremely important that I see this patient. Could you at least help me speak to someone, mister…?"

"Dr. Collins," he corrects. Something like hope sparks. I feel an affinity with him not only as an American, but as a colleague. "And you are?"

I extend my hand. "Dr. Noble."

What am I risking at this point? I need this doctor's trust.

Dr. Collins shakes my hand and nods toward the front doors. "Come on. We'll discuss this further inside. It's bloody brutal weather out here this morning."

A smile flits across my face. "Thank you."

He leads me through a stretch of corridors to his office, where I'm thankful for the heat. "Have a seat, Dr. Noble."

I do, laying my jacket across the back of a cushioned chair. I feel out of place in the clean starkness and sophisticated psychiatric ward. Glancing over my jeans and simple sweater, I wonder why Sadie—with all her education—chooses to work in police precincts. I'm also curious if she dresses the way she does on purpose; to throw others off.

"Coffee?" the doctor asks, motioning toward a machine he has setup in his office.

"Yes, please."

He busies himself with setting up the dispenser. "Where are you from?"

"Maine. I'm a criminal psychologist with my own private practice in Bangor."

He nods slowly. "You've come a long way. This patient must be important. Although I can't help but wonder what a criminal psychologist would need from any of our patients." He sets a white mug in front of me. "Most of them have no more ties to the outside world."

I wrap my hands around the cup, warming myself further. "Rebecca Sullivan could hold potential knowledge of someone's whereabouts, or possibly other information that could lead to this person's arrest." It's a huge leap, but one that doesn't sound so suspicious. Police officials are searching for anyone in connection to Grayson, although his whereabouts have been officially determined.

A groove forms between the doctor's eyes. "Follow me, please."

His rapid shift in demeanor and abrupt request startle me. I hesitate before I'm finally able to stand. "Sorry. I'm still a bit jetlagged."

Dr. Collins only offers a tight smile in response. Did the

mention of Rebecca's name trigger an alarm? I worry I'm being escorted out of the building until he turns down an opposite hallway, guiding me into another wing of the hospital.

"I wish you would've called first," he says as he pulls aside a curtain and gestures for me to go ahead of him. He then inserts a keycard next to a bank of doors, a beep granting us access.

"Why is that?"

"It would've saved you the long trip." He motions for me to enter the first room.

As I go inside, my gaze lands on a shriveled-looking woman curled into a chair. Her aimless gaze stares at the wall, her eyes unseeing.

"Becky has been unresponsive for years," he continues. "I suppose it's now referred to as incomplete recovery, but you'll have to excuse my old habits. I'm still partial to treatment-resistant."

I can't tear my gaze away from the withered woman—the woman who, beneath her frailness and deep-set wrinkles, I can discern traces of Grayson's features. "I'm sorry, but treatment-resistant...?"

"Schizophrenia," he says bluntly.

The floor suddenly shifts, vanishes. I plummet as an intense free-fall overwhelms my senses, my stomach pitching, until I land back in the moment with a crash.

Everything slams together all at once.

I can feel the doctor watching me. I swallow and turn to face him. "Are you all right, Dr. Noble?" he asks, tilting his head curiously.

"Yes, sorry. Again, must be jetlag." As a doctor myself, here to speak with this patient, I should already be apprised of her condition. Clearly, Dr. Collins is surprised by my lack of knowledge. And I'm shocked that it wasn't mentioned in any of the public records I searched.

Floodwaters rush, answers coming at me too fast. The sinking feeling I always sensed near Grayson solved with a blistering clarity. This is what he's kept hidden.

Taking another chance on the kinship I feel with him, I say, "Dr. Collins, I know this is highly unorthodox, but since I have come all this way, is there any possibility I can have access to her patient files?"

He studies me closely. "It is highly unorthodox, but I'm inclined to allow it." He glances at Rebecca. "I feel there's very little harm anyone can cause at this point."

"Thank you—"

"On the grounds that you're completely transparent with me," he says.

A moment of truth. "Her son is my patient."

Understanding settles in the lines of his face. "I wasn't aware that she had a son." He considers something for another long moment, then turns toward a the wall-mounted screen. He goes through a series of actions, where he mutters a curse at technology, then picks up the hand-held phone. "Emily, can you please bring a nurse station to Becky Sullivan's room?"

I hide my amusement. "Again, thank you, Dr. Collins."

He checks his watch. "I trust she'll be in good hands during your visit," he says, the question implied.

I nod. "Of course."

"I'll check back in once I've completed my rounds."

Then I'm alone with Grayson's mother.

I pull a chair up next to her, fold my hands in my lap. "Hello, Rebecca. Or you like to go by Becky, don't you?" She remains catatonic. How long do the episodes last? How often?

The door opens, and a woman—I assume Emily—wheels a cart into the room. She goes over the system with me, giving me access to only Rebecca's files. "When you're done, just exit out here." She points to the program on the screen.

I thank her, then get to work, starting with the earliest records. Wearing my psychologist hat, I review Becky's medical history like a professional. Her behavior over the years, according to her charts, is similar in nature to many suffering from schizophrenia. It was discovered early on, in her adolescent years, as there was an established history of the mental illness. And like so many, Becky went on and off treatment. Finally refusing medication altogether by the age of nineteen.

I evaluate her like a doctor. Understanding her behavior and even her decision to rebuke treatment. But when I set aside my professionalism, I loathe this woman.

On a personal level—because I know and love her son—I want to shake her, demand an answer to why she refused medication, choosing instead to self-medicate. There are numerous ER reports for heroin overdose. The combination of her illness and drugs would make a toxic living environment for a child.

This is proven with the other records, accounts of domestic abuse. Fractures, bruises, broken bones. The charts don't list a name of a boyfriend, or spouse…there's no way to determine whether or not Grayson's biological father was involved. But I can assume, with a hollowed pang in my chest, that Grayson suffered this abuse as well.

It's not uncommon with most mental illnesses to self-medicate, and yet, for Becky, I hold her in a higher regard. I hold her to her actions more severely.

I'm human.

"I've treated your illness with a number of patients," I say aloud, even though I know she won't respond. "Had you been my patient, I would've seen to it that you got the treatment you needed. You might even be living a healthy life today, still in society, functional and contributing."

I change the screen over and open another file. This one dated at around the time when Grayson might've been living with her. "And because you were a mother, I would've made sure that your child wouldn't have suffered. That, I suppose, I should lay at the doctors' feet. Grayson should've had someone who cared to look out for him."

From the corner of my eye, I see Becky blink.

It's the first movement she's made since I entered her room. I swivel my chair to face her. "Grayson," I say again.

Blink.

As inconspicuous as I can, I glance around the room, noting the camera in the corner above the door. Most facilities have video to monitor patients, but not audio. I'm not sure if that's true for this ward, but for me, right now, it's worth the risk.

I wheel the cart closer to Becky. She's gripping the armrest, her fingers white.

"You had a son, Becky. His name was Grayson."

A couple more frantic blinks let me know she's listening.

"You had a wretched family, didn't you. A sister that cared nothing for you once the checks no longer came. A brother who abused and traded children. Who you sold your own son to...for what? Money? Drugs? Or just because the burden to care for Grayson became too much?"

Her mouth twitches, her facial features tic in odd arrangements. Then: "Demon."

The word is barely a wisp of breath, but I heard it. I say his name again, just to be sure. "Grayson."

"Demon," she whispers, her milky eyes latching on to mine.

I nod once. Rebecca Sullivan, amid her delusional state, believed her own son to be an evil force. "What did you do to him?"

But just as quickly as she broke through, Becky is gone. Her eyes glazed, gaze staring past me.

I know enough to make the connections. Just like Grayson works each puzzle piece into place, I can see the beveled edges of the jigsaw tearing through the picture, ripping a life apart.

I tap the keyboard, giving myself some action to do for the camera. Eyes trained on the screen, I talk to Becky. She's still in there somewhere. "Was it all the illness, Becky? Or was it some selfish part of you that made it easy to torture your son? As I said, I've treated schizophrenic patients, most having never been violent. Ironic, considering I've devoted my career to criminal offenders. But it's true. With the right medications and treatment plan, you could've led a good life." I glance her way. "Unless the patient suffers violent tendencies. Then the addition of street drugs in the mix is like pouring fuel on a fire. Madness ravages the mind, an uncontrollable brushfire burning, burning…"

A tremor tics at her lips. Just a small reaction, but it's there.

I lower my voice, more intimate. "I had a patient once who believed he had insects living under his skin. He would claw, nails tearing through flesh, until his arms were bloody. And that's what it's like, isn't it, Becky? Being trapped in there, all the evil things you've seen and done crawling inside you like insects. Wiggling beneath your skin, spider legs tickling your flesh from the inside out…but you can't get to them. You can't move to even try."

One of her fingers jumps. Her nails dig into the arm of the chair, and I smile.

"I don't know which would be worse," I say. "Raking nails over skin until you bleed, or being paralyzed by the fear. Feeling every insect bite into your flesh and not being able to stop it."

I reach out and, as lightly as I can, run my fingers over her arm. She flinches, and for a moment, I think a tear might leak free. But she buries her fear. Trapped down in the tormented depths with her. "Now that I know what he fears," I whisper to her, "I'm going to free him."

I stand and clear the screen. I leave Grayson's mother, giving Dr. Collins another grateful "thank you" as I pass by, and I reenter the world armed. I have just one last stop to make, just enough time before my scheduled departure, and I follow the directions to the house—the address I memorized from Becky's medical file.

I could've done just as Dr. Collins suggested; I could've called. I could've tracked down Becky through searches, hired an investigator if needed. I could've gotten access to her medical history. I would've come to the same conclusion miles from here, having never needed to fly across an ocean.

That's not why I'm here.

As I drive up to the house, I know that I had to see it with my own eyes. I want to look at Grayson's childhood home and envision the boy within, just as he touched the bars in my basement, reverently caressing the iron, connecting to me across time and space.

The house is old—it was probably old when Grayson lived here. Now boarded up, condemned. Abandoned. The ocean breeze whips through the tall grass in the front yard, the gray wood chipped and salted, years of sea spitting against it. This small, winding stretch of oceanfront is called The Burrows.

I tie my hair back and start toward the house. I recall the documents Calvin sent to me on Grayson's ancestry. This address was also listed as the house that was raided—the child trafficking home of his uncle. At some point, Becky must've lived here with Grayson. I'm not sure which came first—the proposition to sell Grayson to her brother, or her brother's insistence to take Grayson from her... But it doesn't matter.

The only truth that matters is that when his mother left, Grayson was left behind.

I walk up to the house and search for a loose board. One finally gives and, when it comes away, there's a strip of yellow police tape plastered against the door. I think about the horror that must have happened here, about how the authorities found the victims, and understand why the house was closed up, forgotten. Set apart from other residents along the street, it's a ghost house.

Once I manage to get the door open, using my body weight to push through, I stand in the center of the main room, allowing my senses to direct my path. Another one of my patients murdered women in his own home, right below his wife and family. Basements make ideal kill spots. Keeping the world and even those closest to the offender in the dark.

This home is near the ocean, however. There's no basement. No garage. I walk through the narrow hallway, peeking into cramped bedrooms, everything feeling too open. Exposed.

Where?

Through one of the cracked bedroom windows, I spot a greenhouse.

I noticed them all over as I drove toward the coast. Just about every house has at least one tented greenhouse in the yard. Some have several rows of the clear-tarp units.

Curious, I make my way out the back and shove open the greenhouse door. Vines and weeds have nearly enclosed the entrance, but once I step inside the unit, I get my answer.

What remains of the rudimentary pendulum contraption is fitted in the back of the greenhouse. Rusted animal traps used to restrain Grayson's victims were confiscated as evidence, as well as the machete. The rope and sand bags required to hoist the machete are still here, along with the large wooden table that held his captors while the weapon swung down to end their lives.

The years gone by haven't removed the blood staining the wood and ropes.

I look away, and that's when I notice it.

In the middle of the ground is a giant hole.

"Oh, my god."

A makeshift cover with locks has been discarded, leaned up against a row of planters. This was the door, and below...

I stare down into the hole.

From this angle, I can make out the boarded walls. They've been padded. Sound proofed. Rusted shackles line every wall.

"Christ."

How long did Grayson suffer here?

I kneel and pull out my phone, using the flashlight to get a better look. Chains dangle from the ceiling of the dark room. It's not just a holding space intended to conceal children amid a trade—it's a torture chamber.

What's left of the room shows clear signs of sadistic, pedophilic cruelty. The heady earthy scent mingles with something more metallic...blood. The noxious smell makes me gag, and it's almost too much. I want to turn away, but something in the corner ices my body, freezing me in place.

Next to a bin of dirty old toys is a stack of puzzle boxes.

Completed puzzles line one of the walls, images of blue skies, oceans, cityscapes. And near the far end, carved wooden pieces with a child's drawings. "Oh, Grayson."

Even as a child, I can imagine how intelligent Grayson must have been. He's an autodidact, self-taught, clearly never having the opportunity for a formal education. Still, he was smarter than his oppressors. How many times did he pick those locks? How many times did he try to run away? How many times was he dragged back here to suffer his punishment?

I close my eyes against the memory of his scars. From his scalp to his chest to his arms. They cover him.

I breathe in a searing breath, and release the pain. This room is another dimension into hell. Grayson was kept here, chained and bound, locked away from the world…

Locks.

A fiery ache clogs my throat. *You're the key*, Grayson told me. I thought it was a metaphor about freeing him…but that's not what he's searching for. He doesn't want to free something—he wants to lock it away.

And who better to choose for that purpose than a psychologist that has mastered the art of forgetting.

19

EPIPHANY

GRAYSON

Every life follows a pattern.

Just as a killer has a signature, there's a clear design within each life that makes it inherently ours. Unique.

History repeats itself.

It's a clichéd saying for a reason. And it didn't take me long to understand that, even at a young age, I could see the framework. The structure. I could suss out the sequence in the puzzle and anticipate the next piece. I knew what was coming.

From my earliest memory, I remember the fear. As I looked into my mother's eyes, I saw my future, the inevitable trap. *My trap.* The finality of me…all in her deranged gaze.

Of course, I tried to escape. I've been on a mission to escape that fear my whole life. Pick one lock only to be captured and locked in hell all over again. A never-ending cycle.

Part of my pattern. My design.

I inhale a deep breath, tasting the rain-covered asphalt amid the humid night. I stop walking when I hit the back entrance to the alley near the Refuge. I want to savor this moment.

A person's pattern is nearly impossible to break.

Like I've said before, I was able to endure a couple years before the compulsions started to drive me mad. Then like winding a watch, I'd turn back the hands, resetting the countdown with every kill.

But that only buys time. It's hardly a healthy treatment plan.

I'm only escaping from one form of prison to the next. Over and over. Until the second hand stops ticking for good.

I bury my hands in my pockets, touch the switchblade. Comfort. Then I turn into the alley. I walk the long stretch with a single thought beating against my skull. I could've killed Detective Foster and Agent Nelson. It would've been the simplest solution.

Once I knew undoubtedly that the copycat killer was one or the other, once I had them both in my city, I could've easily offed Foster before he tracked me to London's office. And Nelson? London could've effortlessly led him to a private location where we both could've taken our time and enjoyed the kill.

But like a puzzle demands to be completed, a game has to be played to the end.

London may choose to believe that I took the game too far, my disorder ruling over intelligence, the compulsion to create an elaborate disaster and witness the turmoil, to snuff out the chaos, too great to overcome. That I jeopardized us both.

There is that…to some extent. It's why I've been caught before. The more elaborate the trap, the greater the risk.

And then there's the issue of my pride. The Y chromosome dictating my actions, the thought of the world believing the copycat murders were done at my hand—destroying my work, a mockery.

I really do loathe the bastard for that.

But in the end, it was none of these things. She's always been my goal, my purpose—even before I fully realized it for myself.

London was my epiphany.

It's such a beautiful word. *Epiphany*. Just the sound of it, the taste of the syllables curling over your tongue, the puff of air across your lips. The moment the word is uttered, it's like a striking realization descends, as if some powerful force beams sheer enlightenment into your head. And for a single moment, everything is clear.

Perfect and pristine.

Every single misstep and tangled web woven was for her.

So she could follow the clues, piece together the puzzle.

She's my key.

There's a pattern to life, and my pattern was designed the moment my mother spit me from her rotten womb. A bond steeped in madness—a prison I can't escape.

I see the small river of blood first. Flowing through the rainwater over the asphalt like filmy motor oil. Then the estranged high-heel discarded in the middle of the alley. My own blood stirs. My pulse picks up speed. The thick scent of death chokes the air.

I step through the blood without thought, as if lured to the body by a magnetic force.

She's propped up against the brick building, her skirt ruched up, her shirt torn, hair a tangled mess covering her face. Distinct bruises wrap her neck. She's beautiful, a gift. I know she belongs to me by the word scrawled across her chest in blood.

Whore.

Even when you know what's coming next, it's nearly impossible to break your pattern. I kneel before the woman, entranced, and reach toward her neck to check for a pulse. Adrenaline slides through my veins like melted wax, thickening my blood, my heart pumping too hard, too fast, drowning out the sounds in the alley.

I almost miss the *click* of the gun's safety.

Atoms freeze. The world halts. The distant sound of cars driving past the alley seems to fade away, leaving only two heartbeats fighting to dominate the void. I begin to pull my hand back from her neck.

"Don't move."

I stop, my hand held aloft mid-action. "Your handiwork, Agent Nelson? The contusions around the neck, right above the laceration—" I chance a look at him "—the signature is a dead giveaway. Pardon the pun."

He levels the gun with my gaze. "Not mine. Yours. Your new MO. The proof that you're devolving. Stand up."

I rise to my feet. "Of course. How else would you have caught me if I weren't coming undone? That makes it more believable."

"My ninety-seven percent capture rate makes it fucking believable. I want the weapon in your pocket. Remove it…slowly."

I keep one hand in the air and reach the other into my pocket. I bring out the switchblade.

"Toss it on the ground," he says.

I sling it in his direction. The blade hits the gravel and clatters at his feet. "What now?"

"Now—" he scoops the knife off the asphalt "—you give

me the rest of your weapons, and we end this like dignified men."

I do so, laying the smaller knife, wire, and tape on the ground.

Nelson kicks them toward the dead woman. Then he flicks the switchblade open and intentionally slashes his arm. "Let's see how this went down. First, I followed a lead to a Rockland bar. A patron recognized your description. Not having enough resources..." He grunts as he cuts another slash across his chest. "Instead of burdening the team with yet another false lead, I set out to investigate on my own." He drops the bloodied knife to the ground. "A fortuitous chance encounter. Catching the criminal himself in the act. You attacked me, and I defended myself. One direct bullet to the head."

I hold his gaze for a moment, then glance at the victim. I recognize her now. Charity. The prostitute. Poor Charity. Maybe I overindulged, too enthusiastic in my endeavors to trigger Nelson's compulsion to kill. He couldn't even wait a full day before he murdered the first person he came across.

Sloppy.

"And also lucky for you," I say, "your lead can't be questioned to corroborate the story."

He smiles. "I don't like loose ends."

"Neither do I. But then you know that, seeing as you studied me, mimicked me."

"You can't really get inside the mind of a killer unless you adapt—try on his skin for a while."

"And how does my skin feel?"

He lifts his chin. "I have to admit, I like it. I'll like it even more when I'm sliding into London's skin."

My hands curl into fists.

He notices my reaction and his smile stretches. "I didn't

get the obsession. Not at first. But I knew she was vital in getting to you." He steps closer. "If not for the doctor, you could've fled the country. Hell, we wouldn't be standing here, right now, your demise a trigger-pull away, if you'd just left. What is it about London that you couldn't let go?"

Jaw set, I breathe out the steely tension from my chest. "If you have to ask…"

Nelson may've said his piece flippantly, but the burning desire to unravel my draw to London flares in his wild eyes.

"You can't copy everything," I say. "London likes her villains authentic."

He raises the gun. "She tastes like lilacs. Did you know that?" he taunts. "I'm rock-hard in anticipation to show her how real I can be—"

The animal in me lunges. A primal roar of possession released into the night. It's not part of the design—but I'm human, imperfect. Carnal and feral, and bloodthirsty.

Nelson is primed for the attack. It's possible this is a part of his design, making the struggle between us all the more believable. I get in a solid punch to his jaw. Satisfaction at hearing the sickening crunch fires through me, blistering my veins, seeking more carnage.

The pistol whips the side of my head, blacking my vision and bringing me to my knees. I feel the cold press of steel to my forehead.

Breathing labored, Nelson says, "Making you disappear would be poetic justice, but I just can't forfeit the capture."

"It's in your blood now," I say, gaze cast up at him. "The lust for the kill."

His finger moves to the trigger, and I close my eyes. London's face appears and, even though this isn't how it's supposed to end between us, I'm comforted by the finality of it. For however brief, she was my salvation.

An eternity passes as I wait for the bang.

A siren *whoop* bounces around the alley. Flashing lights assault my eyelids. When I open my eyes, it's the fear I see in Nelson's face that heightens my senses and feeds my awareness, bringing me back from the depths.

I'm alert, aware of the footfalls echoing off the pavement. Voices shout to "lower your weapon."

Teeth clenched, Nelson pulls the barrel away from my head and sets his gun on the ground. "I'm FBI," he announces.

Two uniforms round us, taking Nelson into custody and searching him, the other wrenching my hands behind my back. "Stand up," he orders. Then a string of profanities fill the air as he notices the dead woman. "We got a vic!" he shouts.

Nelson directs a scathing look my way as the officer removes his badge from the inseam of his suit. His eyes say what he's not able to, expressing the morbid loss of his hard-earned kill.

"Glad we were able to locate you in time." It's Foster's voice that cuts through the chaos. The detective walks right up to Nelson. "For your sake, agent. Can't be too careful where this bastard is concerned." He glares at me.

I'm searched and then cuffed, lowered to the ground forcefully, the gravel digging into my knees. For the second time, Detective Foster has surprised me.

Nelson receives his badge and weapon back, and as he's straightening his suit, he says to Foster, "Just how did you wind up here?"

"What? No thank you?" Foster asks, his voice laced with smugness. A cast wraps his arm, a sling draped over his shoulder. He's still bruised and weathered, but his pride sloughs off about ten years. He beams with satisfaction.

"Don't worry, Agent Nelson. I'll be sure to declare this was a team effort." At Nelson's incensed expression, Foster says, "A crime-scene tech led the taskforce to the Refuge. Said he spotted Sullivan hanging around here. It didn't take long to pick up your scent on the same lead. You're about as stealthy as a bull in a china shop. Luckily for us all, we got here soon after you."

When Foster's gaze lands on the victim, his proud features purse into a saddened scowl. "Not soon enough." Then to me, he says, "But it's the very last fucking time for you, Sullivan. I can't wait to watch you die."

I smile conspiratorially at Foster, and he backs up a step. I sense the disturbed mood rioting through him. He's bumbled his way to this point, a tagalong, not even sure how he got here.

Lawson. If I hadn't left him alive, he would've never had time to think about our moment together to make the connection to me. Ironic. By sparing his life, he in turned saved mine.

Before I'm led away by the officer, I glance at Nelson. "Every hunter has his whale," I say, smiling. Foster has been one step behind Nelson for weeks, tracking the copycat killer just as Nelson has been tracking me. The detective has his Moby-Dick—he just doesn't realize it yet. "Getting caught is an inevitability."

Agent Nelson moves in close. "A lot can happen between holding and prison."

Thrill of the challenge spikes my blood. "Are you worried what I might say?"

His features harden. "Only if you're worried about your doctor. She's been pretty vulnerable lately."

A red haze covers my vision.

The act of murder is intimate in its own right. In the final moments before a person's death, you're given a candid view into them. Open and bare, a secret life revealed. I've never before desired to kill for personal agenda. As close as I become to my victims, I'm still an abstract demon to them—a reflection of their sins.

Revenge. Greed. Even love. All intimate motives to commit murder, and I've felt none of them.

Until now.

As I'm hauled into a squad car, a new awareness settles over me. I've suffered my pattern since the day I entered that dark underground room, and never once did I fear it would touch another life. For the first time in my solo existence, I can feel the shift. The design has changed.

I'm going to enjoy killing Agent Nelson in the most personal and painful way.

20

FOLIE À DEUX

LONDON

By the time my plane is on its descent toward Bangor, exhaustion claims every muscle in my body. A quick layover in DC allowed Sadie and I to make the exchange of documents. She returned my phone with a hesitant scowl, claiming the multitude of notifications forced her to shut it down, worried "this Special Agent Nelson character" would track me down only to find her. Sadie isn't fond of the FBI, to say the least.

Once I was seated on the plane, I turned my cell on, then thought of switching it right back off when the flood of messages and voicemails arrived. Instead, I put it on mute and settled in for the flight home.

My phone vibrates in my pocket. I sigh out a breath, deciding I won't start returning calls until I land. When a notification buzzes my phone immediately afterward, resistance becomes pointless. I ignore the "no cellphone" sign above and swipe open my text messages.

The air leaves the cabin.

My heart stops.

No.

Grayson has been apprehended.

I drag in a breath, forcing my lungs to expand past the constriction as I read the text from Allen Young again, trying to discern a different meaning. My hands shake as I type a message to him, then I stop.

I open my browser and search Grayson's name, my head aching from the pressure. I tap open the first article, and the world tilts.

The Angel of Maine Caught.

The wheels touch down, and the motion rocks through me with a jolting sickness. I only have hours before he's transported to Cotsworth Correctional Facility.

I ignore the calls and messages from Agent Nelson on my way to my apartment, where I hurriedly shower and change into clothes more becoming of Dr. Noble. Sliding into the suit is like sliding back into my own skin, comforting.

A brief thought of Lydia flutters up—what my other, better half would do in this circumstance—but I'm too far beyond her now to feed that insecurity. I tamp it down as easily as I call for a cab, decision made.

I can't flounder one step.

As the taxi coasts toward my building, I pocket my phone with a curse. I've covered every news station report and article, looking for something, anything to contradict Grayson's arrest, and it's not until the cab pulls to a stop that reality fully sinks in.

The car is swarmed as a flood of reporters rush the vehicle.

"Pull around to the back," I instruct the driver. "You can wait for me there."

He blares the horn, forcing camera crews and bystanders to move. "You sure you want to get out here?" he asks as he stops near the back entrance. "I'm not sure I can wait here..."

There's a number of people here, too, but it's not as thronged. "You can wait." I leave my purse in the backseat to keep the taxi waiting, then I jet out of the car toward the door, trying to shroud my face. Cameras flash, and a recorder is thrust in my face.

"Dr. Noble, how do you feel about the arrest of Grayson Sullivan?"

"Do you fear he'll escape again?"

"Are you scared he'll come after you?"

Christ. I wave off the questions and make it into the building, pulling the door closed behind me. Crime-scene tape is layered over the elevator. Irate, I tear it away from the panel. In my mad dash to get here, I hadn't bothered to check if the building had been reopened.

Now that Grayson is caught...

I shut my eyes. Center myself. Then, with renewed purpose, I hit the elevator button.

Grayson has been incarcerated. This is a fact. For officials, whatever investigation my practice or I were under is probably of no more concern. At least for now.

My floor is uncannily quiet when I step out. I curse when I find my office door already unlocked. "They could've at least locked back up."

I push the door open. What's left of my patience ignites a very small fuse.

Agent Nelson is seated at my desk, flipping through my

planner. He doesn't look up, just continues to intrude on my privacy. "I thought you might go to him first." He pencils something into my planner. "But then I figured this is your haven. Where you keep your secrets."

Against my will, my gaze slides to the filing cabinet.

"You would want to check on the status of your office first," he continues, and looks up. "Make sure nothing is out of place."

I smooth the lines of my face, clearing my features of all emotion. It's difficult to maintain an unaffected countenance when I glimpse the wall behind Nelson—my research on Grayson exposed. The Dali discarded to the floor.

"I do plan to see Grayson," I say, moving into my office. "For an interview. Unlike some professionals, I can set my personal feelings aside in order to do my job. His state of mind right now could give us insight—"

Nelson stands abruptly. "You can stop lying to me now."

I square my shoulders. "I don't owe you anything. No explanations. And I'm quite certain that the search warrant is now expired, so I'm politely asking you to leave my office, agent."

He pushes my chair back and turns toward the wall, trails a finger over the pages on the corkboard. "I feel like a fool. Here I was, vehemently declaring your innocence to my superiors, and it wasn't Sullivan who had the obsession—it was you. Fixated on your own patient." He looks at me then. "Are you in love with him?"

This isn't the probing question of a curious FBI agent. Nelson is dropping the guise. His tone seethes with offense. His suit is wrinkled, as if he hasn't slept in days. He's endured some kind of setback during Grayson's arrest.

"Frankly," I say, "that's none of your business. How I

conduct my sessions and therapeutic techniques with my patients is none of the FBI's concern."

He moves around the desk, coming toward me. "I should've put it together with the inconclusive rape exam. What is it about the bad boy that turns smart women into whores?"

I inch toward the door. "You need to leave. Now. You need sleep, agent."

He scrubs a hand down his face. "No. I don't think that's what I need. I need what you gave Grayson. You're his muse. His creative genius is influenced by you."

I grip the door handle, and he halts his pursuit. "With Grayson behind bars, who will take the fall, Nelson? Have you thought this through?"

The farce is over. Nelson never intended for Grayson to be captured alive—that's too much of a risk. An intelligent criminal who's been framed for murders he didn't commit could do serious damage to the guilty party, even from prison.

And I'm Grayson's lover. The proof of my affection is written all over my investigation into him. The hours, days, weeks I devoted to the patient who abducted and tortured me...that's just not natural. I should've been working harder to ensure Grayson's capture, not investing time into setting him free. That's what Nelson sees. The fruits of my labor.

Which means I know about the copycat killings.

I'm as much of a threat to him as Grayson.

"Obsessed fan who finishes what was started," he says, waving a hand thoughtlessly. "Or maybe you just couldn't handle it. The man you love taken away again. The judgment from not only your patients, but also your colleagues. Your career in ruins. Suicide rates are up this season."

I exhale a lengthy breath, thinking how to buy time. "Detective Foster would've been more original. Secretly, I was rooting for it to be him. You're an insult to Grayson's methods."

He chuckles, but the sound is off, disembodied. "Foster is an embarrassment to law enforcement. He doesn't have the first clue."

I crane an eyebrow. "He shadowed you, according to the reports. Followed you right to the scene of the crime. I bet you've been plagued by that—going over it and over it. Thinking if Foster had just been ten minutes earlier..." I trail off, a taunt in my voice. "You shouldn't underestimate people. The number one reason why serial killers get caught is because they start to believe they're unstoppable. They make careless mistakes."

Something in his gaze dims, unseeing. He's staring through me. Gaining an ounce of leverage, I ease away from the door and toward the filing cabinet. I'm not leaving here without what I came for.

Nelson snaps out of his daze, and I stop all movement. "Who slit the rapist's throat?" he suddenly asks.

I stay still. A fixed object, unthreatening. "You're not making sense, Nelson. We can go to my therapy room. I have techniques that can help you—"

"Who slit his fucking throat, London?" He advances on me. "You didn't think that, after all my study and work that I've put into this case, I wouldn't recognize the deviancy in signature?"

He's so close to me now. I can feel his body heat. Smell his aftershave. See every wrinkle in his standard, black suit. I look up into his wild eyes. "I did," I admit. "I placed my hand over Grayson's and, even though we both dragged the blade across his neck, it was my choice."

His nostrils flare. With purposeful movement, he takes hold of my hand and turns it over, exposing the tattooed key I no longer conceal. "A replica of the murder weapon. Your trophy. You killed Malcolm Noble."

"Prove it."

In one quick flash, Nelson strikes my face.

I slam into the door from the force of his backhand. I cover my cheek, vision blurring. The pain hasn't seeped past my shock yet. I watch him with guarded eyes as he hovers near, breathing hard.

"I don't have to prove it," he says, gripping my upper arm and hauling me across the room. He swipes an arm across my desktop. Objects crash to the floor. Then he's pushing me down against the surface. "I just have to get rid of the loose end."

I struggle against his hold and work my way onto my back. Using my feet, I kick at him. "There are witnesses," I say around a grunt as I strike out. "All those people down there…"

My mention of witnesses only fazes him for a second, then he pushes himself between my legs, ending my fight. His hands close around my throat. "Scream," he dares through clenched teeth. "You'll suffer a broken neck from a fall down the elevator shaft. No one will question me. I'm the fucking law."

His fingers tighten, cutting off my oxygen. I claw his hands, gasping for air. "Then why not just do it now," I manage. His hold loosens, gaze narrowed. "You can't. The same way you couldn't allow a trap to take your victims' lives. You had to be the one—you had to feel life drained from them with your own hands…"

Grayson's words channeled through me, but they're true. However this sadistic game started for Nelson, he's embraced it fully now. He's become the monster he hunts. With Grayson locked away, the killings have to end.

And Nelson can't accept that.

His grip around my neck strengthens, tears blur my eyes. Fire snakes through my lungs and curls around my throat. He's shaking, muscles strained. Spittle leaks from his mouth as he squeezes the life from my body.

I'm going to die.

"You'll always be in his shadow," I wheeze out, but he hears me.

Apprehension glints in his crazed eyes. For the briefest second, air finds my lungs, and I grovel for more. I push the panic down and rake my nails across his face. He releases an enraged growl, then one of his hands wrapping my neck is gone. I clutch the air in my lungs like a desperate animal fighting for survival.

"Guess I need to taste the muse for myself, then," he grits out. He works his belt buckle open, and another paralyzing burst of panic seizes my body.

Hand clamped hard to my throat, he wrestles his pants open, and I come alive with fight. I flail and scream, my voice nearly lost, a searing whisper wrenched free. It's not enough. Nelson manhandles me easily, bunching up my skirt and ripping my underwear down my thighs.

He positions himself between my legs, and I can't make sense of this. In spite of the panic, the fear…logic finds a way in. Nelson is going off script. This doesn't fit—the killer he's become in Grayson's wake.

How many perpetrators has Nelson emulated? How many personas does he have trapped in his psyche? He's coming undone.

Just one second. That's all I need.

I swipe my hands along the surface of the desk, anger overcoming desperation. This man will not victimize me. I grasp onto something solid and aim for his neck.

He cries out as my letter opener drives into his shoulder.

A miss, but it's enough. His hand falls away from my throat, and I pull the silver object out and drive my hand down, making contact with his leg.

"Fuck!"

I feel the warm gush of blood cover my hand and, trembling, I roll over. I take half a second to drag an unobstructed breath into my lungs, then I bound off the desk. My legs unsteady, I stagger before finding my footing. Nelson clutches the wound on his thigh, red seeping through his fingers.

Not good enough. I need him immobile.

Every muscle and bone in my body hitched with pain, I brace a hand to the desk and kick. I nail him in the balls. He falls to his knees. Then I attack again, hitting him directly in the same spot, taking him to the ground.

He's spewing venomous curses at me—and I use his angered voice to gauge his presence as I drop before the filing cabinet. I get the key ring out of my pocket. The keys clang in my trembling hands, but I manage to insert the right one and yank the bottom drawer open. I reach underneath and grasp the object taped to the underside of the drawer above.

I close my eyes, lungs struggling to hold in air, as I grip the rusted key in my palm.

I take one last look at Nelson on the floor of my office, then I half crawl, half run toward the elevator. Everything is surreal. Detached from reality. Somehow I calm my nerves enough to fix my hair, pulling it loose from the hair clamp to cover my neck. I straighten my blouse and suit. Wiping any makeup smudges from my face, I ready myself to face the crowd.

The taxi is still waiting for me outside the back entrance. It seems so wrong—how much time has passed? I feel as if it's been hours that I fought Nelson off, but when I get inside the cab and dig my phone from my purse, it's only been minutes.

The driver glances at me in the rearview mirror. "Everything all right?"

No. Nothing is all right.

"Please take me directly to the Rockland Police Department."

His worried gaze shifts to the road ahead, and the car bounds forward. I relax against the seat, my adrenaline tapering off, leaving me drained.

I'm still clutching the key in my hand, the teeth biting into my palm.

I close my eyes. Hear Nelson asking me what happened to the key...the murder weapon. He was right; my practice has always been my haven. My most salacious secrets kept there, safe. Hidden.

It can't be anymore. Grayson is my haven now. My secrets reside within *us*.

I feel along my suit pocket, tracing the outline of a USB drive. I slipped it into my pocket in the elevator, not thinking about it in the moment, unnerved from the confrontation. The drive was taped next to the key. Only one person could've placed it there.

During the ride, I continue to take deep breaths, calming myself further. I gather my thoughts in preparation.

I've been to the jailhouse before, to visit a patient who'd been locked up for public drunkenness. I stood on the other side of the bars, scared to get too near them, thinking how much they reminded me of the cell in my father's basement. I recognized the brand name on the cell door lock—the same name that was on the door to my father's basement cage.

Coincidence or fate?

With shaky hands, I open the locket I brought from home and slip the key inside, then drape the chain over my head. I find a thin scarf in my purse and layer it over the chain and the purpling bruises along my neck.

Then I scrape a fingernail file beneath my nails and place the skin and blood inside my compact. I make the call.

"Young," I say when he answers. "Get me access to Grayson."

He talks on about procedure and regulation and strict enforcement...and I hear none of it. "Make it happen," I demand and hang up.

I make one last call before we're parked in front of the building where Grayson is being kept under heavy guard. I pay my fair and leave the safe confines of the cab, phone pressed to my ear.

I talk hurriedly, keeping the communication short.

Agent Nelson has become more than a complication. He's become a barrier. He's unpredictable. And that frightens me more than the walls between Grayson and me now.

I turn off my phone and adjust my suit, situating myself. If it was just a matter of killing the FBI agent, then it would be less problematic. A single, large dose of succinylcholine, and he'd be one less obstacle to hurdle. But we placed Nelson in a position of power for a reason—and it's too late to change the game.

I lift my chin as I steadily walk toward the jailhouse, arming myself with layers of confidence. Dr. London Noble has the status and authority to overturn any official. I believed this before; I have to believe it now.

Above reproach.

Agent Nelson isn't the only one with the law on his side.

You're his muse.

Wrong again.

From the moment I placed my hand in Grayson's on that roof, everything has been my choice. I wondered when it was that the dynamic between us was established...and now I know. It was then. Right then.

Amid our Folie à deux—our madness shared by two—I am the dominant.

It has always been me.

21

FATED RUIN

GRAYSON

G ray cinderblock and iron bars. A trap of my own design. So familiar it should feel consoling—but I pace the length of the holding cell. A wild animal. This time it's different. Because this time, there's someone on the outside that matters.

I underestimated Nelson.

For that, I deserve my consequences. And I'll willingly serve out my sentence and walk death row with my head held high, as long as London remains free and unharmed.

As long as a disgrace like Nelson doesn't get anywhere near her.

It's the loss of information that's torturing me. Where she is…what's happening to her. If I call the slovenly cop over and tell him there's an unhinged FBI agent out there with his sights set on my psychologist, would he believe me? Or would I put her at even greater risk?

My design is simple: get caught, and escape. It's what I do. The never-ending cycle of my fucking existence. Until I go bleeding mad. With short intervals where I get to touch her…taste her…experience the sweet glimpse of heaven through her—the unexpected variable that interrupted my routine.

She changed everything.

I'm a devil with a heart. Pure lunacy. But then, even the devil loves passionately, ardently, coveting this world…so much so that he rebuffed heaven. A manic laugh starts at the base of my throat, and I'm not sure I can stop it.

They've stripped me of my clothes, leaving me with jogging pants and a plain white T-shirt. Nothing left in the cell that I can use—they're not sure what's safe and what's not—they've taken everything. Only a thin cot mattress and toilet with a sink atop in the holding cell.

I search again, going over every inch. Trying to find a change, upgrade, a revision, or something I overlooked before.

I've studied the schematic of this building, of this cage, for months. I compared every detail and possible outcome. And I know that there's no way out. Not without London.

I was wrong to hinge so much on her, but then this was the least likely result. Planning for a potential outcome is different than expecting it. Truthfully, she wasn't supposed to be involved at all. Just her existence has changed the course, and I don't know if I can ever control it again.

London said our aim was too high. Nelson was too big of a mark. I'm not sure if it was my pride or desperation to be with her that did us in—but here I am. Again. I laugh. Push my palms over my head, as if I can stop the painful webbing cluttering my brain.

We didn't choose Nelson; he chose us. He put himself in our path and made it possible. Only I wanted it too badly—

I've never wanted anything before her, never craved to be free until her golden-flecked eyes really saw me.

And then she appears. My angel of mercy. Clearing the maddening fog.

"Fifteen minutes," the guard accompanying London says. "Three feet away from the cell at all times. Try anything funny, and you're out. You got that, Sullivan?" he directs this toward me.

I nod once, and the guard steps away, giving us the illusion of privacy.

I can't take my eyes off her. In a matter of seconds, I've analyzed every cell of her body, looking for evidence of pain or suffering. She's too well collected, her wall erected to keep everyone out.

"Seems like I'm destined to visit you behind bars," she says. Her voice is raw, strained. I'm not sure if it's the statement or the action of talking that causes her pain, but she's hurting.

"Remove the scarf."

"No," she says, averting her eyes briefly. "Not yet. I need to talk to you first, and I need you to hear me."

Fury boils my blood. I stalk toward the row of bars and link my hands around the cold iron to douse the flames. "I'm listening."

She looks down at her hands. Her thumb traces the inked key and the scar along her palm. "Why did you choose me, Grayson?"

When she finds my eyes again, I hold her gaze, unrepentant.

"I want the truth," she demands.

The truth? Would she believe me if I told her that I didn't realize the reason at first. That I was consumed by her, obsessed with the unknown—that she frightened me as much as she mesmerized me. Scrape the reasons back layer by layer, until only one, blindingly obvious motive sparkles with clarity. "Because you're the best."

My response neither shocks nor insults her. I've confirmed what she's already puzzled out. "Schizophrenia runs in your family," she says, pulling the seams to unravel the truth of me. "After our first session, I decided that you came to me because you wanted me to save your life. I wasn't too far off, was I?"

I breathe in deeply, savoring her scent. I set her free so she could lock my demons away. "There's give and take in every relationship, doc."

"There is," she says on a breathy whisper. Then her eyes drill me. "I've studied your brain scans repeatedly. I've shown you the proof of them. There are no signs of schizophrenia, Grayson. Your fear of inheriting your mother's mental illness only goes so far."

So she's discovered Mother dearest. "And how is Becky these days?"

"Nonresponsive."

I nod slowly, absorbing the information.

London doesn't stop. "After your official diagnosis," she says, "you could've left. Ended the sessions. You didn't need me, not in that way anymore. You're feeding a deluded fear of an illness that doesn't exist. May never exist—"

"It will," I cut her off.

She wets her lips. "And when it doesn't, when you never fall victim to your madness, how will I fit into your puzzle then?"

I can't help the smile that steals across my face. "Do you honestly believe you're expendable to me?"

She shrugs with a shake of her head. "I believe that everyone becomes expendable when their usefulness runs its course. You chose me because I was the best?" she says in a mocking tone. "No, Grayson. You chose me because I was good enough, and I had a secret you could exploit. A means of manipulation for if and when our arrangement was no longer beneficial to you."

I don't deny it.

Her arms hug her slim waist. "Why didn't you just kill me? *Why?*" she demands.

I breathe out slowly. "Oh, London. Don't tempt a man. It's cruel."

"Where are the copies of my patient tapes?" she suddenly asks.

My expression hardens. "With your confession footage, of course."

My admission doesn't faze her, either. I figured she'd eventually put it together; I wasn't hiding it from her—more like saving the best for last.

"Insurance policy?" She cranes an eyebrow.

I huff a humorless laugh. "Not the way you think. I was protecting you."

"From whom?"

"From yourself," I say. "From *Lydia*, apparently. We're human, London. We waver. We doubt ourselves. I couldn't risk losing you."

She nods harshly. "You couldn't risk losing your investment. After all, you put in over a year of hard work. What good would Dr. Noble be to your cause if she was broken?"

I run my fingers up the bar, wishing I could touch her. She's fire right now.

At my silence, she looks down the corridor. The guard is surfing his phone. London lowers her voice. "Manipulation is like foreplay to you."

I chuckle. "I'm sorry. Next time I'll give you flowers."

Her eyes spear me. "Next time?"

The way she says it, so incredulously, sends a current of livid heat whipping across my skin. "Why are you here?"

She doesn't answer right away. The question hovers between us, a livewire that, if severed, will detonate our suddenly fragile connection. "Because I saw your home, Grayson." Her eyes glisten, forcing me to drop my gaze. "I saw where you were raised...*how* you were raised. Since the moment you designed your first trap, setting yourself free, you've been seeking an answer. I understand what my initial purpose was to you. Fear of your mother's illness, of losing your mind, made you cling to the hope that I could treat you. But there's something else. What are you searching for?"

I move back from the bars, putting more distance between us. It's a physical pain that I still have yet to comprehend when she's too far away. The pain feels real. Tangible. I use it.

"Five minutes!" the guard shouts.

"Maybe it's a curse," I say, voice low, searching. "Maybe it's my punishment. Maybe it's fate. Maybe it's chaos theory, and nothing has any rhyme or reason at all. But whatever the purpose of this insanity, it's the design for my life. And I have spent a lifetime reworking that design. Remastering the puzzle...and the only answer I've ever been given is you." I step closer. "You're the closest thing to freedom I've ever tasted."

"You'll never be free. You're doomed to repeat this self-inflicted cycle forever. The madness won't take you—these bars will. You keep putting yourself here again and again, trying to escape, but you're still locked in that dark room."

"Get the fuck out of my head, doc."

She studies me, undeterred. "If you fear it enough, you'll

manifest it. Your mind will make sure of that." She takes her glasses off, letting me see her eyes. "And when that day comes, I'm not sure I can help you."

"You have to."

"Because you helped me?"

"Yes. It's the price. The tradeoff." I tilt my head. "Are you not grateful for everything I've shown you? If you could take it all back, would you?"

She shakes her head. "No. I wouldn't, but I don't know how—"

"You will." My hands clench into fists. "If the day comes where you have to kill me, you will."

A horrified expression crosses her face, but it's gone just as quickly. She's thought of this before. She's had to. We're as much of a threat to each other as we are each other's sick salvation.

Even if my mother's illness doesn't claim me, my love for London might.

Love is madness.

"If you can't help me, then you have no choice but to end me, London. Promise me that now."

"Maybe I couldn't..." She trails off, lost in thought. "But Lydia could."

A slow smile curls my lips. "Then I guess we should keep her around, after all."

"Lydia Prescott is just as important as the boy who's still locked in that dark room under a greenhouse." She swallows hard, wincing. "As your doctor, as the woman who loves you, I'm telling you to embrace him. He's not your enemy. Stop trying to escape, Grayson."

My nostrils flare. Heat creeps up my spine. Resentment singes the edges of my vision in vibrating waves of red.

"Strip all the layers away," I say. "I suppose it's only fair. Seems these bars just bring out the honesty in us, baby."

She nods, as if recalling her experience in the cage where I locked her up, forcing her to remember the past she tried to keep buried. "A lock and a key," she says. "We are an inevitability."

My smile stretches. "Till death?"

She answers by removing the scarf. I notice every nuance, slide of hand, and when she slips her hand under the material to free if from around her neck, she retrieves an object from the gaudy locket beneath.

The guard at the end of the hall missed the action, but I didn't. Only I can't focus on what she's wrapping in the scarf. I can only see the welts, the bruises—the dark fingerprints marking her neck.

I grip the bars so hard my fingers ache.

I will kill him.

I know this as clearly as I know the sky is fucking blue.

London reads the tension thrumming through me and says, "No. We still need him." She glances at the guard. He's watching us. "It's my choice. *Mine.*"

Rage lashes at my insides. "Then you better get to him first."

Despite my attempts to be more than—*better* than—mortal, I'm no god. I'm blood and bone and London is steeped in my marrow. So deep I can feel her becoming a part of me. The pain won't ever stop. The compulsions won't ever stop. I'm human and I'm weak, and she's still my only chance at freedom. My need for her won't stop.

The guard stands.

I release the bars, my hands burning. "Give me the scarf."

Her throat bruised and swollen, London takes a shallow breath. "Did you plan this?" she asks. "Back then. Before.

238

Did you plan all this out in such meticulous detail that every possible outcome had its own contingency? Or are we that fated?"

"Like a bad Shakespearean tragedy," I tell her. I have over a hundred different locks memorized. The second I saw the tattooed key on her hand, I knew exactly which lock manufacturer it belonged to. From there, it was only a matter of obtaining blueprints. Getting a record of which jails and holding cells in Maine used the same manufacturer. "I chose Rockland for more than its scenic beauty," is all I say aloud to her.

Her soft lips part. Her gaze shifts to the bars of the cell, her eyes following the iron all the way up. The cell in her basement is made by the same company who installed the cells in her father's police station all those years ago. I know this, too, because I made sure I knew it. And that jail cell manufacturer is the same one who installed the cell I'm in right now.

She smiles knowingly. "We're a fucked-up kind of inevitability. Not fated. Doomed."

She's probably right. Good things don't emerge from basements and cellars... Dark things do. Demons burned by the light.

"You're still beautiful," I say, my voice thick with the accent I try to conceal. "My dark angel."

Her gaze comes into focus on me. "How did you know I would connect it?"

I shake my head. "I didn't. That's the fated part, London. The variable between us I've never been able to break down and analyze. We're inexorable. Inescapable. The one prison I don't want to escape."

She looks at the scarf in her hand, staring past the material to the key she's hidden within. "It may not work."

No. It might not. It probably shouldn't. The chances that the key used to open her childhood cage would be a match to this cell is highly unlikely. I've already done the math. Calculated the odds. But like us, it can be warped and twisted into something perfect.

With a couple of crude modifications, London's key will be an exact fit.

"We're connected on some deeper level," I say to her. "Through bars and cages and prisons...in the physical sense and the mind. That's why you could never be expendable to me. You're my match."

Does she believe me? Some things can't be manipulated. What I feel for her is real.

"I'm not the hero, London," I say. "But I'm not the villain, either."

"Times up, doctor," the guard calls out.

London moves quickly. She rushes the cell and thrusts the scarf through the bars. "He's going to take me," she whispers. "*Let* him take me."

I grasp the scarf and try to touch her hand, desperation clawing painfully to the surface, before she's snatched away.

"Get her back!"

Two guards push London flush against the wall, giving me only enough time to slip the key between my fingers—like a cheap magic trick.

"Drop it, Sullivan," the officer orders.

I let the thin material go. The scarf drifts to the concrete floor soundlessly.

"Step back," he instructs me.

As the guards escort London out, I keep sight of her for as long as I can. Until she disappears down the corridor. I move to the back wall of my cell as the cop unlocks the barred door and retrieves the scarf.

"Fucking groupies," he mutters as he inspects it. He gives it a sniff. "Smells good, though. You got one hot doctor, Sullivan. I'm keeping this." He sneers at me, and I let him.

Once they leave, I settle in the corner. I run the pad of my thumb along the teeth of the key. Anticipation twists my mouth into a smile. I wait until the jailhouse goes still to start making the alterations to the key, using the edge of the steel sink to file down the teeth.

In less than two hours, an armored truck will arrive with a small army to escort me to prison. They're taking their time, making the adequate preparations. Making sure I have no chance of escape.

And Nelson is going to take her.

London's only chance is if Nelson is terrified to touch her.

I work at the key, sweat leaking into my eyes. The burn satisfying.

When it's time, I go. And I make sure I do enough damage on my way out that Nelson knows I'm coming for blood.

22

THE BETWEEN

LONDON: A MONTH LATER

The rules of psychological warfare are different for everyone. How far someone will go to demoralize and dominate their opponent is dependent on their level of commitment. Their desire and need to win—to make their enemy suffer.

When violence runs in your blood, the compulsion to kill is an inherent part of you. It's intimate and unruly; a lover possessed with only one feeling, one yearning, stopping at nothing to obtain the lead.

For Grayson and I, those lines are blurred more than usual. We can just as easily commit murder as we can make love. Both give us a climactic satisfaction and completion in possessing the other.

Love and murder. The same innate emotion fuels both.

"Dr. Noble? Did you hear me?"

I look up and tuck a loose wisp of hair behind my ear. Warden Marks stands before me in all his lanky, scarecrow glory. "Yes. I'm sorry. I was just thinking we've come full circle."

His smile is sardonic. "We have. Thank you for this." He holds up the file that contains my final patient evaluation for Cotsworth Correctional Facility. "I know saying these past few months haven't been easy for you is a gross understatement—"

A tight smile rims my mouth.

"—but you've fulfilled your obligation to the facility in my book," he says. "I'm happy to sign-off on the early release." He takes a step toward the elevator and pauses. "Where are you planning to go, by the way?"

I glance around the floor at all the partially packed boxes. "I'm taking a few weeks off, then I have arrangements on the west coast."

The warden nods solemnly. "A change of scenery could be good. Well, good luck, London."

I see Warden Marks out, then give Lacy the rest of the day off. With the commitment to Cotsworth fulfilled, and my clients referred to another psychologist, there's nothing left to do but pack.

"Are you sure you don't want any help?" Lacy asks as she grabs her bag.

I shake my head with a sigh. "I can handle the last bit. You should get a jump on your paper. No excuses." I eye her severely, then smile.

Once the floor is empty, I relish the silence, taking my time packing up my office.

Any normal, sane person may feel apprehensive about being left alone in the place where she was previously attacked by a deranged FBI agent—but my questionable sanity isn't the reason why I'm daring the fates.

It's monotony.

Nearly four weeks have passed since I last set eyes on Agent Nelson, and every day I wonder if it's going to be the day that he comes for me. The waiting...the not knowing... it's insufferable.

I'd rather he jump out at me from a dark corner than continue in this morbid limbo.

I toss a box on top of my desk and start clearing off my bookshelf.

The announcement of my practice officially closing released this morning. So if the agent has been lurking on the sidelines, now is the time to strike.

Only the doubt that he'll make any attempt weighs heavily in my steps as I move around the office, the room becoming bare, empty. The job not taking nearly as long as I thought.

I seal up the last box, the harsh sound of tape stretching away from the roll a final note in my life here. I tear the tape and smooth it along the edges of the box, lost in thought.

Grayson has yet to make contact.

After his violent escape from police custody, he apparently fled Maine. I can only speculate as to how it happened, the reports biased and muddled and not having near enough facts. Three officers were injured during the escape, but only superficially—and with the state I left Grayson in, I'm truly surprised there were no fatalities.

I can envision Grayson using my key to unlock the holding cell. Alarmed cops rushing the hall. Shots fired. Batons and Tasers confiscated and used against the officers. A bloody trail in Grayson's wrathful wake.

He's never been capable of extreme emotional outbursts before, but then, I'm not sure if it was reactive or deliberate. Meant to intimidate Nelson.

Which, to be honest, seems to have worked.

When the manhunt for Grayson took authorities toward the south, I was approached by Nelson's superiors and questioned on his whereabouts. I was the last to have seen the agent, to have talked to him. According to the FBI, Nelson was already a loose cannon, having pushed his way onto Grayson's case against their discretion.

Nelson was under investigation at the time, his stellar capture rate not earning him any favors where the FBI was concerned. Although he received a slight pardon for his behavior after the death of his wife and child the previous year, he was required to pass a psych eval before returning full-time.

All the time I spent with Agent Nelson and he never once mentioned the accident that took his family. Then again, revealing a major stressor to a criminal psychologist would not have been an ideal move on his part. To wit, the FBI are the best secret keepers.

Well, almost the best.

I stack the boxes outside my office for the moving crew tomorrow, then I go to turn off the light. A moment of nostalgia grabs me, and I look at the saltwater tank, now devoid of fish, and say a silent goodbye to my practice.

After I lock up for the last time, I set the key on the receptionist desk and decide to walk the scenic route to my apartment. I'm keeping the lease on the townhouse, as Maine will always be my home. I'm just not sure about reopening a practice here. At least, not in the near future.

Time is needed.

Time and distance.

The aviary is beautiful at sunset. Whenever I had a particularly bad day, a detour onto the winding paths through lush greenery always soothed me. I don't even particularly like birds... I come here for the gardens and trails. The ponds that line the boardwalk.

I never really thought about why I might find this place so tranquil. I can't help but wonder if I'm relating to the giant birdcage on a subconscious level. Feeling some measure of comfort in the iron bars. I stuff my hands in my pockets and mentally laugh at myself, mocking my over analytical nature.

This is the first time I've been here since Detective Foster followed me into the gardens. I half expect to see him as I turn the corner. With his hovering cloud of cigarette smoke and derisive expression, ready to scold me for walking home alone.

Over the past few weeks, the ornery detective and I have gotten closer. Oddly enough, Foster has proven to be rather heroic, swooping in to help me evade the press after Grayson's escape when Young couldn't be present.

I even gave him the evidence of Nelson's attack on me—the epithelial cells I recovered from beneath my nails after having scratched the agent. I believe it was that trust I supplied in him, touting a conspiracy to protect Agent Nelson on the FBI's part, which solidified his belief in my having no hand in Grayson's latest getaway.

Before I arrived at the Rockland jailhouse, I called Foster from the taxi, securing a measure of protection against any future attacks from the deranged agent, and insurance for Grayson. If something happened to me, I wanted at least one person to suspect it might not be Grayson.

I kept the truth of Nelson's copycat murders hidden, knowing that, without proof, it would be an empty accusation —one the Feds would hardly be willing to believe or investigate. But I could use Nelson's attack on me to prove his devolving mental state. For now, that's enough.

I'm still pretty good at reading people. And as far as

Foster is concerned, Grayson is a threat to the both of us. Joining us together in some morbid effort to protect each other, as no one else has suffered as we have.

By now, the detective should've returned to New Castle. Yet he's stated that, with the loss of his career, there's nothing there for him to return to. He's taken a job here as a private investigator, claiming he's enjoying the freedom of selecting his own investigations. But I believe, like me, he's waiting.

A feeling of déjà vu assaults my senses, and I stop. Footsteps reach my ears. I whirl around, Taser already in hand.

A young man wearing a blue postal uniform raises his hands. "Whoa—"

"What do you want?"

I'm wary of everyone these days. As I study the man, he appears harmless, but I know how easily one can be deceived. The mini-Taser I keep clipped to my belt loop withdraws back to its place on a retractable cord.

"That's pretty convenient," the guy says, then takes a hesitant step forward. I notice a small package in his hand.

"Don't move," I say. "What is that?"

He holds it out to me. "It's for Dr. Noble," he claims. "I tried your office, but it was closed. Then someone said you just left the building, and I saw you heading this way. Are you Dr. Noble? This package is kind of time sensitive..."

"How much were you paid to deliver it personally?"

A guilty blush tinges his cheeks. "It's important that I get this to you today."

Dammit. This feels wrong. If Grayson wants to reach me, he does so. He doesn't involve others—but maybe he's too far away. Maybe this is the only way he can contact me.

"Who gave it to you?" I ask. When he shakes his head, clueless, I push. "Was it a man? What did he look like?"

"I didn't see him," he admits. "Look. My boss handed it to me and said he'd pay me cash to get it to you quickly. But this shit is starting to freak me out..."

"All right. Give it here." I accept the package and wait for the guy to leave, making sure I'm alone before I start to inspect it.

Regardless of the high foliage and secluded sanctuary of the aviary, I'm too exposed here. The postal worker proved how easy it is to follow someone when you're determined. And all he wanted was some cash.

Nelson wants much more...

I tear the brown packaging open.

The guy said time sensitive, and I've been waiting weeks for something to happen. Inside the package is a small black, cardboard box. Anxious, I ease the top off, and my heart gallops.

A clover rests on a bed of fleecy cotton.

I glance around the garden, my chest tight. "Grayson..."

I close the box and head out of the aviary, the feeling that I'm not alone lingering on the edge of my thoughts.

It started here. It has to end here.

The chest-thumping beat beckons me closer. It's like gravity, drawing me in and through the doors of the Blue Clover. The sultry music engulfs my senses, a hypnotic trance that reels me through the throng of close-pressed bodies.

I've been here before. A familiar, tantalizing promise lingers in the air—the promise of escape. Freedom. I can still taste a hint of it as the mesmerizing colors swirl within a smoky haze over the dance floor.

We had a design. We had each other.

But then, I was sheathed in a disguise, hidden—able to camouflage my desires for a night. There was no question of London or Lydia. There was only my longing to be his.

This time, there's no mask to shield me. My designer black dress suit hugs my curves like perfectly fitted armor. My black-and-nude pumps clash with the wild atmosphere, and probably cost more than every outfit here.

I'm aware of how blatantly I stand out as I move through the dance club. Women size me up, men look too eager to approach me, as if I'm lost, as if I'm on the prowl, a huntress craving flesh.

Which was the whole point when I chose the club as our secret reunion spot. No one would suspect me to come here. Dr. London Noble wouldn't blend.

Maybe I should've donned a disguise tonight. Made sure I saw him first before he noticed me—but that's part of the strategy.

Let him take me.

I stalk the scene on a mission.

The music changes speed, the rhythm faster, matching my rapid heartbeat. Annoyed, I fend off advances, waving away two men in cheap suits, and take up the back wall where I discovered Grayson once before. Smoke rolls across the floor in vibrating neon flashes, the beat climbs higher, and bodies crowd together in a dense mass, obscuring my vision.

For the first time in months, a twinge of pain nudges my lower back. Out of habit, I adjust my posture to compensate for the heels, and a spike of alarm stabs my chest.

This isn't right.

The smoke machine spits vapors at me, stealing my breath. My head spins. The dark club is suddenly too bright.

I'm pushing through the condensed bodies toward the exit, hands snagging my clothes, my hair.

Something's wrong.

The thought hits me as someone presses up against my backside. A strong arm circles my waist. Irritation claws at my defenses, and I clamp my hand around the thick wrist at my pelvis. "Get off."

"I could probably manage that, but I'd love to know what getting you off—*really* off—feels like."

Nelson's gruff voice reaches my ears past the hyped music. My body tenses, my hold on his arm turning to stone.

"Where's Grayson?"

It's the most important question. Every contingency to follow rides on his answer.

He feathers my hair over my shoulder, rough fingers stroking my neck. "*Shh.* You're going to ruin the surprise." Then he presses hard against me, making me aware of the gun tucked in his waistband.

I wrench out of his hold and spin to face him straight-on. "What are you going to do? Shoot me?" I look around at all the people in the club. "This isn't some cliché movie, Nelson. You're not going to stick a gun in my side and lead me to some remote location. If you're going to kill me, do it. Right now. In front of everyone here."

He chuckles. "God, you really are a snotty bitch."

"And you're merely a pathetic imitator," I sling back. "At least we can be honest with each other now."

He stalks forward and lowers his voice. "Do you really want to make a scene? What are your chances to discover what I've done with your lover then?"

The rules of psychological warfare are different for everyone. How far someone will go to demoralize and dominate their opponent is dependent on their level of commitment. Their desire and need to win—to make their enemy suffer.

So the question becomes: Who wants it more?

Me.

"Take me to him," I demand.

I don't give him another moment. We're already drawing too much attention. I start off the dance floor, and Nelson's hand slips into mine. "So we don't get separated," he says.

The cool night air is a strange comfort as I push outside. The chill chases away some of the sickly dread festering inside that the heat of the club allowed to thrive. I remove my hand from Nelson's grip as I start down the steps.

"Your phone, London."

Without turning around, I dig my cell from my suit pocket and hand it to him from over my shoulder. "Is he alive?"

The question leaves behind a sour aftertaste. I squeeze my eyes closed.

I hear the distinct crunch of my phone beneath his boot. Then the former agent moves in front of me. In the dim glow of the streetlight, I discern the scratches I put on his face. Now faint and healed over, but they're there. He notices my inspection with an irritated scowl.

I smile. "Everyone has scars, Nelson. It's what defines us."

Without a rebuttal, he forces me to walk. We're heading in the same direction, following the exact path I took once before. I know he's going to turn the corner into the alley before he directs my course down the darkened lane between the buildings.

"Being on the run from the authorities..." I hedge. "You're really taking this copycat thing to the next level."

Still no response.

"Why do you do it, Nelson? For the rush? For the sheer satisfaction of outsmarting the Feds?"

"You wouldn't understand."

"Understand is what I do. Try me." When he remains silent, I add, "I know about your family. What happened to them."

"You don't know anything," he snaps, driving a hand through his unkempt hair.

"Then explain it to me. Make me understand."

He chuckles, incensed. "You're so fucking annoying." Only he delves into his story. "I was working a case," he says. "I should've been there. But this perp... With all the regulations and red tape, I couldn't bring him in. So I had to sit on him, and wait. Just wait for him to make a move so I could catch him in the act. I thought I couldn't live with myself if he killed another girl while I wasn't looking."

I slow my steps, and Nelson matches my pace.

"I was wrong. I found out that what I couldn't live with was the guilt of not being there for my wife. For my little baby son. Had I been there, that accident never would've happened."

"You don't know that. You can't."

"Oh, but I can. I know that if I'd been there, she never would've been driving late at night to get medicine for him. I would've been behind that wheel, not her. So when it comes to the 'bad guys'—" he makes mocking air quotes "—I no longer dick around. If I know you're guilty, you're mine. No time wasted on protocol."

I look at him. "No matter how far you have to go to catch the bad guy. No matter how many victims—"

"As far as I'm concerned, I did the world a favor. I'm a hero. Every one of my victims had a rap sheet a mile long.

Scum of the earth. They had it coming, and now the world is better for their absence."

Delusions of grandeur. Only Nelson isn't the hero of this piece. He can't be.

"You used your inside connections with the FBI to target victims," I say, analyzing. "Sloppy."

He scoffs. "You're one to talk, doctor death."

I eye him from my periphery. "How did you know about the Blue Clover?"

Silent, he strolls down the alley clad in a white T-shirt and jeans, so different than the put-together FBI agent I remember. He strolls like we're just two people on a walk. No worries. No malice between us.

I'm not a threat to him. At least, not in the traditional sense. Nelson disappeared in part due to the imminent investigation after my attack—but mostly, once Grayson escaped law enforcement, Nelson went in pursuit of his obsession, his need to capture Grayson his primary goal; chasing his objective without the interference of the FBI to hinder him.

Nelson shouldn't be underestimated. It takes a strong will to turn your back on the only life you know in pursuit of another, in spite of all else.

Which also makes him dangerous.

He's a man with nothing to lose.

We come to our destination. The abandoned mechanic garage I selected myself. Nelson finally looks at me and says, "You told me." He brings out a key, and I notice that the lock on the rusted metal door is new. He pushes the door open and sweeps his hands in an invitation, urging me forward.

As I enter the garage, memories of Grayson flood my mind. I feel him everywhere.

Then I see the locks.

I'm thrust back to the mouth of the maze and all the gleaming keys. Only now, every silver and gold and bronze shimmering object stares back at me with the eyes of rusted notches and mouths of keyholes.

"This isn't your trap," I say, my voice breathy. I recognize the construct, the details—all the hours of rigorous study and research I put into the design.

"I can't take the credit," Nelson says, edging closer. "But I can take the prize."

A sharp prick at my neck, and I react. I'm fighting off Nelson and grasping at the needle sinking deep as my vision blurs. Drowsiness claims me, and my muscles go lax.

Nelson captures me before I hit the concrete. My breaths shallow, my racing heart the only part of my body still filled with fight.

"I'm the bait," I whisper.

He smoothes my hair away from my face, gaze cast down as he cradles me. "There was no other way, London."

Grayson is coming.

It's my last thought before blackness takes me.

23

LOOK UPON THY DEATH ~ROMEO & JULIET

GRAYSON

Perfection.

The ultimate assumption that it can be attained if one works hard enough, sacrifices enough, is determined enough to prevail…is the very definition of insanity.

But what is this maddening thing we call perfection?

It's different for everyone.

That one, blissfully high moment of utter and complete satisfaction, of achievement. It's a sweet glimpse of heaven. A split-second where demons depart and the gates inch open, granting us a limited view of something holy.

We have reached the top of the mountain. We have conquered. We reap our reward.

Ah, that reward doesn't come freely. There's a price.

Fear.

Fear governs our life—that soul-sickening dread of loss. Once we've obtained our perfection, anxiety creeps in like the demonic force it is to steal our light.

The truth is a nice dash of salt in a fresh, cavernous wound.

Once we've tasted the sweetest perfection, savoring it on our tongue, everything that follows can only be bland by comparison. Or worse; a sickly sour. Quickly becoming a rotten bitterness that roils our stomach.

The higher we reach, the further we descend immediately afterward. A crushing low.

A torrid pit of hell awaits us at the bottom.

Maybe that's where London and I made our first mistake. Believing we could bottle our perfect piece of heaven. Immortalize it. Exist only for each other.

Maybe we still can.

My ears pick up the low thump of bass as I walk past the Blue Clover. I pull my jacket hood over my head, dodging a drunken, laughing group. Getting back to Maine was harder this time. Before, the authorities assumed I wouldn't return—now they're expecting me.

Luckily, Agent Nelson left me a trail of breadcrumbs. This is where he wants me. Which means he has leverage. He has *her*.

Let him take me.

London's haunting words have set my course since I escaped the Rockland jailhouse. This is her design, and as she's the dominant force, I've conceded to her request. Though it wasn't easy; I caught up to Nelson twice, and both times I waited. And watched.

No one can run forever.

There are only two certainties for men like us. You're either caught or killed.

But unlike Nelson, I have an anomaly—a beautiful dark angel who defies convention.

I notice the shiny lock on the warehouse door. It hangs

open, an invitation. There's no stealthy entrance on my part as I slide the door open. Nelson wants me here, London wants me here…so here I am.

Let the games begin.

I walk inside, and as soon as I see her, my heart lurches. It only ever beats for her.

Suspended above the garage on a hydraulic car lift, London floats there like the angel she is—a vision.

Her mouth and eyes are covered, but she can hear me. She's been stripped of her clothes—her flesh on display, all except for her thin bra and panties. Wire ropes project from her wrists and waist….holding her aloft…like a beautifully disturbed marionette.

The cables are anchored around the lift's arms—the yellow steel beams that support an automobile—and she dangles from just below. The cables flow above the lift, stretched taut above like piano strings, and fold over a second lift bar to drop down like rain. But instead of raindrops, padlocked weights dangle from the cables.

I tear my gaze away momentarily to study the mechanism. Within seconds, I've calculated the system.

The lift is set on a timer. Lowering her every minute. The countdown will end with London submerged in an 8ft shipping container.

It's beautiful, really.

The trap London and I began to design that first night here, now complete, realized to its full potential. A trap I could truly appreciate, if not for Nelson's fingerprints all over it, corroding it.

"I thought to myself," Nelson's voice sounds out, "it's unfortunate that you've never had the pleasure of starring in one of your own traps."

I push the hood off and unzip my jacket. "What's in the container?"

"A concentrated sulfuric acid compound," he replies. "Your recipe."

I smirk and toss my jacket aside. "A copycat down to the last detail." But I realize London's exposed flesh will be submerged in the mixture with no barrier to mute the damage. This sobers me.

"That's just the perfectionist in me. I do have a whimsical side. Like the addition of the locks…just for you. It's a metaphor."

I'm already tired of his voice. "Very clever." I glance around and notice a covered rubber tub beneath the dangling locks.

"Go ahead. Open it."

I stride to the tub and toe the lid open.

Keys.

At least a hundred gleaming keys fill the bottom of the bin…and they've been filed into lethal-looking weapons. The edges knife-sharp.

A hiss echoes through the garage, and the hydraulic lift lowers a notch. I look up at London. She's strong, but her body reacts from the jolting motion, her muscles quaking with involuntary tremors as she sways only feet above the container.

The weighted locks above my head clang together, moving another few inches higher.

"I knew from the moment I found the doctor alive that she was the key to you," Nelson says. "I admit, for a while, you eluded me. You're a conundrum. A psychopathic killer in love… Not only is it ridiculous, but it goes against every FBI profile we have."

"I'm not a profile."

"You will be now. See, I struggled—with every kill—to get inside your head, but I don't have to share your obsession to beat you. I just needed her."

London is so much more than a mere obsession.

"If you try to remove her from the trap," Nelson continues, "I push the button on the lift controls. She might survive the acid dunk...but she won't be very pretty anymore."

I grit my teeth and whirl around, looking for the man behind the voice. "You could just shoot us both. Save us the trouble."

He *tsks*. "Do you think I'm doing this for you? For her? I don't give a fuck how you two twists kill each other in the end. She dies by your hand—by your death trap—that means I get to go back."

"You're not going back, Nelson. You enjoy my persona too much. It might have started out as a way to get inside my head, to hunt me, but as time went on, you got comfortable in my skin. Because otherwise, I'm here." I raise my hands. "You've caught me."

My voice echos around the garage.

I let my arms drop. "You don't want to capture me. You want me dead. So you can continue to use my methods to kill. It's the perfect ruse."

At his intense silence, I have my answer. Nelson doesn't intend for either me or London to leave here alive.

"Being on the run is exhausting," I say. "I know. It wears on a man. Shows us what we're made of. I'm never going to stop hunting you, Nelson. The FBI is the least of your worries."

Another shrill whistle from the gears on the lift, and London descends lower. A warning that Nelson is ready to start the game.

Even if I save her, we're not simply walking away. The only way Nelson gets to be the hero is if we die. He'll become the insulted agent who went rogue to capture an escaped killer.

Except London becomes a victim in the process.

Two deaths have to happen here. That's what's needed.

"Only one key unlocks her shackles," Nelson says. "Dig in."

I look up at London, beautiful and angelic. Her dark hair tangled in disarray, mascara smudged down her porcelain cheeks. Duct tape covers her eyes and mouth, and yet she's speaking to me, urging me on.

It ends here, she said in this very place as I held her in my arms. She saw the design before I could recognize it myself.

I start with the locks, inspecting each one. A Houdini lock and three other puzzle locks. I used to solve these as a kid. I could use the bump key I keep in my pocket to open the locks right now—but that'd be breaking the rules. London would suffer.

Nelson wants blood.

I roll my sleeves up and kneel before the tub of keys, noticing an odd glint beneath the surface. Swiping my hand over the top, I push aside a number of keys.

Razorblades.

"Damn. This is going to hurt."

I fortify myself, and a sort of calm encases me as I sink my hands into the sharp objects. From my peripheral, I see London kicking her feet, seeking the edge of the container. She won't reach it. She only has five minutes before her toes touch the acid.

Five minutes is more than enough time.

I can assume Nelson wouldn't put the keys to the locks anywhere near the top of the pile; he wants me digging, razors shredding my skin. I work my hands all the way to the bottom of the tub, gritting my teeth against the acute pain.

I've had worse done to me. I've done worse—I've scarred my flesh deeper than these razors can cut. I dig through the bin without a single wince for Nelson.

I don't need to try every key here. I know what I'm looking for. I know what the grooves of the teeth will feel like, how they'll slide into the keyhole and turn easily with that satisfying *click*. My favorite sound other than London's soft voice.

This trap was designed for me.

A buzz sounds, then I hear the hiss of the lift. London's body lowers closer to the acid.

Blood stains the silver key as I pull it free. I inspect it quickly, then lay it on the concrete. I dive back in. Fine slashes assault my wrists. Blades carve into my flesh, flaying my skin. But I press on until I find the second, and the third.

Sweat stings my eyes and I'm shaking with adrenaline by the time I unearth the final key.

I rest my forearms on the edge of the tub and take measured breaths. Then I get to my feet, the keys gripped in my bloodied hands.

On the Houdini lock, I twist the beveled screw on the backside loose, then slip in the key and twist. The lock pops open, and I toss it to the floor, the sandbag falls free. "Hang on, London. I'm coming to you."

The next puzzle lock is just as simple. I realize—while I'm sliding the gold flap on the front sideways to align the inner mechanism—that this isn't the trap. Nelson knows I can pick a lock—can pick *any* lock. I'm waiting for the real fun to begin.

The second lock clicks open. The weight releases, and I

grab the cable before it can zip across the lift bar. "Grab hold of the beam above you," I shout to London.

With her wrists freed, she grasps ahold of the lift arm and clings to the steel beam.

I fill my lungs, taking a full breath as I move to the last lock. The key slips out of my hand, slippery from my blood, and I curse. The gears on the lift grind, and I look up to see it drop another few inches.

Her feet hit the acid. London's pained cry is muffled, but the agony of it slices through my chest more painfully than a million razors.

She pulls her knees toward her waist, keeping away from the acid. But she's in pain. She's getting weak.

"Hold on!" The final lock springs open.

I race across the garage and scale a large shipping container to reach the lift. "I'm here." Seating myself on the edge of the beam, I grab ahold of London's arms and help her wrap them around my neck. She's trembling as I bring her to my chest.

I work the wire rope free from around her waist. Then I tell her to keep an arm around me as I guide her across the machine and onto the container. I glance around the shop, seeking Nelson. He remains hidden.

I quickly inspect her feet. Only her toes suffered the acid, but she needs to treat and dress them.

London digs at the tape over her mouth and pries it off, leaving angry red skin behind. "This isn't the whole trap—"

"I know." As gently as I can, I ease the tape from her eyes. She winces at the sting. She blinks a few times to clear her vision. "Are you okay?"

She nods repeatedly, still shaky with adrenaline and her sweat-slicked, exposed skin. "I'll be fine, but I need to get you to a doctor."

At my confused expression, she palms my face between her trembling hands. "The razors—"

"Were tipped with aconite."

Nelson stands at the base of the container, gun aimed up at us. I pull London behind my back.

"That's amazing," Nelson says. "A selfless, heroic psychopathic killer. I believe that's an oxymoron."

I can feel it now—the poison coursing my system.

A clamminess blankets my skin. Spikes of cold and hot prickle my body; nerve endings misfiring. My muscles twitch, spasms starting to set in. Nausea will soon follow. Convulsions. Paralysis. Asphyxiation.

An excruciating death.

How long has it been since the first blade sliced my skin? Five…six minutes?

I don't have much time.

I kneel before London. "Take the switchblade from my pocket."

The panic lacing her gleaming eyes gives way to horror. "What?—I'm not—"

Nelson's deep chuckle grates my already fraying nerves. "Oh, this is priceless. Just perfect." He taps the barrel of the gun to his temple, as if he's thinking. "Yes, London. You have to. A mercy kill…end his pain. You don't want him to suffer an agonizing death."

I swallow as I hold her gaze, resolute. "Put the blade to my throat."

"Grayson…" Her eyes seal shut. She knows this is the only way—but she's fighting fate.

"*Trust*," I whisper. I wet my lips, my mouth running dry.

With unsteady balance, she dips her head and places the softest kiss to my neck. She talks in a hushed tone, her swift words for my ears only. Then her hand slips into my front pocket and grasps my newest switchblade.

"I underestimated you, Nelson," I shout down to him, keeping my gaze trained on London's beautiful face.

When I'm gone, he'll either shoot her or submerge her in the acid, finishing the job. The scene will be set. It's brilliant, really. London and I—accomplices, lovers—destroyed by our own maddening devices. Our own hands.

Such a perfect ending.

Maybe that's where London and I made our first mistake. Believing we could bottle our perfect piece of heaven. Immortalize it. Exist only for each other.

Maybe we still can.

But the higher we climbed, drugged on each other, ruling over a damned world that bowed and trembled before the god-like monsters we'd become, the harder our fall.

We are perfection.

And we are the fear that lurks beneath it.

We feast on each other and exist only for the highs…and even now as I kneel before my dark goddess and pray for her mercy, I regret nothing.

We truly were *happy*.

Maybe we still can be.

The razor-sharp edge of the knife presses into my neck and splits my skin, and I release a hiss. I search her gold-flecked eyes for the spark that tells me she's ready. Her eyes are wild, filled with loathing contempt, her chest heaving as glistening beads of sweat dot her smooth brow.

My beautiful angel of mercy, now my vengeful angel of death.

"Do it," I command.

Her hand steadies. The cold steel a tantalizing tease to my heated flesh.

"Close your eyes, Grayson." Her voice is throaty and raw, wrapping me in her cruel, loving embrace.

I push against the knife, drawing blood. "I want to see the satisfaction it brings you."

Her delicate neck pulses with a strained swallow. I feel the force of it in my throat. My thirst for her never quenched. Even now, as she grips the weapon with both hands and begins to drag the blade across my skin, I yearn to taste her one more time.

Death at my lover's hand. The ultimate reward and punishment for our perfection.

I couldn't ask for a more perfect ending.

24

CORPUS DELICTI

LONDON

"**D**rop the weapon!"
My hands still, the blade trembles with my restraint. A thin line of red beads and drips down Grayson's throat. I stare at the blood, the poison flowing out.

I recognize the gruff boom of the voice. I hold my place, not lowering the knife.

I have to finish this.

"I said, drop it, London," Detective Foster shouts, his gun aimed at me.

"She can't." Nelson turns his weapon on Foster. "She doesn't have a choice. She has to kill him."

I glance at the detective. Foster's confusion results in his aim bouncing from me to Nelson. "What's going on?" Foster demands.

Nelson makes a move to his left.

"Don't—" The sound of the gun safety clicking off reverberates around the tense room. The agent halts movement, the standoff between them thickening the air, suffocating.

I use the distraction to gauge Grayson's condition. He's weakening. Sweat dots his forehead, his facial muscles tic, muscles spasm. I know the symptoms; I memorized them. Soon, convulsions will take hold.

He doesn't have long.

This scenario has two contingencies: Foster's arrival sets the first in motion.

"I'm ready," Grayson says. "*You're* ready."

I suck in a fortifying breath. Then: "You've been chasing a copycat," I tell Foster. I catch and hold his gaze. His Glock is still directed at Nelson. "The murders in Brunswick and Minneapolis. The second Rockland victim. Even the prostitute that you stumbled on to…" I let the truth of my words drift over him. "And you've been so close to catching the killer. Working alongside him nearly every day of the investigation."

His thick brows draw together. As realization sets in, he focuses on the man in his sights. "I knew something was off with you."

Nelson adjusts his stance, rolling his shoulders and lifting his chin. "You're not a part of this, Foster. You're a bumbling, reject detective, and you're officially off the case."

A gunshot fires.

The silence breaks. Gunfire cracks with a resounding echo, leaving behind a muted ringing in my ears. On startled reflex, I drop the knife. Grayson pulls me down against the container and positions his body over mine.

A loud groan of pain, and then another shot rings out.

"I hate guns." Grayson's voice is barely audible through the gauzy stuffing filling my ears. "This how you want to announce your legacy, Nelson!" he yells. "Gunning down your victims... Not very original."

Then, Grayson's comforting weight disappears. He releases a grunt as a booted foot makes contact with his ribs, then a sharp pain lances the back of my head. I'm yanked backward, my bare skin burning as I'm dragged along the cold steel.

"Get up," Nelson seethes, pulling me to stand by my hair.

I lash out, nails aimed at his face, but he easily blocks my attack. He smashes the butt of the gun against my temple. Pain splinters my head, darkness blinks before my eyes. He draws me against his chest. Pushes the muzzle to my throbbing head.

My feet kick at the steel despite the pain it causes my injured flesh, seeking purchase as he drags me over the container. Nelson grips my shoulder, securing his forearm across my chest. Grayson watches the moment through a haze of pain and helplessness as the aconite ravishes his system.

Incensed, I regain my composure and latch on to Nelson's arm, digging my nails into his skin. "Let me go—"

"Not happening," he says near my ear. "You're good at being a hostage, London. Don't let me down now."

As my vision clears, I glimpse Foster below. Leaned up against a support beam, he uses it as a shield. He's holding his casted arm. Red seeps between his fingers. He's been shot.

Grayson is dying. Foster is injured. How badly, I'm not sure—but he won't be able to make a stand against Nelson. I'm a sacrificial lamb for Nelson's escape. Fighting to live only long enough until I transition into a burden. Where he'll dispose of me.

The moment is crystal, pristine. So clear, I can taste the acid infusing the air.

I catch Grayson's gaze and stop struggling. The clarity I feel is reflected in his sheer blue eyes. He's losing the battle, his awareness slipping away. *Now.*

When Foster steps from behind the beam, gun drawn and aimed, I act.

I go limp like a rag doll. Nelson growls his frustration as he tries to hoist me up. Foster takes his shot. The bullet wizzes past Nelson, just missing its mark. Nelson abandons the fight for a hostage and releases me. He takes aim at Foster.

Grayson is forgotten in the chaos.

He rises up now, the last of his strength concentrated into one final burst. Nelson notices too late. Grayson attacks Nelson, and the gun skitters across the container. I crawl toward it, but by the time I've closed my hand around the weapon, I've already lost too much time.

Grayson has Nelson locked in a vise-grip, his arm latched around his neck. "The knife," Grayson says.

A moment—one clear moment—where our eyes meet, and I know what I have to do.

The knife is in my hand. I look for Foster. He's ascending the side of the container, slowly. His broken arm a hindrance. Steps deliberate, I approach Grayson. His struggle with Nelson is diminishing him further. He can't restrain him much longer.

I meet Nelson's eyes and, with a smile, drive the blade into his sternum. He sputters a shocked, incomprehensible admonishment—something with a muttered *bitch*. I twist the blade deeper, up beneath his rib cage.

From my peripheral, I glimpse Foster's hand reach over the top of the container.

Only seconds now.

As Nelson quickly becomes dead weight, Grayson nearly topples over. "I'm too weak..." He trails off.

"I'll see you soon," I tell Grayson.

"In hell, baby." He winks.

I brace my bare feet against the metal and slam my hands into Grayson's shoulder.

Grayson and Nelson go over the edge together. The momentum knocks me off balance, and I slip on the blood coating the container. "Grayson—"

It happens so quickly, in a blink.

I scramble toward the edge of the container and look over the side, my hands gripped to the metal like it's the only solid force holding me together.

I flash back to how fast the predator in the maze dissolved —how, within minutes, I could no longer distinguish his body parts. Flesh and bone liquefied.

Below me, the mixture of sulfuric acid churns violently. The fumes irritate my eyes. A thick film already bubbles over the top, blocking my view of the carnage happening within.

Then I'm pulled back. Foster's thick arm locks around my waist as he wrangles me away from the edge. He's telling me not to look. *Don't look.*

I fold myself against him, my bones weak. Every ache and pain alive and fueling my oncoming breakdown.

"Don't look, London," Foster says again. He grunts from the pain of his gunshot wound. "It's over now. They're both gone. You're safe."

I squeeze my eyes closed. I'm not sure if he's trying to reassure me or himself. He puts the call in, and within minutes the police arrive, followed by the FBI. I'm soon draped in a coarse blanket, just like the morning I awoke and Grayson was gone.

Death and freedom are sometimes described as one and the same. Death is a form of freedom—freedom from the prison of life.

I aimed to set Grayson free. In the end, I succeeded.

WHEREFORE ART THOU

LONDON

A villain. A hero. And a sacrifice.
That was the missing element—*sacrifice*—the reason why the story was never complete before. The finality of events tie it all together. The end.

As far as the reports go, the hero of the story echoed my account of the night, declaring the death of both villains. Foster is a credible witness.

And authorities needed a credible witness.

Forensics couldn't reconstruct the remains for identification. By the time they arrived to extract Nelson and Grayson from the container unit, the acid had dissolved the bodies. There was no DNA to analyze. What bone fragments they recovered were too degraded and disintegrated upon examination. No teeth to match to dental records.

There was only a psychologist and an ex-detective to account for the remains—what was left. A sludge of mutilation.

After twelve hours of questioning, I was released and,

bags and office already packed, left immediately to escape the infatuated press. I heard there's already a book in the works, and possibly a movie script.

The world is enthralled with what is impossible to comprehend.

A special agent with the FBI goes off kilter and resorts to killing criminals to better understand the killers he hunts. A convicted serial killer who murdered the deviant and sadistic, who in turn defeats the disturbed agent by taking both their lives. One obsessed detective who arrived in the nick of time to help save the psychologist that both deranged men were transfixed by.

Sounds like a ridiculous work of fiction.

Only I lived it—and now my name is synonymous with the Angel of Maine.

We're a duet. Forever linked.

I breathe in a deep inhalation, filling my lungs with the dry, warm air of San Francisco. We're experiencing an Indian summer, and the weather is temperate and the air clean. Denoting a new beginning.

I make sure I walk the same path every day. Developing a pattern. I take the same route to the coffee shop, and then the park, and then back to my three-story townhouse. It's seated on a corner, not far from the bustle of the financial district. I live in the top apartment. My new practice is on the bottom level, after I converted the garage into an office and therapy room.

It's easy to get lost in this city.

I turn the corner and head into the park. Coffee in hand, I make my way to the bench under a large oak that I've claimed for the past six weeks. I watch mothers stroll their babies along the paths. Dogs race the grassy hill as their owners toss toys to be fetched.

I'm nearly done with my coffee and turn to toss the cup in the bin when a rare breeze floats over the park. A chiming pricks my ears. I freeze, waiting to hear the clanging notes again.

They sound, and I look up into the branches of the tree.

Two silver keys twinkle above.

My heart lurches.

I stand on the bench and reach high overhead. I clutch the keys, snapping them free from the branch. The small objects feel heavy in my palm, the cold metal quickly matching my heated skin as my heart knocks painfully against my breastbone.

So as not to deviate from my pattern, I slip the keys into my jacket pocket and walk the familiar route to my townhouse. My fingers touch the keys along the way, tracing the grooves, the imprint of letters and numbers.

Once inside my office, I lower the blinds and dim the lights. Then I place the keys side-by-side on my desk, and study the numbers. "A storage unit," I say aloud.

It was my choice to select the puzzle locks. And once that idea took root, it only made sense to complete the trap design with a magical element that paid homage to one of the greatest escape artists.

A combination of Houdini and Shakespeare. I've always harbored a flare for the dramatic.

Juliette planned to fake her death—but she didn't put in enough planning beforehand. Had she had a little more patience, she and her Romeo would've ridden off into the sunset together.

I open my laptop and connect to the secure connection. The one Grayson developed and left for me on a USB drive that I discovered taped next to my key in the filing cabinet. I search the numbers on the keys, locating which storage facility they belong to.

When I questioned Nelson about how he discovered the Blue Clover, he said I told him. This is true. I led him there with the notes I kept behind my Dali. I planted the clue in the one place I knew he'd find, and that he'd keep hidden from the FBI. I even left Nelson the design for the trap itself. A basic contraption I designed myself using all the elements of Grayson and myself combined. A trap so perfectly enveloping our team dynamic, that Nelson wouldn't be able to resist the compulsion to make it his own. To steal it. To use it against us.

It was a huge risk.

I wasn't sure Nelson would take the bait. He was devolving faster by that point, and by the time he sent for me, requesting my appearance at the Blue Clover, I knew any number of things could go wrong.

Not all the details were worked out the night Grayson and I made love in the abandoned garage. Only one finite aspect needed to be secured in order for the rest of the pieces to align—for the dominos to topple accordingly.

I gather my purse and stuff the keys inside, then lock up my townhome. This time, I make sure to use a route I've never taken before. I catch a trolley to the other side of town. I stop into a coffee house, noting every person who enters after me. When I leave, no one follows.

I contain my smile. I'm not clear yet.

By the time I enter the storage yard, sweat trickles down my back. I pull off my suit jacket and drape it over my arm, making my way cautiously toward the guardhouse.

"Excuse me," I say, gaining the guard's attention. The man is relaxed in the booth, his feet kicked up as he plays with his phone.

After a few seconds, he says, "Just go on in."

I do smile now. "Thank you."

I walk around the gate that the guard couldn't be bothered to raise, and locate the unit that corresponds to the keys. With a determined breath to steel myself, I push one of the keys into the lock.

I lift the roll door.

It rolls back with a deafening clatter that jars my nerves.

The unit is empty. All except a snow globe in the corner.

Glancing over my shoulder once, I note that I'm still alone, then enter the unit. I pick up the globe and laugh.

"Of fucking course."

The ferry ride to Alcatraz Island is a short fifteen minutes. I clutch the railing, my nerves a tangle of excitement and fear.

I left my cellphone behind at my townhouse. The only way for anyone to know of my location is if they've been following me. I've learned how to sense this; strengthening those dormant hunter skills that lay buried in us all.

No one is concerned about Dr. London Noble anymore. My part is too boring, too cliché, to be of interest. The story is far more exciting if I'm just the victim, giving the stage to the main players—the villains and heroes.

I coordinated an elaborate scheme, but I believe the most impressive bit of magic I performed was in becoming invisible.

I step off the ferry and am guided to the tour hosts, where they section off tourists to visit the different parts of the island.

I select the prison.

A giant red sign reads: Tour Starts Here

And that's where I start. The tour guide leads us through corridors, pointing out the many cells. A familiar pang of nostalgia grips me, acute in its haunting clutch. I've lived within a cell my whole life. In one way or another.

He couldn't have picked a more perfect location.

By the time the tour is coming to an end, I'm worried I missed the mark by a day, or even hours. No. I didn't stray from my pattern.

Trepidation slithers around my bones, slowing my steps. I didn't share every aspect of the trap with Grayson while I was designing it. Some elements—like the aconite—was decided later. We never got the chance to prepare beforehand.

Then a terrible thought: He might not be coming to me, but *for* me.

A hand slides into mine.

I stop walking. I'm held back from the rest of the tour group as they progress ahead.

For a few beats, I let the coarseness of his palm speed my heart. Adrenaline pours into my veins and skitters along my skin. Then I turn to face Grayson.

26

THE END

GRAYSON

What beats a perfect death?
Faking a perfect death.
It's not an easy feat. It takes time.
Preparation. Skills. And an accomplice who is apprised in
manipulation tactics that rival the most intelligent law
officials.

I pull London inside one of the cells.

"We might get trapped in here," she says. But her eyes are
wide in excitement. Those golden flecks sparkling.

"I could do time with you." I wrap her in an embrace,
bringing her close, and try to conceal the pain touching her
causes me.

She's never fooled. She immediately rolls my sleeves
back to inspect.

The scars on my arms are covered in new red and silvery
slashes. The razor cuts are still sensitive, the poison leaving
behind a permanent imprint on my nerve endings.

"The pain will subside with time," London says,

tentatively touching the wounds. She looks up. "Any lingering side effects? Dizziness, paralysis?"

A grin curves my mouth. "Always the good doctor."

She goes to say something more, and I cover her mouth with mine. Stealing her breath and inhaling her deeply.

It's ironic that, what got me tried and found guilty, would also set me free. *Corpus delicti.* Body of the crime. It's difficult to prove a death occurred without a body—but not impossible. Substantial circumstantial evidence is needed, and a witness.

A witness to observe the death is always helpful.

The psychotic FBI agent, obsessed with his capture rate, designed a death trap in the copycat manner to end my life, and he did. Grayson Peirce Sullivan is no more.

I now go by Cain Owen Hensley. That's what it states on my fashioned ID.

I thought it was fitting, seeing as Cain killed Abel and then was doomed to wander the world aimlessly. Except I'm not aimless in my wandering. Not anymore.

I have a very specific destination.

"I can't believe you chose Alcatraz," London says as we board the ferry back to the mainland. "You're disturbed."

I smile. "I was always curious if I could escape it."

As we watch the island get smaller in the distance, London turns to me. "Well, lucky for us, you'll never have to find out."

I place a lingering kiss to her forehead. "I'll try to stay out of prison."

"Oh, I know you will, *Cain*. Because I'm setting the ground rules now."

My smile widens. "Yes, doctor."

I have no choice but to trust her on that. She's the one

who designed my death, after all. I owe every bit of my freedom to her.

While London was crafting the trap, I rigged the container unit with an inner-glass chamber that not only provided a stabilized environment for the concentrated acid concoction, but also housed a separate compartment, obscured from view. Once the lift arms lowered beyond a certain level, it pulled a cord that dragged the container lid farther back, exposing the compartment. Which to anyone else, simply looked like part of the contraption.

But it was my safety net for the fall.

Being off by even an inch could've killed or exposed me. I had to be angled precisely, so that Nelson tumbled to the acid, and I could use his dead weight to propel myself away and land in the compartment.

I then had ten minutes to make it to a storage unit in London's name and administer the antidote she concocted. Seems she had a scientist friend in the forensics' department who enjoyed a challenge. And who enjoyed money even more.

The key to the antidote is under the container.

Her whispered words to me right before she pressed the knife to my neck.

Then she sank the blade into Nelson and pushed us to our deaths.

Perfectly planned and executed.

Yet, it was more than a gamble. Anything could've gone wrong. Foster may have not arrived in time, responding to London's urgent text too late. He could've brought police with him, giving us too many witnesses to construct our narrative.

Foster's broken arm might not have delayed his climb to

the top of the container, giving us less time to eliminate Nelson, or for me to make my escape.

I'm still uneasy about the way it went down; trusting too much to chance. But change and acceptance are a part of becoming a couple. A duo. A team.

And that's all there is. *Fin*.

Endings suck. Why shouldn't they? We're sad when life ends. We're disappointed when something good comes to an end. No one wants an ending; we're designed to want to last forever. So very difficult to bring an end to something brilliant that's taken a lifetime to build.

For London and I, it should've been tragic.

All epic love stories have a tragic ending. The classic failure of two great souls is what makes their brief union passionate. Intense. Epic. And everyone enjoys a good love story. Give the audience what it wants, so the story can end without dispute. A finale with a standing ovation.

I study London's profile as she stares across the bay. She is stunning, beautiful. My dark goddess. My angel and savior.

There is one loose end…but I've decided not to pull that thread. London was the architect, and she waited until we were in the moment before she revealed the poison aspect of the trap.

I smile to myself. Maybe she thought I'd enjoy the surprise. Maybe it was a late addition to the trap. Or maybe she was waiting until the big reveal of my life before she made her final choice.

She won't talk about it. And I won't pull that thread. But I believe she went to Ireland to find that answer. She knew there might be a chance she'd have to sever our relationship.

I take her hand in mine and lace our fingers. Locked together.

The madness is held back for now. The fear that my genes

will ravish my mind one day is never too far from my thoughts. Even so, London's presence helps hold the compulsive thoughts at bay.

Because I know, if that day ever comes, London won't fail me. She'll give us the tragic ending we truly deserve.

EPILOGUE

LONDON

Hawthorne Cemetery sits on a pocket of rolling hills in my family's hometown. Fall leaves, fading from lively green to hues of red and orange, dust the corner of the graveyard, covering mounds of dry grass.

I've now visited twice. Once to see where my parents lay in rest, and today to see my sister, Mia, in her final resting place next to them.

Jacqueline and Phillip Prescott—my biological parents— share one large alabaster headstone, so I had Mia's designed in the same marble finish, and purchased the plot next to theirs.

I walk toward the headstones with my wool coat pulled closed, my dark hair whipping my cheeks in the unforgiving Cincinnati wind. I stop at the foot of their graves.

The branches rustle in the breeze above, stirring the only sound in the otherwise silent cemetery. I'm alone, and I realize with a startling truth that, when my time comes, there will be no place for me.

Just as well. I don't really belong here, with them, after all.

My life awaits me back in San Francisco, where Grayson is pursuing our newest patient, getting to know our soon-to-be victim. David Lyman has a preference for young girls. He sought out my services because his daughter is about to turn thirteen. He didn't admit as much to me during our introductory session, but Grayson knows where to look to uncover the truth.

I plan to exercise David's demons, making sure that he ends his life before he has the chance to get at his daughter.

Then, Grayson and I will move to another country for a time. Our plan is to keep relocating. Leaving behind no more than one victim in each place.

My death… Well, hopefully that's further off.

I walk toward the middle of the plots and place a single sprig of lilac on my mother's grave, then white roses on my father's and Mia's. I learned that my mother loved lilacs; it was her favorite flower. My first home—the one I can't recall—still has lilacs planted below the windows.

Some things are inherent in us. Some memories buried so deep, our subconscious mind clinging to them, even when tragedy tries to strip us of our identities a trace remains.

I'm making peace with Lydia.

A noise to my left—the snap of a twig.

I whirl around to locate the sound and spot a squirrel. My held breath releases in a whoosh, fogging the air. I turn to leave, and something catches my notice between the trees. A hulking figure…

I look again, but other than the squirrel, there's nothing there. Just the shadow of a pine cast over the graves.

It's not the first time I've thought I've seen Foster nearby. Every once in a while my paranoia creeps up, usually when it's too quiet, too still. Like now. I brush the eerie sensation off and start toward the pebbled pathway.

I met with Foster right before I moved away from Maine. He checks in on me every now and again, just to make sure I'm all right, as we still remain friends in a sense.

He asked me about the knife.

Although he corroborated my account in the garage, he wasn't—technically—present during the final act. For that one minute while he struggled to climb the shipping container, when Grayson and Nelson went over the edge, Foster didn't have sight of us.

During our conversation, I played confused, but I knew what he wanted to know: How did Grayson's switchblade end up at the bottom of the container of acid? It was gnarled by the time forensics pulled if free, but it could still be identified. Unlike flesh and bone, steel is rather resistant to sulfuric acid.

I told Foster that it's possible Grayson stabbed Nelson before they went over. Everything happened so quickly…

He accepted my answer with a nod. But I could still see a trace of doubt in his eyes; that lingering need he has as a lifelong detective to close out every angle of the case.

Should Foster prove to be a problem, we'll manage him. Maybe Foster even realizes the danger in this…or maybe it's nothing at all. My mind playing tricks on me.

Pebbles crunch beneath my heels as I progress along the path, and then I feel it—his eyes on me. His presence near.

An arm wraps around my waist, drawing me to him.

"You have got to stop that," I say to Grayson as I sink against his chest.

"You have got to be more aware of your surroundings," he retorts. Then his lips find my neck, chasing away the chill and sending a shiver over my skin at the same time.

"Do you think…?" I hedge.

"No," he answers simply. "We're safe, London. We're free."

I breathe a little easier, accepting this. In another few months we'll be leaving the country, and then I can finally relax, too far away for my demons to follow.

As we leave the cemetery, I study Grayson's profile. Thinking about how, if I was truly safe, he wouldn't be here. Then I shake the thought from my head and take his hand in mine.

Grayson says I'm his angel, but it's he who watches over me. My dark protector.

Not all demons are born to the dark. And not all angels seek the light. Sometimes our circumstance demands a fusion of both. There is no good and evil, only the time spent between both heaven and hell, where we find our peace.

And love.

Even the vilest of monsters deserve to be loved.

Thank you, lovely reader, for taking this journey with London and Grayson. I hope you enjoyed their dark and twisted story. If you did, please consider leaving a review, as it helps authors so much. Truly, thank you.

Want more London and Grayson? If you've made it this far, I hope you'll continue down the rabbit hole with me even further with my next thrilling romance duet *Cruel Malady*. Here you'll follow Grayson's twisted web as he and London entangle Dr. Alex Chambers and Blakely Vaughn in their mind games. Both Grayson and London make cameo appearances. Read a teaser from Alex below.

ALEX

The VIP lounge accommodates its exclusive patrons with private restrooms. I spot Lilah coming out of the women's bathroom and head in that direction. The narrow hallway is set back from the main area, offering the illusion of privacy.

"Lilah—" I call out. When she doesn't respond, I put myself right in her path. "I didn't think that was your name."

"You're a clever one." She tucks her clutch under her arm and squares her shoulders. "None of the girls go by their names."

None of the girls. As if she's just simply one of them. "What is your name, then?" I demand.

"Whatever you want it to be, baby," she fires back.

My mouth slants disapprovingly. That line doesn't work for her. My presence here is bothering her. I'm an interference for some reason.

I step closer and slip my phone into my front pocket. "I noticed you don't seem too bothered to entertain your clients."

"You seem to notice a lot," she says, her gaze tracking over me deliberately. "I notice a lot, too. Like the fact your name isn't Lawson. Not according to your credit card, *Alex.*"

A heated spark shoots up my back, a current of electric excitement. She just ticked up the score a notch on her assessment.

"You're extremely observant," I say. "Maybe I wasn't comfortable enough to give my real name, either."

Her gaze narrows. She doesn't believe me. "Look. My time is better spent *entertaining* in private. That's what my clientele pay for. Which"—she makes it a point to look at my clothes—"I'm sorry to say, is very out of your price range." She levels me with a severe glare. "You should leave, whoever you are."

Those eyes…that stare… It's unnerving.

I lean in toward her and lower my voice to an audible whisper. "You're not a whore."

Her blood-red lips tip upward. That smile is disarming. "Is that supposed to be a compliment?"

"You're not an escort," I clarify. "What are you, undercover? FBI? Trying to take down an escort ring, underground MMA fights? Or does it have to do with Ericson and his firm?"

The value of a predator is unrecognized, unappreciated. I am not one to take predators for granted. Her skills far outweigh those of one simply offering physical indulgence. Whatever this woman's purpose here tonight, it's not to bring pleasure to men. In truth, I'm probably doing Ericson a favor.

Our moment is disrupted as a guy comes around the corner. Lilah uses the opportunity to inch closer to me. Her body presses against mine, her curves mold perfectly to the contour of my form. She's a distraction in all the wrong ways, and she knows this. She uses her body as a weapon.

"Whatever your kink is," she says, "I'm not into it. Maybe Sophie or one of the other girls would be interested."

"I don't think Sophie is my type." No—none of them are the type I need. I've found what I'm looking for.

The first step in the scientific method is to identify, and I've just identified my new subject. A thrill courses my blood as I stare into the eyes of a psychopath.

She's the one.

"Trust me," she says. "I'm definitely not your type." As she turns to walk away, I grab her arm, and that's a mistake.

The realization comes with a shock—a literal electric shock that sends a pulse of 20,000 volts into my body.

I hit the floor, my body convulses with spasms. I stare up at her, noting the small Taser in her hand too late.

Christ. That was unexpected. Every muscle in my body seizes with intense cramps. The sudden and immediate sensation of needing to vomit follows the pain. Then, just as suddenly, the torture subsides.

As my muscles begin to relax, I take measured breaths, thinking about getting to my feet, only my reaction time is delayed. She's on me in seconds, and a biting pinch stings my arm.

The beauty with lethal moves looms over me, those intense green eyes peering down with callous disregard, before the world dims black.

Start reading Blakely and Alex's story now in *Cruel Malady*

Special gift to Trisha Wolfe readers. Receive a FREE bonus story featuring your favorite dark romance couple, London and Grayson, from the ***Darkly, Madly Duet***.

We weren't born the day we took our first breath. We were born the moment we stole it.

~Grayson Sullivan, *Born, Darkly*

He's the devil. And she's his wicked game.

After I'm called to a crime scene to investigate the most gruesome act of violence to descend on the legendary town of Hollow's Row, I have no choice but to turn to Kallum, to the man I had locked away in an asylum for the criminally insane.

Sadie Bonds appeared in the *Darkly, Madly Duet* as London's colleague and college friend. Follow her dark and twisted journey on the hunt for a serial killer in ***With Vision of Red***

TRISHA WOLFE READING ORDER

All Trisha's series are written to read on their own and pull you in, but here is her preferred reading order to introduce worlds and characters that cross over in each series.

Broken Bonds Series

With Visions of Red

With Ties that Bind

Derision

Darkly, Madly Duet

Born, Darkly

Born, Madly

A Necrosis of the Mind Duet

Cruel

Malady

Hollow's Row Series

Lovely Bad Things

Lovely Violent Things

Lovely Wicked Things

Dark Mafia Romance

Marriage & Malice

Devil in Ruin

Standalone Novels

Marrow (co-written)

Lotus Effect

Cellar Door
Five of Cups

ABOUT THE AUTHOR

From an early age, Trisha Wolfe dreamed up fictional worlds and characters and was accused of talking to herself. Today, she lives in South Carolina with her family and writes full time, using her fictional worlds as an excuse to continue talking to herself. Get updates on future releases at TrishaWolfe.com

Want to be the first to hear about new book releases, special promotions, and signing events for all Trisha Wolfe books? Sign up for Trisha Wolfe's VIP list on her website.

Connect with Trisha Wolfe on social media on these platforms: Facebook | Instagram | TikTok